The Fadeaway

REBECCA JENSHAK

Rebecca Jenshak
www.rebeccajenshak.com
Cover Design by Emily Wittig Designs
Editing by Ellie McLove at My Brother's Editor

The characters and events in this book are fictitious. Names, characters,
places, and plots are a product of the author's imagination. Any similarity
to real persons, living or dead, is coincidental and not intended by the
author.

Paperback ISBN: 978-0-9997820-8-8
eBook ISBN: 978-0-9997820-7-1

For Michelle – Thank you!

1

JOEL

Four Months Ago

I need caffeine.

Typically, I run just fine on four hours of sleep, a slight hangover, and aching muscles but last night's marathon fuck fest was unlike anything I've ever experienced. Or want to experience again. The chick wore a cat ear headband (in retrospect that should have been my first clue) and she actually meowed while I went down on her. Yeah, like a cat. My back and ass bear the marks from her long fingernails shaped like claws that completed the whole cat-like persona she had going on. And don't get me wrong, it was sort of hot and kinky, but what the actual fuck? It's like every girl is trying to outdo the last and sure I'm down for some kink, but what happened to good old-fashioned boning where the only thing that's crossing my mind is how good it feels to be buried inside a warm, wet pussy?

I push through University Hall to the small campus café. Blair is nowhere in sight. Bummer. I was hoping she'd throw in about twelve muffins. She's hooking up with my teammate and roommate Wes and the perks of my buddy banging a girl who works at the café include free coffee and pastries. I can afford it, but that's not the point.

When I reach the counter, I still don't see anyone.

"Hello," I call out.

A blonde head pops up and I step back as cups and sugar packets go flying. My eyes catch on her name tag first. Katrina. *Kat*-rina. I wince and shudder at the memory of the *cat*astrophe from last night – pun, totally intended. But as my gaze moves up, all memories of the chick last night, and every other girl for that matter, disappear.

"Holy sh– crap." She straightens and looks up. Long dirty blonde strands of hair fall in her face and she brushes it back with a hand as she meets my eyes. "What can I get for you?"

Damn.

Brown and blue eyes assault me. The left iris is totally blue, and the right nearly all brown with just a hint of blue in the middle dancing around the pupil. I stare at each one individually, back and forth, trying to decide which I like better.

I don't know how long I stare at her multi-colored eyes, but when someone clears their throat behind me, I finally remember why I'm here.

"Yeah. Coffee. Large." I'm incapable of stringing together a sentence, which is definitely new for me. I can talk the panties off anyone. Damn, that chick last night must have really done a number on me.

"Want room for cream and sugar?"

I nod. "Blair working today?"

She sighs. "Not until this afternoon. Sorry, no quotes this morning."

Better to let her assume I just wanted a quote on my cup – something Blair is known for doing when she works at the café, then let her know I really wanted to wipe out the pastry counter on the house.

As she gets my coffee, I take in her slim frame, the leggings that fit snug against her giving me a preview of the terrific ass her apron tries to hide. She's not short, but I'm six foot six so there aren't many people I don't tower over.

When she turns back to me and sets the coffee down in front of me, I decide the best way to shrug off last night's weird sex is to move on to someone new. And this girl, name aside, is perfect.

"What time do you get off work? Can I buy you lunch or coffee?"

Her brows raise. Yeah, coffee was a fuck shit idea, but the only thing I plan on doing is her, so it's just semantics.

"No thanks." She presses a few buttons on the register. "One fifty-eight."

I pass over the money. "Well, how about we exchange numbers and we can make plans when you're not busy."

"I didn't say I was busy. I said no thanks."

The guy behind me clears his throat again.

Look there's no way to not sound like an asshole when I say that girls don't turn me down... like ever, but they don't. Ever.

"You got a boyfriend?"

"Seriously, man. I gotta get going or I'm going to be late for class," the guy behind me says to my back. I turn, prepared to death glare him, but he looks down and his face goes red.

"Coffee?" I hand out the cup I just bought in his direction.

Without lifting his head, he nods but makes no move to take the cup.

"Here." I practically shove the coffee in his hand. "Sorry, but I need more time so unless you want to be late for class, I suggest you take this one and go." I tilt my head in the direction of the door.

Swiping the coffee and running off, the guy hauls ass out of University Hall leaving me alone with Katrina. Shudder. That name. I can't call her that. Kat? Hell no. Trina? Nah, she doesn't seem the type. Rina? Eh.

She makes a little sound somewhere between a scoff and a laugh that sounds like the sweetest purr. I smile. She's not a Kat, she's a cute, playful *Kitty*.

"Where were we, Kitty?" I lean against the counter and she rolls her eyes and crosses both arms against her chest like she's annoyed by the nickname. Too bad the movement only draws more attention to her tits that push out from the contact. She's got a nice rack, bigger than average. When I meet her eyes, I don't miss the heat and a hint of amusement in them. She may not like the words that are coming out of my mouth, but she likes *me*.

"I was trying to blow you off and you weren't taking the hint."

"Just trying to save you from making a huge mistake." I lean in to see if she's bluffing. She is. Her breathing hitches and she stills as if she's holding her breath. I don't know why she's playing hard to get. "And it would be a *huge* mistake."

"You're wasting your time, Joel Moreno. I know all about the carnage you leave behind."

She first and last named me. She's as good as naked.

"Whatever you heard, forget it. The only thing I've left in my path is happy, satisfied women. What's wrong with a little fun? Only live once. Yolo, and all that. How about dinner tonight?"

"Sorry, I'm going to be washing my hair."

"What a coincidence I've got a shower and I'll even let you stay after to use it." My gaze rake over her again. "I think I might need one too after I'm through with you."

She snorts and uncrosses her arms. "No, thanks."

No clue why she's putting me off when I can tell the attraction is mutual. I shrug and push off the counter. Her loss. Although, as I take one last good look at her it feels a little like *my* loss.

2

JOEL

*N*athan plops onto my unmade bed. "Party at Theta house tonight, you in?"

I toss my cell on the bed, ignoring the three text messages from Shelly aka cat girl. "I don't know. Might just stay in."

He raises both eyebrows. "Sick?"

"Nah, just not feeling it."

My roommate leans on one elbow waiting for an explanation. If it were any one of my other roommates, I'd get a pass. Wes is too caught up in Blair and Z operates like a full court press. Only the most aggressive and determined get past his intimidating front – which it totally is. Guy's a teddy bear underneath, just don't tell him I said so.

"You ever go into the café at University Hall?"

"Nah, I don't like coffee. This about Blair?" His face pales and he looks legit nervous. "Please don't tell me you slept with her. Wes will kill you – like actually kill you.

Fuck, it'd be entertaining to see that guy get worked up over something besides basketball, but I'm pretty fond of our pad here. Beats dorm living."

I never had the privilege, and yes, I say that sarcastically, to live in the dorms. Parents live about twenty minutes from the university and when they were convinced I was capable of managing college and ball without flunking out they bought this place just off campus. I glance around my room which is about three times larger than the dorms I've seen. I got the master suite, but all the rooms are big. Everyone calls it The White House. Aside from the obvious, it's white and big, my dad is the university president. Could be worse. They could call it Moreno Hall or some shit.

"There's a chick there named Katrina. Never seen her before."

"I'm sure Blair knows her."

I nod slowly. "Probably. Anyway, I asked her out today."

"Ah, so you've got a date tonight."

A rush of warm air makes my face feel like fire and my throat gets tight. Is this what embarrassment feels like?

"She turned me down."

Motherfucker laughs.

"No shit?" he asks, attempts to keep himself from laughing more. Fails.

"Whatever it was one girl." I walk toward my closet.

"Don't worry, buddy, it was bound to happen eventually. Chicks are weird. Maybe she's on her period."

I survey the shirts in my closet. Grab one, put it back.

Pull another out. I start to put it back but fuck why am I stressing about what to wear?

"You could sound less happy about it," I say as I walk out of the closet. "Besides my average is still waaaay better than yours."

"I think I like you better taken down a notch. What's this girl's name again? I want to buy her a drink."

"Forget it. Forget this whole conversation or I'll tell the guys about the shit you're selling for Frank. They're not stupid, man. Word is gonna get around."

"It's just until I get enough saved up for next year."

"There are other ways to make money." I shoot him a hard look. I feel bad for the guy. I don't know what it's like to not have money, but I know selling drugs is a terrible idea. "You're still keeping that shit out of the house? Don't take us all down with you."

He shakes his head and locks his stare on mine. "I'd never. You know that."

I do, but it's good to hear him say it.

"Alright, let's do this."

"I thought you were staying in." Calling me on my bull-shit, he stands, and I follow him out of my room and downstairs. When we reach the living room, I'm only half-surprised to see Blair here, feet pulled up on the sofa, earbuds in and notebook on her lap.

When she sees us she pulls one bud free. "Hey."

"Where's Wes?" Nathan asks as he takes a seat in a lounger.

Blair shrugs, but Z enters from the direction of the

kitchen, protein drink in hand, and says, "He was checking in with PT."

He shakes the cup in his hand reminding me I need to grab something to eat before we hit the party. And make sure Nathan does. Guy has a tendency to skip meals when we don't have food in the house. My mom knows this and tries to keep us stocked, but that's a near impossible feat. Z alone eats enough to feed a family of four. He's a big guy even by athlete standards which means he takes in a lot of extra calories to keep on the muscle he carries. We're close to the same height, but Z is built like a cross between a linebacker and bodybuilder.

"Blair, what do you think of this shirt?"

She looks to each of the guys, who chuckle, before answering. "Umm. It's fine."

"Fuck. I should change, right?"

Their continued laughter is the only response. Nathan tosses me a basketball. He doesn't say anything, but I read the "chill the fuck out" written on his face.

But I can't. Katrina knocked me off my game.

I palm the ball for comfort and look back to Blair. "Well?"

She sits forward and gives me a slow once-over. "Turn."

"Excuse me?"

She motions with her finger for me to spin. Fuck me.

Not letting go of the basketball, I turn with arms held out.

Wes' voice is amused when he walks in and asks, "What the hell is going on in here? A fashion show?"

I toss the ball at his head and then regret it immediately because now I'm just a dude standing in the middle of the room twirling.

"Blair is helping me pick a shirt for tonight."

"Why the obsession over attire tonight?" he asks as he takes a seat next to Blair.

"He struck out getting a number this afternoon and is now all bent out of shape." I shoot Nathan a glare that reminds him I've got dirt on him. It's too late though. My rejection is out there.

"Aww, you poor, poor schmuck," Wes says, not sounding the least bit sorry.

"That isn't what this is about. It was one girl. One girl." I jab my finger in the air for emphasis. "Fuck you all." I don't have enough fingers to count their rejections. I look down at my shirt and pants and then decide to roll the sleeves. It's nice out. "So, this one is good?"

Blair bobs her head enthusiastically this time. "You look hot. Black is a good color for you. It gives you the whole dark and mysterious thing with your skin tone and dark hair."

"Easy, now." Wes sounds jealous and that makes me happier than I've been all afternoon.

I shoot her a wink. "*Muchas gracias, linda.*"

"Yeah, definitely do that." Her eyes light up.

"Do what?"

"Talk in Spanish. Not all the time. . . but drop it in casually. Accents are sexy."

Flash her a smile in appreciation for the tidbit. She's

not the first girl to tell me that, but I guess I'd sort of forgotten. Been using my jock and overall God's-gift-to-women status to pick up chicks and now I've got no game when it counts.

Blair and Wes make plans to see a local baseball game later tonight, which makes me question his idea of romance but then she looks at him all heart eyes so what the hell do I know? She says her goodbyes to the group, off to do some studying or something else super boring. I wait until the door is closed behind her before taking an opportunity to point the jabs at someone else.

"Soo. . ." I ask innocently. "You and Blair. . . things getting serious?"

Wes' face pales. "What? No, it's just. . ."

"If you're having sex, then it's getting serious. You wouldn't be mixing business with pleasure unless it's serious." Wes hasn't dated as long as I've known him, and random hookups have been few and far between. He likes Blair. Not sure why he can't admit it. We all know.

"I'm not mixing—you know what? I'm not even gonna go there." He looks like he's going to be physically sick. Well shit, he hasn't boned her.

"Wait, wait, wait. You haven't slept with her?"

"Is that really so ludicrous? I've only known her a few weeks."

"Uh-huh. Uh-huh." I'm not sure why I'm suddenly feeling hopeful and romantic that these two are going to hook up, but I am straight giddy at the prospect. "So, does that mean tonight is the night?"

"We're going to a high school baseball game, not looking to do jail time for indecent exposure," Wes throws back. I'm not buying it. Lame excuse.

"Don't bullshit me. Tonight's the night."

"She completes you," Nathan adds. We just watched *Jerry Maguire* a few weeks ago in Z's quest to see every single one of Tom Cruise's movies.

"Fuck off, both of you." Wes tosses the ball from hand to hand.

"I gotta shower," Nathan announces.

"Hurry up. I'm leaving in fifteen, and I need to make a stop for condoms." I look to Wes. "You good? Need me to put some in your nightstand?"

He throws the ball back to me.

"Okay, fine. I'll lay off. You probably need to go take care of business anyway. Since she bailed on dinner, you have time to rub one out before and after your shower."

"For the love of all that is holy," he whines.

"What? Please tell me you aren't planning to show up to the game without clearing your head? Dude, you go in there without taking care of business, and you're gonna embarrass yourself and the whole male population."

He shakes his head and lets it hang down.

"What the hell is wrong with you?" I mean honestly, the dude doesn't get laid in months and he's just gonna show up fully loaded? He'll be coming in his pants by the time he gets her clothes off. Rookie move.

He stands and ambles toward the stairs.

"You know I'm right," I call after him. He doesn't look

convinced. I pull my phone from my back pocket and set an alarm for later tonight. Good thing for him, I take orgasms – even when they're not mine – very seriously. I'll text him later to make sure he heeded my advice.

In fact, I'd be doing the same thing if I hadn't already jerked myself raw trying to work Kitty out of my system. Those blue and brown eyes haunted me as I came so hard, I saw stars. Twice. Even picturing her now I can feel myself getting hard again. The fact that Kitty not only said no but did so with such disdain has gotta be why just the thought of her has my pulse racing and a smile spreading across my face.

Blow out a breath and pull up my text history. One hot girl is the same as any other – at least for what I'm looking for. I don't do romantic gestures or long walks on the beach. Well, unless by long walks you mean sex. Sex on the beach is awesome.

While I wait for Nathan, I scroll through the chicks that have messaged me about hooking up tonight. They said hang out, but every time a girl texts me to "hang out" it ends with her undressing me. Chicks don't like to come right out and ask for sex.

Busty blonde? Sassy redhead? Freshman good girl looking to break out of her quiet shell? The options are endless, but I am bored.

"Knock, knock," my sister's voice calls out from the back entrance.

I hurry to greet her. The smell wafting out of the casserole dish she's carrying makes my stomach growl.

"That smells amazing," I say, taking it from her and pulling the foil back.

I grab a fork and plate, give myself a generous serving, take a bite, and then look up.

"Game night?" I ask around a mouth full of pasta and point my fork toward her green Valley High t-shirt and matching green pawprint painted on her cheek.

"Playing Pinnacle tonight. They're even bigger and meaner than last year."

"Go easy on them," I say with humor lacing my tone because even from the stands, Michelle is a force. She is the definition of crazed fan, razzing players and coaches alike. She loves watching basketball maybe as much as I love playing it. And she does it with as much flair as I do.

"Hey," Nathan calls out entering the kitchen and pulling a clean shirt over his head. "Good to see you, Smelly."

Michelle rolls her eyes. She hates that my friends have adopted my childhood nickname for her. She's at that age where she wants everyone to think she's mature and capable instead of the sixteen-year-old naïve kid that she is.

I push a plate and fork in front of Nathan, and he helps himself to the food.

"What are you two up to tonight?" Michelle asks, pulling a beer from the fridge, popping the top and taking a long pull.

"Give me that." I take the beer for myself. "Want one?" I ask Nathan.

"Theta party tonight," Nathan answers for us and shakes off the beer.

"Just the two of you?" She motions between us with a frown. "Aren't you supposed to take dates or something?"

Ah, innocent Michelle.

"Joel tried and got shot down."

They laugh and I shoot them both a glare.

Michelle studies me. "Wow, someone actually turned down the great Joel Moreno. What happened? How'd you ask her?"

"Uhh. I just asked if I could get her number so we could hang later." I shrug. "She said no."

Let me tell ya, talking about it *again* is not making me feel super.

My sister groans in exasperation. "Wow. It finally happened."

"What's that?" I question, sure I'm going to regret asking.

"Your ego got so big you forgot how to put in the effort to ask a girl out the right way."

"Oh, shiiit." Nathan covers his mouth, but it doesn't hide the huge ass grin on his face.

"I mean, did you put any thought into it at all or did you just wing it and expect her to fall at your feet?"

Nathan doubles over with laughter. Glad he's amused.

Regarding me seriously, Michelle's voice is full of sympathy. "Not every girl is a lying, backstabbing, no good cu–"

"Alright, I think it's time for you to go," I say, screw my

eyelids shut and hope I've cut off her rant for good. The fact that my baby sister knows just how badly relationships can blow up in your face is all on me. But at least it doesn't seem to have made her any less of a romantic.

She laughs softly and I open my eyes and sigh in relief as she heads toward the door. Thank God. "I hope your bruised ego won't affect the game this weekend," she adds, waves, and disappears.

"She has a point," Nathan says. "I mean, when's the last time someone made you do more than ask nicely before they were volunteering to bounce on your penis?"

"Work for it," I say, mostly to myself. Sadly, the thought hadn't even occurred to me. Damn. Well, challenge accepted. I mean, honestly, how hard could it be to convince a girl I *know* already wants me, to go out with me?

3

JOEL

Present Day

The sound of an incoming text is my second alarm of the day. The first came five minutes ago when Z pounded on every door of our house.

The second, though, always comes precisely at five thirty in the form of a text. Specifically, a meme. Nathan loves them. Hand to God the guy sends me like ten a day. He must spend a good portion of his free time combing through Imgur to find the best ones. They're funny as shit so I don't tell him to stop even though ten texts a day from another dude is a bit much.

Slide my finger over the screen and tap on the text. Squinting through the bright light of my phone, I kick off the blanket and prop a hand behind my head. The meme reads "How do I sleep at night knowing I'm an asshole?" The white words are on a plain black background. Disappointment flickers because I prefer funny pictures to a wall of text, but I keep reading anyway. "Butt-ass naked with the fan on."

This earns a gruff chuckle and I snap a picture of my junk, angled so the black fan beside my bed is visible. Dude knows me too well. I hit send and jump out of bed. Pull on boxer briefs, shorts, and a shirt. I brush my teeth while I piss – multitasking like a pro. Once I've finished in the bathroom, I grab socks and shoes and pad downstairs. The rest of the guys are already in the kitchen eating breakfast. Z is the only one that's sitting. His big frame is seated at the dining room table with a plate and glass in front of him – using manners the rest of us reserve for mixed company. By some unspoken agreement we take turns making breakfast and by the slightly burnt toast splayed out on the counter with various condiments – butter, jelly, Nutella, and peanut butter, I know this is Wes' doing.

"Breakfast is served," Wes says as he pulls four more slices of blackened bread out of the toaster and drops them on the counter. Then he grabs a hand full of butter knives out of our silverware drawer and sets them beside it.

"Coming to practice today?" I ask, and daggers are shot in my direction from everyone but the man I'm talking to.

A grunt and head nod are my answer. After a season-ending injury, the senior point man just recently started coming back to practice. It's damn good to have him back, if only on the sidelines. Not the same without him on the court with us, though.

I pull on my socks and shoes, then grab a cup and fill it with water. Dump a scoop of protein powder in it and mix with a knife because that's what's out on the counter for the toast.

I raise the cup to my mouth just as Nathan steps beside me, grabbing another piece of toast as he shoves what's left of his last piece in his mouth.

"Dude, don't you know every time you send a dick pic it shrinks by an eighth of an inch?" he says, mouth still full. Then he proceeds to slap my junk. I groan instinctively before the pain even registers. Spill my drink down my shirt and onto the floor. "That's for the visual of your small prick I can't get out of my head."

"Not cool," I grit out. "So not cool."

I cup my balls through my shorts and give them a protective squeeze. "The opportunity was too good, man. And if my dick is small then yours is microscopic."

"Time to go," Z says as he stands and takes his dirty dishes to the sink.

I grab two pieces of dry toast for the walk over and guzzle what's left of my protein drink. Wipe the back of my hand over my mouth and follow the boys out the door.

It's quiet out. Early, dark, and cold. We move at a clip across the street to Ray Fieldhouse where we practice, workout, and play games. It's my favorite place on all of campus. The fact that it doesn't have my last name plastered all over it is a definite bonus.

Might be a new semester, but we're deep in the season. Final Four is less than two months away and everyone is feeling the pressure and excitement. Coach Daniels doesn't need to yell at us about being lazy or sloppy, although he does, because we're as hard on ourselves as he is. We want this. Maybe more than ever now that we've seen Wes go out with an injury.

We practice for two hours before classes and then most evenings we're back in the gym for workouts or drills. We've got a big game on Sunday, so today's practice is particularly grueling. Shooting drills, one-on-one maneuvers, full-court press scrimmage, conditioning, and then more shooting drills. By the time we're done I'm almost looking forward to class just so I can sit and relax.

Walking into the locker room for a quick shower before I head out, I pause as Coach yells out from his open office door, "Moreno, see me before you leave."

I lift my head in acknowledgment. After I'm showered and changed, I stop in Coach's office as requested.

"What's up?" I slouch into the chair on the opposite side of his desk and grab two granola bars from my bag. These things are worthless. I'd need to eat like twelve to satisfy my hunger, but two is all I have left. Need to tell my mom, the saint who keeps our pantry stocked, to get something more substantial next time for snacks.

Coach stares down at his phone, a mixture of confusion and excitement in the way his mouth curves into a smile but his eyes scrunch together. "One second."

I'm amused as he proceeds to make me fucking wait while he's lost to whatever he's got going on.

I give in and comment on his weird actions when the

man actually snickers at the ping of an incoming message. "Sexting during office hours?"

It takes a moment before he lifts his head and meets my gaze. "Sorry, what?"

"Nothing. You wanted to see me?" I lift a hand for him to get to the point.

He sets the phone on the desk and then leans back in his chair. "Right. I want to switch things up a little bit on Sunday and have you up top of the zone instead of in the back. Shaw is still finding his place and we're going to have to play the ball more aggressively if we want to rattle them."

Makes sense. I'm taller and faster than the other options and Z is a beast down low.

"All right. Anything else?"

His phone pings again and he glances down before answering. "Yeah, what about local restaurant suggestions? Something nice but not too pretentious."

I feel my left eyebrow arch up in question. "Team dinner?"

"Uhh. No." He shakes his head. "Just thought you might know somewhere good. Since moving to Valley five years ago most of my dining out has included In-N-Out I'm afraid."

"We talking restaurants of the romantic variety?"

The embarrassment that spreads across his features throws me off. Coach Daniels is not the kind of guy I expected to be looking for dating tips. "I said nice, not romantic."

"When it comes to dining, those two things are synony-mous." I decide to put him out of his misery. "Araceli's. It's got great views, good menu, but it's not over the top."

"Araceli's," he repeats the name back slowly like he's trying to remember it.

I toss the granola bar wrappers in the trash and pull my phone out. "I'm texting you the details. Shouldn't need a reservation on a Thursday, but if you have any problems, just tell them you're a friend and you want my table on the patio."

"*Your* table on the patio?"

"I have a standing Thursday night reservation."

He cocks his head to the side looking at me like the twenty-one-year-old kid he thinks I am.

"You better hope tonight isn't the night I finally need it." I stand and grin leaving him before he can ask me more.

4

KATRINA

I was never particularly fond of mornings. Looking back that seems ridiculous. I mean how hard was it to get only myself up and out the door? Mornings now, though, are torture. Someone should warn you before having kids that getting up before the sun lasts way beyond the baby years. And those little Energizer Bunnies don't understand the concept of not speaking until you've had a cup of coffee.

Nope, Christian barreled into my room before the sun even thought about rising and he's been going nonstop ever since, chattering away all the while.

"Christian, we're leaving in two minutes." I don't know why I give him a warning like that's somehow going to hurry him up. My three-year-old son has no concept of time.

I grab my books and laptop and shove them in my backpack running through a mental checklist making sure

I have everything for school, and he has what he needs for a weekend with his dad.

"Don't forget to grab your soccer ball in case you guys go to the park." Highly unlikely but if he takes the ball, there's at least some chance that Victor will feel obligated to spend some time with his son. I'm so far beyond subtle manipulation at this point.

"Alright let's load up." I heave my backpack on my shoulder and grab the soccer ball that I spot laying on the living room floor. I mean honestly it isn't like I wasn't going to have to carry it anyway.

Christian comes running out of his room, messy blonde hair and a smile that doesn't understand his mother isn't a morning person. "I need to pack some treats for Rex!"

"Already done. They're in your backpack. Did you brush your teeth?"

Instead of answering he looks up like he's trying to remember that far back. That's a no.

"Come on, let's brush them real quick." I put my backpack and the soccer ball back down and he skips off down the hallway. I follow behind, picking up toys and dirty clothes in his path. I can hear the faucet turn on and then the unmistakable sound of him karate chopping the water with his toothbrush. I resist raising my voice, it doesn't do any good, but gently correct him as I enter the bathroom. "No playing in the water. It makes a mess, remember?"

"It's just water. It'll dry."

Fair point.

Wordlessly I help him brush his teeth, clean up the water with his bath towel, and then I grab my stuff again. It usually takes two or three tries to get out the door. I plan for this by adding a fifteen-minute buffer.

"Do you think Grandma Nadine will let Rex sleep in my room this time?" Christian asks as I head for the door, hopeful this time we'll make it to the other side.

I bite back a smile at how much he loves that silly dog. I'm pretty sure she bought it just for Christian, but hard ass Nadine would never admit it. Christian loves animals. Always has, but it became a full-blown obsession sometime over the last year. We can't have pets in our apartment building, but even if we could, there's no way I could give a dog the kind of attention it deserves.

"You can ask her when we get there, okay?"

He nods excitedly.

"Daddy is coming down late tonight, so you'll get to see him this weekend too."

He races back to his room for a toy he *has* to take. I feel bad that he's more excited to see the dog than his dad, but in his defense, the dog is far more reliable.

It's less than an hour drive to my hometown where Victor's parents, and my own, still live. When we arrive at Nadine's house, she's coming out the front door, Rex at her heels, before I can get Christian out of his car seat.

"There's my favorite grandson."

"Grandpa told me I'm your *only* grandson."

"Did he?" She puts on her best fake disbelieving voice. "Well, that makes you even more special then, doesn't it?"

She manages to get a quick hug before he wiggles out of her grasp and starts to chase Rex around the front of the house.

"Stay away from the road, buddy," I call as I grab his suitcase and hand it to Nadine.

"Thank you."

She waves me off. "Don't need to thank me for watching my own grandson. We love having him here."

And I know she does, but still, I'm thankful for the role she's played in Christian's life.

"The feeling is mutual," I say as I watch my son run around carefree and happy. Kids are resilient. That's what the doctor told me when I'd asked how being raised primarily by one parent would impact him.

Victor, Christian's father, makes it down for a weekend about once a month to see him. As far as my son is concerned this is normal, he hasn't gotten to the age where he compares his situation to others, but I know it's coming. He's in daycare and started preschool last fall and though he's seen a diverse group of kids from all sorts of families, eventually my son is going to ask me the hard questions about his father.

Still, Nadine takes him every other weekend, even when Victor doesn't come down, and she's gone above and beyond what I could have imagined. The woman wasn't my biggest fan when she found out that Victor knocked me up, but she's never held that against her grandson.

"Congratulations on your play." My gaze shoots up to

hers in surprise. "I saw your mother at the grocery store. She's very proud."

"Thank you."

She nods, and we stand there awkwardly.

"You want me to come get him on Sunday?" I offer.

"Nonsense. Bill and I will drive him back after Victor leaves, like we always do." She huffs like my offering is the real imposition. "And besides, Christian likes to go to that pancake place in Valley so we'll take him for pancakes and then drop him off after. Unless you'd like to join?"

That pancake place is IHOP, but she refuses to call it by name, another Nadine quirk. I mull over her invite. I never know if the correct answer is yes or no. We have a decent relationship, but I don't want to intrude on her time. Christian races by me and I grab hold of him to hug him before I leave. "I think I'll leave the pancake party to you guys."

He bounces at my side. "Are we going to IHOP?"

Oops. I shoot her an apologetic look.

"Not until Sunday, but if you go inside, you'll find blueberry muffins waiting for you. Say goodbye to your mom first."

She takes a few steps toward the house to allow us to say our goodbyes.

"You be good for Grandma and Grandpa, okay?"

He nods once, but his eyes are already darting toward Rex. "Hey, look at me." He does, albeit reluctantly. "I mean it. Listen to Grandma and promise me you'll have lots of fun with Daddy when he gets here, okay? You can show him your new soccer skills."

"What about you? You won't have any fun without me around."

My chest hurts at the idea he worries about me while he's supposed to be having fun with his dad. "I promise to try if you do, deal?"

He smiles and bobs his head, and I step back. "I love you. See you on Sunday."

"Bye," he calls out as he runs toward the house. "Loooove you."

I watch him disappear into the house before I get in the car, already missing him. I know the time he spends with his father and grandparents is good for him, but it makes for a long weekend for me.

The only silver lining? It's Thursday, my favorite day of the week.

5

KATRINA

I work at the campus café twice a week – Tuesdays and Thursdays. With my scholarships and some student loans to help cover the remaining of our living expenses, it's enough money to cover the necessities without keeping me away from Christian at night. And honestly, I like the time to myself. Especially Thursdays.

At exactly ten fifty-three he walks through the door into University Hall. Every Thursday is the same and every Thursday I wait eagerly. His eyes find mine and a cocksure smile lifts the corners of his stunning mouth. His confident stride is long but unhurried.

I don't allow myself to ogle his body because that would be giving in to the battle of wills we've been engaging in for months. But I know what I'd see if I did.

Black hair, light brown skin, a lean but muscular body that he covers in clothes that hug his body and look like they've been selected by a freaking stylist.

He's always somehow totally put together and still manages to exude masculinity and panty melting prowess. It's not fair for a guy to look so effortlessly handsome.

Joel Moreno. Valley basketball player – actually, scratch the first two words – he's just an all-around player. And I can't even blame him. If I were a guy and I looked like that, I'd be sleeping my way through coeds too.

What I wouldn't give. I resist making that "mm-*hmm*" noise guys make when they see a girl that they think is super hot. That noise is exactly how I feel.

Look, I haven't had sex in four years.

That's right. Four years. Oh, and the last time I had sex, I got pregnant. Good times. That'll make you trigger happy. And leave you with a present that scares off guys in their twenties forever after.

I give in and meet his gaze which I regret immediately because his grin grows impossibly wider and mocking. I don't have to look around to know every eye in University Hall has turned in his direction. He's a magnet.

I straighten behind the counter of the university café and busy my hands by retying the blue apron around my waist. My body overheats as he walks closer. Even if I were blind, I think his presence would fire every neuron in my brain and alert me to the danger. Because that's exactly what this guy is – dangerous.

He doesn't say a word as he steps up to the register and places a hand on the counter.

Looking at his chin, I say, "Hi, what can I get for you?"

"Ah, don't be like that Kitty, you know how I like it."

Always Kitty, never Katrina or even Kat. The nickname should rankle. It *should*, but it doesn't. There's something about the way he says it like he knows it's ridiculous and he just wants to get a rise out of me.

When I don't acknowledge his comment – and yes, I know exactly how he likes it – tall, cream, two sugars, and a side of tits and ass to go, he speaks his order, "Tall house roast with cream and two sugars."

Wordlessly I grab a cup and fill it with coffee, leaving an inch for the creamer and sugar I add next. I know he's staring at me as I complete the task and I know when I turn around it'll be appreciation I see in his eyes. That look gets me through the week.

When I turn, his dark eyes lift slowly until he's studying my face.

"Anything else?"

"How about dinner tonight, Kitty?"

Direct and to the point. Interesting approach. I've gotta give it to him he's been far more persistent than I ever predicted. My heart thumps rapidly against my brain's better judgment. My body sings, but I lift one shoulder noncommittally. "Sorry, not interested."

We play this game every week. He hits on me and I turn him down. He thinks we're playing the longest game of hard-to-get ever.

We're not.

Or, I'm not anyway. I have no intention of being had. The pickup attempts, which I actually sort of love, will never be good enough. I mean if things were different, I probably would have pulled him over the register the first time we spoke. Being with Joel would be fun and crazy hot, I'm sure. But things aren't different. I'm not the kind of girl that Joel Moreno dates, if he seriously dated at all. Casual seems to be all he's interested in and my life is scheduled, routine, and doesn't exactly lend itself to quickies in the stock room.

But for two minutes every Thursday, I get to pretend I'm just a regular college girl flirting with the most popular guy on campus. And I'd be lying if I said I don't also indulge in a little harmless daydreaming about what those quickies in stock rooms, bathrooms, alleyways (hey, they're fantasy) might be like.

I'm not sure why he keeps coming back when I've given him no indication I'm going to change my mind, but I think at this point he just wants to prove he can have any woman he wants. He's clearly not used to rejection.

He probably thinks I'm making this a challenge for sport's sake, but if he really stepped back and thought about it, he'd realize that he doesn't even really want me to say yes. Maybe he's already figured that out. He never pushes – never asks me twice or calls me out on my lame excuses. Subconsciously, I think he looks forward to me shooting him down every week.

I'm quite possibly the last loosely hanging thread that holds his ego in check. The next time he's banging some lucky girl he's going to do so with a satisfaction that couldn't be found if he didn't have my weekly 'no' to ground him to the possibility of rejection. When you win all the time, the game isn't fun. I'm the pesky loss each week that makes him work harder and appreciate the wins all that much more.

My legacy at Valley U may very well be the motivation that urged Joel Moreno to win over every other girl on campus. You're welcome, ladies.

With a nod, he hands over his credit card for the coffee. I take my time, drawing out the process to delay his departure.

"See ya next week."

As he walks away, I finally take him in – every gorgeous inch – and I let myself believe it's all real. That he really did ask me out hoping I'd say yes and that he's going to spend the next six days mulling over how to break me down. I want him to fantasize about me the same way I fantasize about him. That's all he can ever be. All I can be to him. I'm okay with that. Fantasy is almost always better than reality and Joel Moreno is my perfect fantasy. Why mess with that?

After my morning shift at the café, I sprint across campus to Adams Theater. It's the first day of rehearsals for the spring play. Every semester the screenwriting department teams up with the theater department to put on an original performance written and performed entirely by students for a Spring Showcase. This year is the first time a junior's play has ever been selected. My original play, The Tragic Love Story of Hector and Imelda will be performed in just a few months and I'm so nervous I feel like I'm going to throw up any time I stand still long enough to think about it. Which is thankfully not often.

My advisor, Professor Morrison, the screenwriting department head, is standing just inside and greets me. "Katrina, I was just talking about you. Meet Brody Bradley."

Brody Bradley. His tongue twister of a name works because he's the kind of guy that couldn't possibly have a normal name. Someday he'll be on Broadway or starring in an Oscar-nominated movie and crowds will go wild for him.

"Nice to meet you." I shift my backpack up higher on my shoulder and offer my hand.

"Brody here is going to be your Hector."

My Hector.

Anxiety on high, I shiver when his big hand encloses mine and bright green eyes take me in. If I hadn't seen him perform, I'd be worried. His personality is big and charming – loud. Nothing like Hector's understated appeal. But I've seen Brody pull off crazier. Last semester he played the phantom in a re-telling of *The Phantom of the Opera* and brought me, and the rest of a sold-out show, to tears.

"I'll leave you two to chat. Excuse me." Professor Morrison places a hand at his waist in an almost bow-like gesture and steps away from us.

"So, you're the screenwriter huh?"

"Aspiring. Yeah."

"Not aspiring anymore. I've read the script, it's good. I'm really excited about it."

"You are?"

One side of his mouth lifts and he cocks his head to the side like he's trying to figure me out. "Of course. Come on, let me introduce you to everyone else."

The next hour is a whirlwind as Brody introduces me to the entire theater department. Faces I've admired and some others that work behind the scenes. I'm awe-stricken and totally inspired. And the smile on my face is large and genuine when I exchange numbers with Brody and Tabitha who is playing Imelda.

"A bunch of us usually go out Friday night after rehearsals," Tabitha tosses out as we're leaving. "You in?"

"Oh, I..." My voice trails off as I reach for an excuse and realize I have none. The few times I've been invited out to parties I've had to say no because of Christian. We don't have family in Valley so that means no mom's nights out unless there's daycare provided. That's not something you see listed on the campus bulletin board.

But there's no Christian this weekend and Tabitha looks at me with such contagious excitement at the prospect of hanging out. I surprise myself by saying, "That sounds fun."

And it does.

6

KATRINA

I sit at the front of the stage with my notebook in my lap and the printed script in front of me. Brody and Tabitha are running through the opening scene where Hector and Imelda meet at the Día de los Muertos, or the Day of the Dead. It's a nod to the movie Coco, where my inspiration emerged, but I also chose it because I knew how beautiful the stage could look lit up with fake candlelight as the backdrop to the start of an epic love story.

The stage crew is working on the creation of the large canvas that will eventually be painted and have lights strung through it and it's already more beautiful than I ever could have imagined.

"It needs something."

I glance over at Willa's words to find her studying the stage intently, playing with her lip piercing. She continues, "I'm not getting the historical or the Mexico vibe."

My stomach drops at her words, which were said

kindly but don't make me panic any less. She nudges me with her elbow. "Hey, it's a great story and it's going to be amazing. I'm sure the costumes and props will bring it all together."

I sigh. "No, you're right. It feels contemporary and American because that's what I know."

"What made you decide to write a historical play anyway?"

Bite the corner of my lip and wonder the same thing but don't say it out loud. I can only shrug. Honestly it wasn't intentional. I never dreamed it'd be so difficult to translate the culture and time of Mexico in the early 1900s. Apparently a lot was going on in Mexico, the whole world actually, that I failed to consider.

"What we need to do is research." She claps her hands together. "Ooooh, let's plan a trip to Cabo. We can get a tan and ask around about history and whatever."

I smile at her wide-eyed excitement. Willa writes the most beautiful and insightful words, primarily poetry and short stories, but she talks like a nineties valley girl which makes me laugh. I adore her.

She's also probably the closest thing I have to a college friend. We're in all the same classes and are both part of a critique group that meets once a week to share our writing and bounce ideas off one another. Her enthusiasm and creativity make her a great critique and brainstorming partner, but I wonder how she's able to put her thoughts on paper so poetically when she ends sentences with things like "and whatever."

"I think I'm gonna have to solve this problem from Valley, but that's not a bad idea. Maybe we can chat with the Spanish department and see if they have some recommendations. In the meantime, I need to work on the ending. I can't figure out the last scene where Imelda receives the last letter from Hector a month after his death."

I bring the end of my pen to my mouth as I try to visualize it. I want it to be perfect.

When rehearsal is over, Tabitha bounds down from the stage.

"Hey, Katrina, you still in for tonight?" Her gaze flits over to Willa. "Hi, I'm Tabitha."

"Sorry. Tabitha this is Willa, she's a screenwriting major too."

"Well, you both should come out tonight. I just need to swing by my place and change."

Willa stands. "I'm out. I've gotta work tonight."

"Katrina?"

"Oh, I..."

Willa nudges me. "Go. You have to go."

She's right, but I'm suddenly more nervous than I anticipated. "Okay, yeah, I'm in."

Willa's excitement is far greater than mine as we pack up and follow Tabitha out of the theater. She knows how seldom I go out and I'm sure Monday I'll be under intense scrutiny to get every detail.

"Have fun. Get drunk, kiss boys or girls... just kiss

someone." She purses her dark purple lips and kisses the air.

"I really don't think that's going to happen." I huff a nervous laugh, but the excitement of the unknown makes butterflies dance in my stomach.

"See you later." Willa waves. "Nice to meet you, Tabitha."

Tabitha returns the wave and then turns to me. "Why don't you follow me to my place and we can pre-game and then catch a ride with Brody to the party. He takes longer to get ready than anyone I know so we should have plenty of time for a drink or two."

This slightly embarrassing dirt on Brody somehow puts me at ease and a drink before walking into my first college party sounds great.

Tabitha's apartment is just a few blocks from campus. It's smaller than the place I rent for me and Christian, but I'm still jealous as I take in her cute décor – white couch, light pink throw pillows. The thought of a white couch anywhere near my son makes me cringe. And the toys and kid stuff that always seems to make its way to the living room no matter how many times I tell him to put it in his room doesn't make for a very chic space.

"What do you want to drink? I've got wine, tequila, vodka, rum, a bunch of mixers."

"Whatever you're having is fine. I just need to make a phone call real quick."

"You're not bailing on me already, are you?"

I shake my head. "I have to call and check in on my son."

"Get out, you have a kid?"

"Yep," I say, and she doesn't look surprised or weirded out, anything really. Just accepting. "A son, Christian. He's three."

"Well, call him, do what you need to do. I'm going to pour us two very strong glasses of rum and diet."

She pours the drinks as I settle on to her couch. Dropping my glass down on the side table, she carries hers toward an open door I assume leads to her bedroom. "I'm gonna change. Holler when you're done. I want to hear your story, Katrina Phillips."

I take a small sip of the rum and diet. I can't remember if I've had rum before, but I'm pleased to discover I don't hate it. Pressing send, I take a larger gulp hoping it'll ease my nerves. Nadine answers on the second ring. "Hi, Katrina. Christian was just asking about you. Well, you know before he darted off to the next thing that caught his attention."

"He was?" I smile into the phone. "How's he been?"

"Busy. Just like his father always was. I always used to tell Victor I hoped someday he'd have a kid as busy as him. 'Course I assumed he'd be around to raise him.'"

She goes quiet which is more alarming than her rant.

"Victor isn't there? I thought he was coming down tonight."

She sighs, and I breathe through my nose and let it out slowly trying to erase the irritation I feel. "He had a slight change of plans, but he'll be here tomorrow. Christian's out back with Bill filling the bird feeders. You want me to call him in to talk?"

"No, that's alright. Can you just tell him goodnight and I love him and that I'll call him first thing tomorrow morning?"

"You don't want him to call before bed?"

"Well actually I'm just getting ready to go out with a friend so I'm not sure..." I know it's not the same, but suddenly I feel like Christian has had two parents flake on him tonight. "Actually, yes, have him call me."

"How about I have him call first thing in the morning instead? He really should be getting to bed."

"Oh. Okay. Yeah, that's fine."

"Enjoy your night, Katrina," she says, and I think it's pity I hear in her voice.

We say our goodbyes and I toss my phone into my purse as if it's some symbol of the responsibilities of my real life.

Tabitha is in her room holding up two dresses when I walk in. "What do you think?" She moves the one in her right hand in front of her. "Little black dress?"

It's a simple dress – short, low cut. It's more barely-there-dress that just so happens to be black, but with Tabitha's long legs and tiny waist, I have no doubt she could pull it off.

"Or the pink?" The way she practically squeals with excitement I can tell which she prefers. And when she holds it up to her face, it compliments her pale skin tone and auburn hair. She's like a hotter coed version of Molly Ringwald in *Pretty in Pink*.

"That one," I say and then steal a glance down at my outfit. I'd opted for an off the shoulder top, leggings, and boots. I look good but next to Tabitha I'm better prepared to teach preschoolers than go to a college party. "I suddenly feel really underdressed."

She holds the black dress out to me. "It's all yours. I mean, you already look hot. You always do. I've seen you a few times around campus and in the café, you're always so put together."

In this case, I think put together means doesn't show enough skin.

Tabitha was right about Brody and we've already finished our second drink and I've told her more about my life than anyone but Willa before he texts that he's on his way. She makes one more attempt to get me in the skimpy dress. "Last chance."

"I don't think so."

She rolls her eyes dramatically. "You might as well make tonight count. If it's going to take another three years to get you out for a night..."

"It's only been a year," I say as I laugh. "Willa took me to a local poetry reading and mixer."

"Oooh so wild," Tabitha mocks, but her tone is playful.

"Alright, fine. I will wear the dress but promise you won't leave my side. I have a feeling I'm going to feel very exposed."

She grins victoriously. "I promise not to leave your side,

but that's only because if I stand next to you, there's a slight chance guys might notice me after they're through checking you out."

When Brody finally arrives, we giggle our way to the curb and pile into his beat-up station wagon. It's a good thing Brody is such a popular guy because this car would not score him any points with the ladies. Not that mine, covered in crumbs that I can never seem to vacuum up and complete with car seat, would pass as cool.

"Katrina, wow." Brody's eyebrows shoot up as he sees me. "You look... wow."

"Not too naked?" I ask with a nervous laugh.

"Is that a trick question?" His smile is reassuring. "You look great."

"Where are we going anyway?" I ask from the back seat while Tabitha and Brody fight over the radio.

"Jock central." Tabitha claps her hands and turns back to me. "Baseball guys are having a party tonight and their parties always attract the other teams on campus."

"Their record is shit, but they're good guys and they're cool with everyone, so their parties are always awesome. You been?"

I shake my head and take deep breaths hoping that'll calm my rapidly beating heart.

I see people walking toward the party before I see the house itself. It sits just up the street and across the road from the baseball field which makes sense although I hadn't given it much thought before.

Brody parks along a side street and kills the engine.

Confused butterflies that flutter with excitement and then nose dive with intermittent anxiety rid me of any remaining false calm from the alcohol. I follow along silently as we walk up to the baseball house in a steady stream of people. I'm doing it. Only took three years but I'm finally attending a real college party. The thought of beer in a plastic cup never sounded more appealing.

No one seems to look at me funny, so I take that as my fitting in. But where they're all moving with purpose and ease like they've done it a million times, I'm hesitant and watch Brody and Tabitha closely to mimic their movements.

We walk through a living room and into a small kitchen that has liquor bottles lined up on a counter with cups and mixers. I spot the silver barrel and do a little mental happy dance at seeing my first keg in action. I watch a group of guys huddled around laughing and taking turns pouring beer from the metal drum.

I accept the cup Brody pushes in my direction as he says, "Pick your poison."

Tabitha eyes the bottles carefully before pointing at the rum. "I'm not mixing my alcohol tonight."

Brody hands her the bottle. "I'm gonna take a lap, see who's here before I commit to a drink for the night."

He walks off as Tabitha pours rum and diet into her cup. "What about you Katrina?" She stops. "You go by anything else? Kat? Trina?"

I lift a shoulder and let it fall as I shake my head. When

I was younger, friends tried to call me different things, but nothing ever stuck.

"Nicknames?"

The only one that comes to mind is...

"Kitty." His voice, *that* voice, it's husky yet smooth and when he says my nickname, the ridiculous nickname that makes my body tingle, it feels like a brand.

7

JOEL

"Kitty." Her name is out before my brain fully acknowledges it's her.

You could knock me over with a feather. Maybe it's one of those weird dissonance things where your mind fails to associate a person outside of the usual place you see them or maybe I'm just that hammered. I've never run into Katrina anywhere but the café, but it's clear I'm also drunk because it's the only reason I'd be using nerdy words like dissonance. Even in my head.

The dress she's wearing shows off long, toned legs, and the tits I've been admiring under the layers of material she usually has on are happily not the result of a miracle push-up bra. Her profile is to me, but I watch her react to my voice. She stills and her lips part as she turns toward me. She doesn't respond until the girl next to her, a dark redhead who eyes me with a mixture of confusion and intrigue, elbows her.

"Joel Moreno." The way she says my name is like a double shot from the bottle of Jack I hold in one hand. It burns so good.

"What are you doing here?"

One brow raises and a hand goes to her hip. It's the same mocking look and stance she gives me every week, but tonight she looks nervous without the counter between us. "It's a party. What do you think I'm doing?"

"Good point." I give her friend, who looks familiar but thankfully not in an *I've seen her naked* way, a small head nod and step closer to Katrina. I grab three cups and fill each of them with a healthy shot from the bottle I've nearly finished off. I hand a cup to Katrina and her friend and then lift the other toward them. "Cheers to doing what people do at parties."

Her friend smirks and looks between Kitty and me. Katrina lifts her cup to her pink lips but pauses before drinking. She grimaces at the smell, proceeds to take a sip, coughs, and then forces the rest down like a champ. "That's disgusting."

"Shots usually are," the redhead says and takes hers all at once. She consolidates the cups in her hand and chases the shot with whatever she's drinking.

Kitty watches and does the same. "What's the point of drinking something that tastes bad?" Her face flushes. "I don't drink very often."

I file that tidbit away. "First of all, don't talk about my boy Jack like that. Secondly, depends on what you want from the night. Different kinds of alcohol make people feel different ways. Wine drunk is emotional. "Oh my God, I love you *so* much," I say in a mock high-pitched voice that pulls a small laugh from her friend. Beer drunk is loud and obnoxious..." I wave my hand toward the keg in the dining room. The guys around it push and shove while they take turns filling their cups, smack talking so loud you can hear their taunts above the rest of the noise in the house.

"And this." She lifts her empty cup. "What kind of drunk will I be?"

"Fun and invincible."

The girl next to her snorts. "Until tomorrow morning anyway."

"Some truth to that," I admit.

"Tabitha," the redhead introduces herself.

Katrina glances between us. "Sorry, I thought maybe you two already knew each other."

"Joel, nice to meet you." I extend a hand to Tabitha.

Before she can shake, Nathan butts in. "Shots, shots, shots," he sings in his best Lil Jon impersonation, which is fucking terrible.

He has an empty pizza box he's using as a serving tray and it's filled with shot glasses of whatever party concoction he's created.

He offers it first to Tabitha and Katrina who both take one.

I hold up a hand to pass. I know my limits. I like to teeter right on the brink of wasted. I'm toeing the line as it is. The mixture of booze and the adrenaline pumping through me at the sight of Katrina right here when I least expected it has me lit.

"Shut up. You're not pussing out. It's only ten o'clock. Party's just getting started."

"I'm pacing myself," I say, annoyed, but take one anyway. I lift it to my nose and sniff, try and get some idea what I'm getting myself into. All I smell is a fruity punch of some sort.

"What is this?"

His smile is fast and wicked.

Ah fuck. "There Everclear in this?"

Fuck that. I place the shot back on his tray. And no way in hell I'm letting Katrina drink this. Girl will be blackout drunk before she knows it.

Too late. I look over in time to see her pretty face contort in a mixture of confusion and disgust.

"Oh God, what is that?" she asks after she's taken half the shot.

I swipe it from her hand and drink the rest of it before responding. I catch only the slightest hint of the ridiculously high proof alcohol, but my body shivers as if it knows I've just fucked it.

"Hey, I was gonna drink that."

"Trust me. I did you a solid."

Tabitha sets her still full shot glass down and glares at Nathan. "What's in that?"

"Relax." Nathan bumps my shoulder. "It's only got a little bit of Everclear in it."

"That shit will mess you up so fast you don't even realize it."

I'm pleased when Katrina makes no move to get another cup from Nathan's tray, but instead lifts her empty cup and says, "I'm going to get a beer."

Nathan is already off on his quest to get everyone shit-faced, so I follow Katrina to the keg.

"I can't believe you're here. I've never seen you out before."

She attempts a pour. Flow is weak and she messes with the tap and gives it a shake like that'll help.

"Needs to be pumped."

"Uh, what?" She drops it and looks to me helplessly.

"I'm starting to think this might be your first time pouring from a keg." I step forward and give the keg a couple slow pumps. "The key is not to over pump. You pump too much, and you'll be able to ski on the head."

I motion her over with a head tilt and hold out the nozzle. She places the cup underneath and I fill it like a pro.

"You're staring," she says as I hand her the cup and do indeed keep watching her.

"Sorry. I'm just... surprised to see you. Come on, let's go outside. It's quieter out there and we can talk."

Talk, make out, whatever.

"I should get back to Tabitha." She motions with her head and I look over to see her friend watching us carefully. "We came together."

Girls are weird as shit about sticking with their friends

at parties. Typically this is when I'd offer they both join me outside, but I'm not in the mood for a three-way. My attention is focused solely on Katrina. But she's not getting out of my sight, either. I'm afraid she might be a hallucination or maybe I've already passed the fuck out and I'm dreaming.

I place an arm around her shoulders, enjoying every inch of bare skin that heats my forearm. "Tabitha," I call out as we approach. "How do you feel about drinking games?"

Her expression doesn't look the least bit staged or put off at my domineering their plans. "I love them."

I let my arm drop and grab Katrina's free hand. Her small palm is limp for the briefest of moments before she relaxes and curls her fingers around mine. I lead them to the table in the middle of the kitchen and thank karma or God or just dumb luck that there are three empty seats.

Mario and Vanessa are seated with some other baseball guys and girls I recognize as baseball house regulars. "Yo, Mario, cool if we join you?"

He groans as Vanessa shoots a quarter into the shot glass in front of her and raises both arms overhead in victory. "Sucker, drink again!"

"Fair warning, Vanessa is unnaturally good at shooting quarters," he says as he fills his shot glass with the Captain Morgan bottle in front of him and then shoots it back.

"It's true," Vanessa says with pride. Her eyes land on Katrina and her smile widens. "Hey, you're Katrina. You work at the café with Blair... or well, did before she quit."

Katrina nods. "I thought I recognized you. You're her roommate, right? It's not the same without her."

Vanessa is hot but ruthless. I wouldn't cross her for any amount of money, but right now she smiles so sweetly as she motions for Katrina to take the seat next to her that I'm at a total loss. My Kitty seems to have a weird effect on everyone. The remaining seats are on the other side of the table, so I pull out a chair for Tabitha and then take the one directly across from Katrina. At least this way I can watch her more carefully. So much for getting handsy, though.

We play quarters and Vanessa destroys us as Mario predicted. My eyes stay glued to Katrina who watches and copies the movements of everyone else. I can't get a read on her. She's not a party hopper because I've never seen her out, but she seems to be enjoying herself if not more timidly than everyone else.

"Okay, I'm out," Mario says after he's forced to take another shot.

Vanessa scrunches up her nose at him. "Good call. I don't want you to have whiskey dick later."

"TMI, V," I say with a chuckle and watch as Mario hangs his head and mumbles something under his breath.

"How about Drunk Jenga? You still got that one?" I ask, not having any interest in playing anything, but suddenly feeling like I need to be Martha-fucking-Stewart playing hostess and ensuring everyone has a good time. Well, not everyone, just Katrina.

"Good call," the jersey chaser next to me says with more enthusiasm than Jenga deserves.

"What's Drunk Jenga?" Katrina asks hesitant and quiet, directed to me.

"You'll like it," I promise. And she will. Her having a good time has become my only goal for the night. Well, and getting her home with me.

We set up Jenga and Katrina laughs as she reads out some of the tiles. "Flash the table."

One of my personal favorites.

"Make a rule for the table." And "Dare two people to kiss."

I read the look on her face that asks if we're seriously going to play such a ridiculous game that could have been made up by middle school boys. Yep, sweetheart, college is just puberty on steroids. Playing games like Spin the Bottle, Truth or Dare, or I've Never is totally legit because there is alcohol involved. Tomorrow people will blame their actions tonight on being drunk when the truth is they were super horny and looking to get laid.

"I'll go first," the girl next to me says, side-eyeing me. Ah, hell. I hadn't considered that I might have to partake in the festivities. I mean, I'm usually game, but with Kitty here – no fucking way I'm wasting time making out with some other girl.

"Actually, how about we let Kitty go first seeing as how it's her first time." I stand and move around the table. With one hand on the back of the chair, I lean down.

"I know how to play Jenga," she says with a smirk.

"I just want to make sure you choose wisely." I point to a tile in the middle of the tower.

She eyes me suspiciously but pulls at the one I picked anyway. I try and hide the smile pulling at my lips as she reads it to herself.

"What's it say?" someone asks, but neither Kitty or I answer.

She finally looks up and around the table and I can almost hear her weighing out her options. I step back and wait. When I've almost given up hope, she sighs, turns to me, stands, and says, "This doesn't count as a date."

There's laughter from the table as Vanessa reads the discarded tile aloud. "Seven Minutes in Heaven."

When we're upstairs in Mario's room, she finally speaks. "I'm not sure if I should be insulted or impressed that you got me in a bedroom within an hour of my arriving at the party."

"Impressed." I walk all the way in, hoping she'll follow, and place the bottle of Jack I'm still carrying onto the desk. She hovers in the doorway, and I step back to her and brush her hair away from the side of her neck. Leaning in, I press a kiss just below her ear before murmuring, "Definitely impressed."

"I'm not having sex with you," she whispers in a shaky voice. I pull back. Indecision wars in her eyes. She wants me, I've always known this, but something still holds her back. Even here with no one else and no barriers between us, she's throwing up a stop sign with the way she looks almost guilty.

Somehow, I manage to step away. Her scent follows me, and I try and find some semblance of sanity as I pick up the bottle of Jack. "We don't have to do anything except stay in here for seven minutes."

I settle onto Mario's bed with the alcohol and pat for her to follow.

She looks around the space which is clean and not at all what she pictured judging by the look on her face. I'll have to thank Vanessa for that. I see touches of her all over the room, including the bed that has been made and sheets that smell like they've been washed recently.

"Come on. I've been asking you out for five months. Throw a guy a bone."

Or, you know, let me stick mine in you.

"Okay, but door stays open and I'm not touching that bed."

She moves into the room and stands, arms crossed, eyes guarded.

My head is heavy, probably from the alcohol, but I wrack my brain for an idea. Anything to keep her here and all to myself. "How about we do something else to pass the time? We could get to know each other. Seven questions in heaven." Look at me all clever. Won't exactly be adding this one to the game though. Seven minutes in heaven shouldn't normally be altered. Drastic times and all that.

She seems to consider this. "I can ask you anything?"

"Sure. As long as I can do the same."

Her arms go to her sides and she moves to the bed and sits on the edge. Progress.

"Okay."

I lob her a softball. "What's your major?"

"Screenwriting. Yours?"

"Communications," I answer and then fire back to keep the game going. "What made you decide to come out tonight?"

She shrugs. "Tabitha invited me out."

"Yeah, okay, but I've never seen you out so why tonight and not before?"

Her lips part and her chest rises and falls before she answers. "I guess the stars just aligned. I was free and she asked. I honestly don't get invited to that many parties. And that was two questions."

I hold my palm out in a gesture that it's her turn.

"How many girls have you brought up here? Ballpark."

I'm pleased this is a question I can answer honestly and to my credit. "None."

She narrows her gaze. "I don't believe you."

"It's true. The official Seven Minutes in Heaven room is actually the closet downstairs."

Rolling her eyes, her stance closes off a bit. "You know what I meant."

Yeah, of course I do.

"I don't know. A lot. Does it matter?"

"No, I guess it doesn't. That's four questions." She holds three fingers in the air with a smirk. "Why do you keep coming to the café asking me out every week? You have to know that I'm never going to say yes."

"That's where you're wrong," I argue. "You want to say

yes. I don't know why you keep saying no, but I know I'm not wrong about the attraction between us being mutual."

"And you're what? Hoping to wear me down by buying coffee?"

"Winners want the ball."

"Excuse me?"

"You heard me."

"I don't understand how that fits this scenario. Am I the ball?"

Reaching out, I let my fingertips graze her arm – elbow to wrist. Goosebumps meet my touch, but she doesn't pull back. "It means that I'm willing to risk you turning me down every week because there's always a chance you'll say yes. I might fail ninety-nine times before I succeed, but I'm going to keep trying because I want you. You're not the ball, Kitty, you're the goal."

She scrunches up her nose. "The goal? You can 'score,'" —she air quotes the word— "with any girl you want. So, I'm not sure I buy it. If I'm just a goal..."

"Don't twist my words. You're not *just* anything."

Our eyes lock and the air shifts. I don't dare move even though I'm dying to taste her, to show her how good we can be together.

She lets out a long breath and shakes her head. "Can I have a drink of that?"

I hand over the bottle and watch as she tips it back and proceeds to grimace as the liquor meets her tongue. She hands it back with a cough. "Thanks."

"Lo que tu quieras hermosa."

Her eyes widen. "You speak Spanish?"

Damn. I haven't pulled out the Spanish on her? In all my attempts to get her to go out with me, I'd forgotten Blair's advice that tossing out my ability to speak Spanish was the ultimate panty dropper. Admittedly it doesn't usually come to that. My handsome mug and the body that comes with the workouts and practices of being a college athlete do practically all the work for me.

"My parents wanted us to be able to communicate with our extended family in Mexico."

She shifts so she's sitting fully on the bed. "Did your parents grow up here or in Mexico?"

"Both. My father's family moved here when he was a baby. My mother came over with her sister after high school."

Whatever hesitation and block she'd been throwing up is down as she leans forward and asks the next question. "How'd they meet?"

I shake my head and click my tongue against the roof of my mouth twice. "Oh no, you've used up your seven questions. It's my turn."

She holds her hand out for the bottle.

I pass it over, watching mesmerized as she takes another small drink and hands it back. "I'm ready. Shoot."

"Admit you're attracted to me."

"That's not a question."

"Fine. Are you attracted to me?"

Her face pinks. If I'd been doubting it, which I haven't, I'd be certain now. Katrina is attracted to me, but I need to hear her say it. I need her to admit it to herself. She rolls her eyes. "You know you're hot, you don't need me to pad your ego."

"That's not the same thing. I asked if *you* were attracted to me?"

She throws her hands up, exasperation bouncing off her. "Of course, I am. I'm pretty sure the entire female population is attracted to you." More eye rolling.

I take a drink to hide the cocky grin that is threatening to spread across my face. The burn of the alcohol and the excitement of her admission has me lightheaded.

"Final question."

"I'm pretty sure you still have at least two left."

That cocky grin I was trying to hide? Yep, no hiding it now. It pulls across my face and, thank you, Jesus, this night is about to get good. Good and dirty. "I only need one."

She arches a brow, looking at me suspiciously.

Leaning forward, I hear the intake of breath as my thumb moves to the corner of her mouth and I trace her full, bottom lip before moving up to the center of her perfect cupid's bow. She's coated them in a glossy, light pink, and I want to taste it and smear it in equal measures. She trembles under my touch and it's such an honest reaction that my pulse quickens.

I drop my hand from her face to neck and thread it through her hair, watching the path and admiring the goosebumps that rise on her ivory skin. "Can I kiss you?"

When I meet her beautiful multi-colored eyes, they're

wide and dark like maybe she's as jacked about this finally happening as I am.

"Your eyes..." Her lips part as I get closer and her gaze darts from my mouth to my eyes. *"Tienes los ojos más bonitos que he visto."*

She still doesn't respond with words but nods ever so slightly as I hover so close our breaths mingle. Her eyes stay locked on mine until our mouths meet. Lashes flutter closed and she meets my kiss tentatively. I want to fucking devour her, but I hold back, refusing to rush this moment. Her kiss is soft and unassuming like she's trying to savor this moment too. Maybe I'm projecting.

She opens wider and I sweep my tongue in tasting the lingering liquor and a sweetness that I want to bottle up and gulp. In fact, my head spins and as my hands find her hips and dig in, the kiss turns frantic. Her moans meet mine. When did I become a moaner? I feel the blackness creeping in as I push away all questions and try to hold on to her and to the moment, not wanting it to end.

———

"Ojos bonitos," I whisper the words against her neck. My hips search for contact, dick so hard it's painful.

"Wake up, Moreno." Something hits my face and I register the pillow and the loss of her at the same time. Without opening my eyes, I let my other senses play catch up to the situation. I'm not in my bed, or any bed. The lumpy cushion beneath me and the pillow I spoon. My pulse throbs between my eyes.

"He alive?" I hear someone ask followed by a chuckle.

"Yeah, he's alive." I recognize Mario's voice this time. "Probably nursing a hangover to rival all hangovers."

I groan in response, all I can manage without fear of my head exploding.

"Wes called looking for you. He said to tell you to get your ass moving. Practice in thirty minutes."

Well, that's not good news, but I'm less concerned about that than I am with what happened with Katrina last night. A vague recollection of her getting a text and insisting she needed to go is the only thing I remember after kissing her. I sit up slowly and take in myself and the situation around me. I'm passed out on the living room couch.

I check the time on the cable box underneath the TV. Assuming it's right, I'm hella fucking late. Our usual morning practice got bumped to mid-day, hence the night of drinking. From November through April we don't get a lot of nights to let loose. Early morning practices, after-noon workouts that sometimes go well into the evening. Then there are game tapes and oh right I'm also taking a full load of college classes.

So, when Coach moved our morning practice, Nathan and I took full advantage.

"Nathan crash here too?"

"Nah, he stumbled out last night. You were passed out

in my room. Took everything I had to get your tall ass down the stairs and onto the couch."

"And Katrina?"

"The chick you took up to my room?" He shakes his head. "Didn't see her after you two went upstairs to do the nasty on my bed. Vanessa insisted on changing the bedding and then burning your sex sheets."

Normally she'd be right on the money, but the way I feel right now? Something tells me there wasn't any sex to be had.

"Sorry, man. I owe you."

I feel for my phone in my pocket, relieved when I find it, but disappointed when I see the battery is dunzo.

I pocket it and pull my ass up off the couch. With a salute to Mario, I'm out. When I walk the two blocks to my house, the guys are already out the door as I'm heading up the sidewalk which means I've got shit for time. Looks like I'll be wearing whatever rumpled, smelly clothes I left in my locker.

Wes hobbles toward me all grumpy and pissed off – his new MO. The boot on his right foot from the injury that ended his college career thunks on the pavement and echoes like a cannon in my goddamn head.

"Walk of shame? Really?"

"I hate that phrase. This is the walk of awesome. Don't be jealous I had a good night and you probably tucked your lame ass in at eight."

The smallest lift of his lips makes me second-guess my

assumption. "Ah, you stayed in with Blair. Nice. You lock that down yet, make it official?"

He doesn't respond, but he doesn't need to. Wes' silence tells me everything.

"Good for you. 'Bout damn time."

Nathan hustles forward, taking his walk to a jog and leaving us behind. I lift my head in his direction. "He was drinking Everclear last night and now look at him. He's either got an unbelievable tolerance or..."

"Don't finish that sentence," Wes instructs. "I'm putting in for that coaching job next year. The less I know, the better."

"Coach Reynolds," I try it out. "Coach Wes." Shake my head. "Nah, how about Coach Dubya – ya know like George Dubya Bush."

"Those all sound super weird, but if you call me Coach Dubya, your ass will be doing a lot of extra miles."

"Cold, Dubya. Cold."

8

JOEL

"Relax, I talked to the owner. It's cool."

Wes looks unsure despite my words as we enter The Hideout. It's the first time we've been back since he got into a bar fight with Blair's ex-boyfriend last month. Cops were called, it was all very dramatic, but I paid for the damages – a couple broken chairs and glasses – and promised we'd be on our best behavior from now on.

Blair follows behind Wes looking just as nervous. Her gaze goes to the bar and she scans the length of it. Vanessa nudges her. "Hottie bartender doesn't work here anymore."

"How do you know?" Mario asks with enough bite in his tone that it makes me chuckle.

She wraps her arm through his all reassuring like. "I overheard the other bartenders talking about how he left them short-staffed right before March Madness. They're expecting the turnout to be big with everyone following the basketball team this year."

The five of us settle into a table near the bar. Z opted out like he typically does, and Nathan played it off like he wanted to rest up for tomorrow, but I'm pretty sure he just didn't have the funds to cover dining out.

The Hideout is packed and it's still early. Too early for the Saturday night drinking crowd. We've got an away game tomorrow, so it'll have to be an early night for us. While we wait for someone to take our order, I look around the place weighing my options. Being the fifth wheel sucks. Don't get me wrong, I don't envy Wes or Mario, but they're shit for company when their girls are here.

I wonder what Katrina is doing tonight. Did she make it home alright? What does she do on a typical Saturday night? I'm annoyed that I'm still thinking about her. Any ideas I had about fucking her out of my system are gone. I kissed her senseless last night and all I can think about is doing it again. This girl has my curiosity begging to be satisfied. My dick too.

"Yo, Blair, can I borrow your phone for a minute?"

She's distracted by Wes, who has a hand so high up on her thigh I wonder if maybe they should just skip dinner and go bang. Godspeed and all. But it works in my favor that she's here and distracted because she unlocks the screen and pushes it toward me without a thought.

I scroll through her contacts, holding my breath until I

see her name. Katrina Philipps. Jackpot. I transfer her number to my phone and then stand.

"Be right back," I announce and head toward the hallway that leads to the restrooms.

I tap out a bunch of different texts, over thinking it and finally saying screw it.

ME

Plans tonight? I want to kiss you again.

I pace, watching my phone for a reply that comes only a few minutes later.

KITTY

Who is this?

ME

How many people did you kiss last night?

KITTY

Depends on who is asking.

ME

The guy who kissed you the best.

KITTY

How did you get this number Joel Moreno?

When most people say my full name, it comes with expectations, intrigue, and guarantees that I'm about to get laid. With Katrina, however, it seems to be a barrier between us. What do I have to do to get her to see me as just Joel?

> **ME**
>
> Tell you what. Meet me at my place in fifteen minutes and I'll tell you anything you want to know.

> **KITTY**
>
> Shouldn't you be resting before the game tomorrow?

> **ME**
>
> Keeping tabs on me?

> **KITTY**
>
> No. It's hard not to know the game schedule of the legendary Valley basketball team.

> **ME**
>
> I'll sleep better after I've thoroughly kissed you. You'll be doing the team and university a service.

> **KITTY**
>
> Good luck at your game tomorrow.

I growl at the phone and shove it in my pocket before rejoining the table. Looks like I'm back to square one with Katrina. Taking a drink of the water that's appeared and picking up the menu, I try and push the girl out of my mind. I'll just call someone else. Answer one of the many texts or DMs. Why am I not already doing that?

"Dude, you okay?" Wes asks. The whole table is staring at me. Perfect. Now they decide to notice me?

"I'm fine." I feel their eyes still on me as I look over the menu. I set it down and stand. "Actually, I'm not hungry anymore. Mario, can you drop them off?" I point to Wes and Blair, and he nods. "See you guys back at the house."

I drive to Ray Fieldhouse and walk inside. The women's basketball team is just finishing up and I wait until they're gone to grab a ball and dribble onto the court.

If you asked any of my teammates, they'd probably say I prefer game day to practice. I like the roar of the fans, the way that all eyes are on me and my team, and the rush knowing I can bring an entire stadium to their feet with the perfect shot. But being on the court alone, just me, the ball and the hoop – there's something almost religious about it. No fanfare, no applause, no expectations.

I lose track of time as I shoot. The routine of it soothes me and I've nearly forgotten about the girl wreaking havoc on my sanity.

"Moreno, what are you doing here?" Coach's voice booms across the court. I rebound the ball and turn to find him on the sidelines giving me a confused look. He walks toward me, and I can't help but notice that from far away he looks like he might be part of the team. Tall, still built, wearing shorts and an old Baylor basketball shirt that's cut at the sleeves. The year nineteen ninety-nine proudly displayed on the front is faded from being washed too many times. He's not one of those coaches that looks like he enjoys a big steak dinner every night with boosters and alumni with big pockets. He doesn't go as far as to scrimmage or workout with us, but I'm certain he could give us all a good run for our money on or off the court.

"Just getting in some shots. Big game tomorrow."

He eyes me in that way that tells me he knows it's bullshit, but he doesn't call me out. "Should go home and get some rest."

The phone he's carrying in his hand pings and he grins as he reads whatever is on the screen. Coach lifts his phone in a salute. "Alright, get out of here. I'm gonna do the same."

Seems everybody has someone to get to tonight except me. Which is bullshit because I could have a dozen different girls waiting for me at home if I wanted. Anyone but her.

Damn her.

9

KATRINA

I watch the end of the Valley game on TV. I've never been to a college game in person, but since our basketball team went to the Final Four last year, I guess I've got caught up in the excitement as much as the rest of the university.

And it doesn't hurt that the object of my every thought is wearing jersey number thirty-three and dancing around on the sidelines like he doesn't have a care in the world. I mean Valley did win, but the rest of his team looks serious and focused despite the victory. Joel looks as comfortable as if he were celebrating a pickup game at the local park.

My mind wanders to Friday night and that kiss. *That* kiss. Never in my life have I been kissed so... thoroughly. Joel kisses like I imagined. No, better. My lips tingle and I bring my fingertips to them wishing I could bring the memory to life. My face warms and I shake my head hoping to clear it. A million and one things to do and my brain replays the look of desire just seconds before he kissed me. He looked at *me* that way. Like kissing me was as important as taking his next breath.

Joel's Valley basketball roster picture splashes on the TV and the announcers discuss his season and daily stats. They continue talking about him until they're forced to a commercial break and I finally get a second without the greatness of Joel Moreno all up in my grill.

I busy myself around the apartment, folding laundry, doing dishes, and picking up toys until my mind is focused. I grab my laptop and sit on the couch to finish editing the dialogue in the last scene of the play when my phone pings. I reach for it absently, bring it up to my face and glance down ready to dismiss whatever notification or news alert has interrupted my writing.

And stop short.

Jaw gapes.

Body flames.

It's the second day in a row he's shocked me by reaching out.

Four little words pummel my heart as I read the notification: JoelMoreno33 wants to send you a message. My social media accounts are locked down and I've never been so glad.

I'd be lying if I said I'd never checked out his, which are very much public. His posts and interactions are as entertaining as he is. And let's not even talk about the photos he's tagged in. There's an actual Joel Moreno Fan Page.

My thumb glides over the notification and before I can make too big a deal of it, I press Accept and open the message. It's a video of a guy taking a shower. You can't see anything but the guy's legs until a cat walks into the shower and starts rubbing against him getting all wet but clearly happy for the attention and completely undeterred. I'm sure there's some sort of message here but instead of engaging I close out without a response.

Not five seconds go by before a text pings.

> **JOEL**
> You're still up. What are you doing?

Crap, I forgot Instagram shows when the other person has read the message. Rookie mistake. I laugh a little at the way I worked a sports reference in and then groan because I just laughed out loud in my quiet apartment. Christian's been asleep for hours after the longest no nap day in history.

> **ME**
> Writing. Congrats on the game.

> **JOEL**
> Thanks. Tell me a bedtime story, master storyteller, I'm tired as fuck but buses were not meant for tall people.

> **ME**
> Once upon a time there was a very tall boy...

JOEL

Man, sweetheart. Tall man.

I roll my eyes but smile as I correct the intro to the story.

ME

Once upon a time there was a very tall man-boy with hair the color of coal.

JOEL

And the body of Zeus.

ME

Who is telling this story?

JOEL

<smiley face with zipper lips>

ME

His mouth was clever. His words charming. So charming that when he spoke women fell to their knees. But the strong man-boy, simply swept the women up and took them to his lair where he ravaged them. Later, he left them alone and cold to find more women to bring back. For he was greedy and wanted all the women for himself.

JOEL

<chuckle> Lair, badass.

ME

But as the years passed, he grew a terrible hunch on his back from continually bending down and sweeping the swooning women into his arms. Disgusted by the now ugly and hunched man-boy, all the women in his lair stood, pulled themselves together, and went about their lives like the man-boy had never existed. The end.

JOEL

Weird. Is that supposed to be some sort of cautionary tale?

ME

Just an impromptu bedtime story, man-boy. All persons in this story were fictional.

JOEL

Now I'm going to have nightmares of hunchbacks, thanks a lot.

ME

I do what I can.

JOEL

Come over tonight.

ME

You never give up, do you?

JOEL

Never.

I'm typing my sign off for the night when another text comes in and I laugh into the silence of my apartment for a second time tonight.

> JOEL
>
> If I ever do get you to my lair, I'm totally going to ravage you.

> ME
>
> And leave me cold and alone?

> JOEL
>
> With you in my lair, I don't think that would be possible.

———

BETWEEN CLASSES AND THE PLAY, the week flies by in a blur. I haven't heard from Joel again and I'm wondering if I should have just slept with him the night of the party or taken him up on his offer to go over to his house this weekend. I mean if that was my last shot, should I have just gone for it? I watch the clock like a hawk in a futile attempt to speed it up or slow it down – alternating feelings depending on the minute. I'm not even sure he's going to show up to the café again. He may not have gotten exactly what he wanted, but maybe that kiss and my continued refusal to sleep with him was the last straw.

Is that what I want, to get rid of him? Or did I honestly think he was going to chase after me forever?

I groan audibly.

Before I can work out my feelings, he pushes through the door and locks onto my gaze with an intensity that I feel in my toes.

"Morning, Kitty."

"Coffee?" I ask, and he nods.

"And maybe dinner tonight?"

A small, okay a large, part of me jumps for joy that he's not given up on me. But then that makes no sense because I'm not going to say yes. But how do I justify the relief I feel that he's here? Guess that answers my question if I wanted to get rid of him. I don't.

"Sorry, I can't."

"*¿Por qué mierda sigo torturándome?*" he mutters under his breath.

His exasperation makes me smile. My saying no has never seemed to bother him before. Not really. Not like this. And there's something seriously sexy about a man speaking in another language.

"But," I say quietly, and his head snaps up and something that looks like hope flashes across his face. "I have a project I'm working on that I could use your help."

"A school project?"

"A play I'm writing. It's set in Mexico."

"Ah." He seems to consider that. "I could help you during our date."

That seems unlikely, but maybe I can barter. I mean, honestly, a date with Joel in exchange for help with the play that might make the difference on job applications next year is hardly an unfair trade. And worst case, it'll be the most entertaining night of my life. Of that, I have no doubt.

"I'll make you a deal. If you help me, then I'll go out with you. *One* date."

"Done," he answers without hesitation. "Pick you up tonight at seven?"

"Oh, uh, tonight's not good for me." Oh God, am I really doing this? Once I go out with him, the fantasy will be gone and there'll be no going back to Thursdays where Joel waltzes in and tries to sweep me off my feet. I'll have been swept and he'll move on to someone new.

And I still haven't told him about Christian. I realize now I should have just told him the first time he strolled in and hit on me, but I'd wanted to stay in fantasy land. Now it's all weird because I haven't told him and how do you just blurt out, I have a kid, without sounding like a weirdo or like you're asking for a blood signature relationship oath? It's a tricky situation that I've mostly avoided in the past by not letting men in at all.

"How about Sunday afternoon?"

"That's three days away." He raps his knuckles on the counter as he thinks. "Sunday afternoon. I've got somewhere I need to be at noon. How's ten?"

"Ten is good." Or I hope it is. I need to check with Nadine and my mom and see if one of them can watch Christian for a few hours. They're always insisting it's no problem and it *is* technically for school.

"Perfect."

I grab a cup, mostly to have something to do with my hands. "The usual?"

"Ya know what? I think I'm good." He smiles and steps back. "I finally got what I've really been coming in here for all these months... a date."

"Sunday isn't a date, it's a study session," I call after him.

He places both hands over his ears. "La, la, la, la."

I shake my head slowly at his antics, but my heart beats faster.

———

"GRANDMA NADINE IS GOING to be here in five minutes."

Christian doesn't move from his spot in the middle of the living room floor. He's got an elaborate race track set up and pushes cars around in circles and up ramps. My son may be chill about the day, but I am not.

Books, check. Laptop, check. Notebook and pen, check and check. Satisfied that the third perusal of my backpack hasn't changed the fact it's ready to go, I step toward my bedroom so I can look at myself in the mirror again. I've not even made it over the threshold when the doorbell rings. Guess this is as good as I'm going to look.

I open the door as Christian stands and runs to greet Grandma Nadine.

Except...

"Victor, what are you doing here?" The edge in my

voice is uncalled for and I try and recover. "Sorry. I thought Nadine was coming."

"Daddy," Christian says and throws himself at Victor's legs.

Victor gives him a pat on the head and walks in. "I drove back yesterday, so she sent me. Thought I could take Christian for pancakes – heard it's a Sunday tradition."

Christian squeals with excitement.

"Christian, can you go put your toys in your room while I talk to Mommy?"

My internal alert radar goes off and my body tenses waiting for what must surely be bad news. Victor has been to our apartment exactly once before and that was because Nadine came down with the flu and couldn't bring Christian home one weekend.

"What's up?" I ask when Christian's arms are full of toys and he's headed to his room.

"I'm moving back. Well, moved back, I guess."

"With your parents?" I cringe at the judgey way it comes out.

"For now. I'm going to get a job and then finish up my degree at the community college."

"That's great." I think? I'm completely thrown. "Everything okay?"

"Yeah." He shifts uncomfortably. "You know school was always hard for me."

The smallest bit of pity washes over me as I realize he probably dropped before he flunked out.

"Well, Christian will be glad to see more of you."

He nods once curtly. "Mom thought... *I* thought maybe I could keep him for a week or two. I'll be free until I find a job and it'd give you a break."

"I don't need a break from my son," I whisper-screech.

Victor runs a hand over his jaw. He's sporting a short, trendy beard that's new since the last time I saw him. "Look, Katrina, I just thought it'd be nice to spend some more time with him while I'm not busy."

So many snarky comments sit on the tip of my tongue. Like, yes it would be nice if you'd spent time with him... the past three years. And, while you're not busy? How self-less of you. But I bite them back as Christian comes racing out of his room.

"Let me think about it. He's got preschool and soccer. We have a routine here." I grab my backpack, tell Christian to have fun with his dad and squeeze him hard. "I'll be back by two."

At the library, I snag a table on the second floor in a back corner that gives me a view of the stairs. I'm hopeful with my vantage point I will see him before he sees me. With Joel, I'll take any advantage I can get. The guy seriously throws me off kilter. I'm nervous for a study session which is ridiculous, but there it is.

I pull out my notebook and laptop and get lost in the world of Hector and Imelda. I'm chewing on the end of my pen cap, imagining a scene in my head when he drops into the chair in front of me. So much for my advantage. I startle and he grins.

"Writing more stories about me?"

I was, in fact, imagining him as Hector, but like I'd give him the satisfaction of knowing that.

"No. Far more interesting heroes."

He glances at my notebook. "What are you working on?"

"The play I told you about. I'm still working on some dialogue. I'd love to get your feedback when it's ready, but for now, maybe it'd be more useful if I asked the questions I prepared?" I ramble, so nervous the words spill together, and Joel looks at me like he's utterly confused.

10

JOEL

"You said your mother came to the United States after high school. What made her decide to leave Mexico?"

I stare at Katrina for a solid five seconds without comprehending the words that have come out of her mouth. For starters, when did I tell her about my mom coming from Mexico after high school? And then the obvious follow-ups like why the hell does she want to know personal information about my family? I thought this was about a school paper.

I'm not proud that my first thought goes to her selling information about me to some tabloid or maybe she's started her own blog on my awful pickup lines, but her followers got bored and now want more juicy details.

"I'm sorry, what does this have to do with my helping you?"

She stares back blankly before responding. "Everything."

Her gaze narrows while I continue to grapple for what the fuck is going on. I think back to the other night. It's blurry, but okay yeah, I broke out the Spanish and I vaguely remember her wanting to know more about my parents and their immigrating to the US, but I thought this deal was just a charade. I'd pretend to help her for an hour or two and then I'd convince her to come home with me. Is she seriously expecting me to help her with Spanish?

"You don't remember." She crosses her arms and leans back.

"Sorry." I've never been more embarrassed to have gotten memory fog drunk. "I drank a lot before you got there and then I took that Everclear shot... it's fuzzy after we went upstairs."

She laughs, taking me by surprise and earning a few annoyed stares from nearby tables. "Oh my God. That's so..." She stares up as if she's searching for the right word. "Serendipitous."

"How's that?"

"You've been trying to get me to hang out with you for months and I finally do, and you don't even remember it."

I run a thumb at my temple. "I remember."

She doesn't look convinced.

"I remember I was glad to see you and we had a good time – I think. I remember kissing you was nice."

She smiles sweetly. "Except that weird thing you did with your tongue." Then glances down to her crotch and cringes like she's remembering the worst oral sex of her life.

The hand at my face goes still and I swear to God my heart stops. Did this girl just call my oral skills weird? And damn, I really wish I remembered going down on her.

"I'm totally messing with you."

"So, we didn't..."

She motions between us with the pen in her hand. "We didn't have sex."

I nod.

"Of any kind," she adds.

Relief and disappointment shoot through me. I want her, but damn I want to remember it too.

Amusement twinkles in her eyes.

"Wanna tell me what we did do?"

"You mean did I let you get further than first base?"

"Wrong sport, Kitty."

She thinks for a moment. "What's the equivalent to first base in basketball lingo?"

"In basketball, it's all or nothing. You score or you don't."

Her lips part and cheeks pink. When she speaks her voice is tight. "No one scored."

"Damn shame. Although, probably for the best."

She arches a brow in question.

I lean in. "*When* I score with you, I'm going to be stone cold sober and I'm going to remember every second."

Letting out a breath, she breaks eye contact. "Ooookay. Maybe we should get back to the questions."

"Wait. First, I want to know what I agreed to. You writing some tell-all piece on the Moreno family?"

"Would people read that?" She looks disbelieving.

"Damn straight they would."

They would.

"No. I wrote a play that takes place in Mexico in the early 1900s." She stops and pulls out a couple of books that look like they might have been printed in that time-frame. "I got these Mexican history books but honestly history is not my jam and I think, or I'm hoping, that learning more about your parents will help me under-stand a little about what it would be like growing up in Mexico."

As she finishes explaining, disappointment mars her face like she's just realized it's a long shot. It is, but I have an idea.

"Okay."

"Okay?" she asks hopefully.

I let out a breath like this is gonna be tough – a real imposition on my part. "I'll help you the best I can." This is gonna be cake. I can't even try to hide my smile. "Admit it. You were just looking for an excuse to go out with me."

She rolls her beautiful eyes.

I lean back in my chair. "Let's get this done then. I'm capitalizing on my date immediately."

"It's Sunday."

She stares blankly. I don't give one single fuck what day it is or even what time. I'm cashing in now.

Pulling out her notebook she re-asks the question

without looking up. "Why did your mother decide to leave Mexico?"

I think for a few seconds. The obvious answer is more opportunities, but I don't want to give her a bullshit answer that she could have gotten without my help. She really should be asking my mom.

"How about we grab lunch and I can get you your answers at the same time?"

"Does this count as your date?"

I shake my head. "Nope."

"That's cheating. You're trying to get two dates out of this."

I shrug. "Nothing wrong with eating while we discuss. Besides, the place I have in mind is rich in Mexican culture."

Her eyes light up and I know I've got her.

Standing, I reach for her bag and toss it over my shoulder. "Come on."

She's silent as we walk to the parking lot behind the library. I head straight for my car and open the passenger side door. She stops in her tracks and looks at me.

"I'm over there." She points across the lot.

"But you don't know where we're going."

No movement.

"I promise to return you to your car."

"I have to be back by two."

I smile in agreement and wave a hand for her to sit. Semantics. Just get in the car, woman, so I can call this date as good as on. "Whenever you want."

Once we're driving out of the parking lot, I finally give myself the props I deserve for commandeering this study sesh to a date. Damn, I'm good. Quick lunch with my family where she can ask her questions and then I'll convince her to a proper date that will hopefully end with us naked.

It's as good as done.

11

KATRINA

"Where are we going?" I go for curious, but I'm a little panicked as Joel pulls off onto a road that looks like it goes nowhere but up the mountain. This is where I die. Okay, that's dramatic, but my palms are sweaty, and I think I've got a contact high from being enclosed with Joel like this.

"Lunch."

"Are we going to hunt rattlesnakes and mountain lions?" I laugh awkwardly as I clutch my purse like a lifeline in my lap. Not sure about cell reception out here, but maybe I can get a text to go through. I have no idea who I'd call in my hour of need. That's a shitty realization.

"Not today, Kitty, not today."

When the house comes into view, a wave of relief washes over me and then it hits me. "Oh my God. Are we at your parents' house?"

A cocky grin pulls up one side of his mouth and he

settles a big hand on my leg and squeezes. I'm sure it's meant to be reassuring, but my body tingles and clenches at the contact that's gone before I can even properly enjoy it.

"This is the best way I know to get you your answers."

"Couldn't we have just called your mom and asked her? This seems like overkill. I can't just barge into their house and interview them."

"Relax. The whole family is over for lunch. We do it every Sunday. *Cuantos mas seamos, mejor.*" He winks. "The more, the merrier."

Since it looks like I'm not getting out of this, I take in the beautiful Spanish-style house. Joel parks under the port cochere and kills the engine. I glance out my window and down the mountain looking over Valley. "This view is incredible."

He nods in agreement without looking and opens his door. "Ready?"

"Anything I should know? It's been awhile since I've met a guy's parents. And not usually before we've had our first date."

He shrugs like it's no big deal. "Just don't let Dylan saw you in half." I give him a quizzical look. "You'll see."

He leads me through a house which I silently catalog with amazement like I'm on an episode of MTV Cribs.

"My mom will be in the kitchen," he says as we walk toward the sound of voices.

It's in this moment that I realize I should probably have checked my hair and makeup, maybe had him swing by my apartment so I could put on something besides leggings and an open back t-shirt. There's no time for any of that now, though. I'm pulled into a room and all eyes are on me before I can even think through what it is I would have worn had I known.

There are at least ten women in the room and one by one they each notice the girl next to Joel. Unfortunately, that girl is me. The room feels too quiet and too concentrated on me for two whole seconds before Joel breaks the silence.

"Hey, Ma," he says and walks us toward a gorgeous woman standing on the other side of a huge island in the kitchen. Joel's mom is hot. I've never called someone's mom hot, but it's the best way to describe her. Hair the exact same color as Joel's, she's tall and fit just like her son but in a feminine way. Her eyes are a shade lighter, and her smile holds none of the arrogance his does.

She drops the scissors she was using to cut the stems off what looks like two dozen white roses. The rest of the room has gone back to whatever it is they were doing and ignoring me – thank God.

Mother and son embrace and then Joel drops a kiss to her cheek. Her face lights up with such happiness it makes me miss my own mother.

I'm frozen watching the interaction when Joel steps back and places his hand back at my side. "Ma this is Ki – Katrina."

"How lovely to meet you, Katrina."

"It's nice to meet you too, Mrs. Moreno. You have a beautiful home."

"Thank you, dear. Call me Isa." She shoots her son a look that I can't decipher.

"Katrina is working on a school project and had some questions about Mexico in the early 1900s – you know about the time you were born."

She swats at him, but her smile stays intact. "That's wonderful. What sort of school project?"

"Oh, I—" I wasn't prepared to give my elevator pitch. What if they think it's the dumbest idea ever? Will they still help me? "I wrote a screenplay based on the great, great-grandparents in the movie Coco – Hector and Imelda, and it was selected to be this year's Spring Showcase performance."

"You didn't tell me that part," Joel says, astonishment in his tone. "That's incredible, Kitty." He doesn't catch the nickname that rolls off his tongue. "I love that movie."

"You do?"

"Dylan made us all watch it many, many times," Isa adds.

"My son did the same thing. That's actually where I got the idea."

My face warms and I feel the man beside me turn to stone. Sh– crap. Well, that certainly isn't how I imagined telling Joel I had a kid. I look over at him with what I hope is an apologetic smile.

He clears his throat, but when he speaks, it's gruff and stiff. "Katrina these are my tias, Lupita, Opal, and Bonnie, and my sisters Bree and Michelle. Those three over there are my cousins Karla, Anita, and Celeste," he rattles them off as if there is any chance I could possibly remember all of them. Each one smiles or waves in hello.

"It's so nice to meet all of you. Can I help with something?"

His mom looks to Joel who motions toward the back of the house. "Dad outside?"

"You know he is." She pulls two waters from the fridge and hands them to Joel. "Make sure he doesn't throw another putter into the mountains."

"You good?" he asks quietly, turning so his back is to the rest of the women in the kitchen and shielding me from their gazes.

I nod, but he doesn't budge. The look in his eyes is intense as he studies me as if he's really seeing me for the first time. All of me. Katrina Phillips, twenty-one-year-old college student and mom.

"Go on. We'll take good care of her." Joel's mom's voice cuts through the moment.

His fingers brush mine as he takes a hesitant step toward the door. "I'll be out back if you need anything."

Isa calls out orders as I watch him go. "Katrina you can help me with the buñuelos as soon as I get this arrangement done."

Lupita, the only name I remember because Joel introduced her first, steps forward and holds her hand out. "Let me finish the centerpiece. You're cutting those roses too short for the vase. *Desastre.*"

Joel's mom hands her the scissors and motions me to follow as she walks into a large pantry. "I've been hoping she'd take over for the last half hour. I'm afraid I'm terrible with flowers." She hands me a pan filled with rows of tiny balls of dough and takes two others herself. "But cooking I can do. And this is an old family recipe so it's perfect that you're here to help."

"Thank you for being so great about this. I hadn't meant to intrude on your family lunch, but Joel insisted it'd be easier if I asked you directly."

"*Cuantos mas seamos, mejor,*" she says repeating the same words Joel did in the car. "The more, the merrier."

We take the trays back to the other room, and without prompting, Joel's sisters take the trays and begin rolling out the dough into thin circles about a hand's width wide. I can't exactly jot this down in my notebook while I help so I mentally catalog it all. Including the way his sisters work like they've done it a million times, despite looking a few years younger than me. In fact, the whole kitchen works this way. There's no bumping into each other and asking what needs to be done next. They've all been here in this kitchen every Sunday just like Joel said and it shows in the ease of their routine.

"How long have you known Joel?" One of the aunts whose name I can't remember asks with a knowing glint in her eye.

"Not long."

I hope that is a safe answer. I still don't really *know* Joel. But when no one replies, I ramble on. "I mean he comes into the campus café where I work so I've talked to him lots of times, but I just ran into him the other night and that's when I found out about your family. He agreed to help and here I am."

He agreed seems like a nicer way to put it than he bartered because he wants to get in my pants. The look these ladies give me, though, I think they're well acquainted with Joel's motives.

"That's very nice of him," the talkative aunt says. I wish I could remember her name because I have a feeling she's the one who has the dirt on every member of this family.

"Too nice of him, don't you think Michelle?" the older of Joel's sisters pipes in, looking to the other. Well, that's one more name to the list. I really need a refresher on who's who.

"I think it's hopelessly romantic. You ran into each other and just happened to be writing a play based on Mexican culture." Michelle looks around as if she's waiting for everyone to agree. "And we're a Mexican American family."

"That hardly makes us unique," older sister retorts.

Michelle isn't deterred, and I want to hug her in hopes some of her idealistic views rub off on me. "But it was Joel she ran into at just the right time. I mean of all the people you run into every day it's amazing that one of them has just the thing you're looking for."

I don't argue that he's been running into me on purpose for months now. I like her thinking better.

"In this case, I think that thing he was looking for was —"

I'm certain I blush at the words about to come out of Joel's older sister's mouth, but his mother, God bless her, intervenes. "Fate or not, we're happy to have you here." She looks from me to the sisters. "Bree, bring the buñuelos over here. Michelle, you and Katrina can sprinkle the sugar and cinnamon on."

Michelle moves next to me with a pleased smile. "You're really pretty. Your eyes are so cool."

"Thank you."

"You and my brother would have pretty babies. Do you like basketball?"

I choke on my own spit to the point everyone side eyes me in concern. I don't think they heard Michelle because no one jumps in to tell her how crazy of a thing that is to say to a near stranger.

"Sorry," she says when I've nearly gotten myself under control. "I have a bad habit of saying what I'm thinking. But it's true, you would. You're not married, are you? I mean I checked for a ring, so I'm thinking not."

The first buñuelo is placed in front of us and I follow her lead and sprinkle a generous amount of the sugar and cinnamon mixture on both sides.

"No, I'm not married," I confirm, and she rewards me with a big smile that gives away her visions of little nephews and nieces. "And I do like basketball, but your brother and I are barely even friends. He didn't even know I had a son until today."

She waves me off. "Joel loves kids. He—" She pauses, bites her lips and then repeats herself, "Loves kids."

Uh-huh. Everyone loves kids when they can return them. Having a kid or dating someone with a kid is a whole different thing. Or so I believe. I've not dated anyone with a kid or really dated since I had Christian sooo I'm guessing at best. It feels true.

We're moving the food outside to a covered patio before I realize I've completely neglected to ask any of my planned questions. Being in the Moreno household is a bit like how I imagine it would be to ride a magic carpet. It's exhilarating and cool and so magical that you forget to do anything but be in the moment. Well, hey, that's what it looked like for Jasmine anyway. I really need to expand my movie watching beyond cartoons.

I spot Joel crossing the yard toward me. Long legs covered in athletic pants eat up the space and it transports me to the times he walked through the door at University Hall. Except there are no barriers between us now. No café counter to hide all the truths I was afraid to say.

I like him. There I've admitted it. He's sort of sweet under all that suave charm, and though I have zero expectations that he wants anything besides sex, I'm not as put off as I'd been initially. He may be a total player, but he's been respectful and attentive and the amount of effort he's put into getting me to go out with him shows a level of commitment I've never had from a guy before.

A little boy about Christian's age barrels past me at full speed and launches himself into Joel's arms. I watch in fascination realizing it's exactly what I want to do. Joel carries him toward me as the boy clutches his neck and chatters happily. "Tio Joel, I learned a new trick. Wanna see it?"

"After lunch okay?" The boy looks absolutely crest-fallen. "Dylan, this is my friend Katrina."

He eyes me carefully and I give a little wave.

Joel leans in and whispers something in Dylan's ear and he nods excitedly before reaching behind Joel's back and pulling out a white rose seemingly from thin air. He hands it to me and I'm rightly impressed.

"For me? Thank you."

"I'm a magicianan," he states, butchering the word, but stating it so very matter of fact that I know better than to laugh.

"What other tricks do you know?"

A devious smile spreads across his adorable face. "I can cut you in half."

Joel laughs. "No chopping up people today, little man. Go wash your hands before we eat."

Joel motions toward the food. "Ready to eat?"

I follow his lead and fill my plate with everything – wanting to try it all and experience every bit of his world. Everyone sits outside and for the almost buffet style dining, it's still intimate and homey.

The large backyard has a pool, an outdoor grill, a TV, a putting green, and a large grassy area where several soccer balls and hula hoops have been abandoned. The older family sits at an outdoor dining table and the kids opt to take their plates and sit on the grass. Joel leads us to the table. "Did you get your questions answered?"

"Oh, um..." I really mismanaged my time. "I guess I got a little wrapped up in the food prep." I take a bit of the buñuelo. "This is amazing."

Joel's father appears beside Isa. I know this even before he leans down and kisses her softly on the mouth and says, "Everything looks amazing, *mi reina*. As always."

Joel's father has the presence and command that his son does, but where Joel's charm seems deliberate his father's is not. He's just got an air of importance and charisma.

"You must be Katrina?" he asks when he spots me sitting next to his son.

"Yes, sir."

His eyes crinkle with a smile that has me rethinking the differences between his son. "Call me Dax. Tell us more about this screenplay you've written. What's the title?"

I answer their questions. The entire lunch conversation revolves around it and they seem truly fascinated. So much so that I forget to be nervous. They even answer some of my questions, but I'm enjoying our easy conversation too much to pry too deeply into their lives.

I learn that Isa and Opal are sisters. Isa is the youngest and they came from Mexico City to the United States as soon as Isa was eighteen because Opal had met Joe – a pecan farmer turned businessman who traveled between Mexico

City and Valley for work. Opal and Joe have three kids – Lucas, Will, and Karla. Karla is the only one here today with her husband Pete and Dylan the magician is their son.

Dax has two sisters, Lupita and Bonnie. They moved here with their parents at a much earlier age. The exact reasoning is a bit fuzzy but the general consensus seemed to be more opportunities. Lupita is married to Jose and they have two kids Anita and Celeste – neither married. Bonnie is also Dax's sister, but she's unmarried too as far as I can tell.

"How did the two of you meet?" I ask Isa and motion between her and Dax. It's hard to tell what the age difference is. Isa could pass for thirty, but if I've gotten the timeline right by the various dates they've thrown out, she's around forty. I think Dax is older, maybe as much as ten years older, but the way they look at each other I don't think anyone could call him a sugar daddy or her a gold digger.

"I met her first," Lupita announces proudly.

Isa and Lupita share a smile that hints at years of friendship and sisterhood. "I applied for a job at the university."

"I didn't know you worked there too."

"I don't," she says with a laugh. "I didn't get the job, but I did meet Lupita and she found me a job with Jose's real estate company."

The man I can only assume is Jose raises his drink to her. "Best agent I ever had."

"I met Dax at Jose's thirtieth birthday party about six months later."

Isa reaches over and places a hand on Dax's cheek and the moment is so intimate I force my gaze elsewhere. Looking over at Joel, he watches his parents with such love and appreciation it's hard to reconcile this side of him with the guy who has been slinging cheesy pickup lines at me for months.

"When is the play, Katrina? I'd love to come see it." Lupita's smile and voice are sincere.

I have the date memorized of course, but I stumble over my answer because I hadn't anticipated that level of interest. "Oh, it's not until April."

"Opening night is April fourth," Dax adds. "Isa and I attend the Spring Showcase every year."

The youngest family member barges over to the table, face covered in cinnamon and sugar. "Can I show you my new magic trick now?" He looks up at Joel with big pleading eyes.

"Does it involve cutting or fire?" Joel asks in a serious tone.

Dylan shakes his head. "Nope. Mom says no more magic that requires anything sharp or flammable." The last word is said in his mother's tone and with total disregard for the meaning.

I steal a glance at Karla who gives me a, "Oh the stories I could tell" look that I try and flash right back at her.

"Tio Joel, I need your watch. I'm going to make it disappear."

Dylan waves a wand he's been clutching in his right hand and Joel takes off his very expensive looking watch and hands it over without protest.

Holding it in one outstretched palm, Dylan closes his fingers around it as much as he can and then waves the wand three times before opening his now empty hand.

"Where did it go?" I ask.

"On your wrist."

I look down to discover my wrist newly adorned. The watch isn't clasped, but it is draped on my right hand. "Oh my goodness. How did you do that?"

"Magic," he answers simply.

Joel reaches for my wrist and thumbs my pulse just below the metal band. "Thief."

I watch the movements of his thumb entranced with the way his touch warms my entire body.

"It's a nice watch," I say finally and reluctantly move to take it off, seeing the time in the process. "Oh no. No." I stand and pull my cell out of my back pocket to verify. "I'm late. I'm so late." I tap out a text to Victor.

Joel moves to action at the urgent tone in my voice. "Ma, we gotta run."

I calculate the time I think it'll take to get back to the university to get my car and then to my house. Ugh, how could I be so careless?

Hastily, but forcing as much appreciation and sincerity in my tone as possible, I say goodbye to everyone on the way out feeling genuinely regretful to be leaving this family lunch.

I'm lost in my own thoughts as we head back. I can't help but compare Joel's family with my own. My pregnancy put a strain on our families – mine and Victor's. The families supported us, of course, but it hasn't been an easy road. There's a loss of dreams that parents face when they realize their kid has to grow up and be an adult before they should.

And then with Victor moving away so soon after Christian was born, it added to the burden our families felt. And I'm not even sad for the ways that changed me, I just want Christian to have the best. He's such a special kid and I only wish Victor could see the way his actions impact Christian. I know he can't miss what he's never had, but I want him to have *more*. For the first time since he showed up at my door this morning, I'm wondering if I should go easier on him. I can't change the past and if he's showing up now for Christian, isn't that all that really matters?

I steal a glance over at Joel who stares out into the open road lost in his own thoughts.

"Thank you for today. Your family is incredible."

His smile is easy. "Did you get what you needed?"

I consider what I learned today. I didn't write down a single note, but I do feel like I got the tiniest peek into their lives. "I'm not sure," I answer honestly. "I got so swept up in your mom and aunts that I found myself listening more than asking any of the questions I intended."

"Send me the questions and I can email them to my mom, or you could always come back next week. Standing invitation."

"You guys really do that every Sunday?"

"Yep. I don't make it every week. Practice and away games sometimes interfere, but every Sunday at noon lunch is served at the Moreno house for anyone who shows up."

My phone beeps and I read Victor's message telling me it's fine that I'm going to be a few minutes late.

"Late to pick up your son?"

It's the first time he's mentioned the bombshell I dropped, and I don't miss the tightness in his voice. I wonder if he's disappointed because I have a kid or because I didn't tell him. It's better not to ask. The first option is soul crushing and the second is completely valid and all on me. I should have told him and avoided this whole awkward tension.

"Yeah, I'm supposed to be home in..." I check the time. "Three minutes."

"Where do you live?"

"West side of town. Columbia and Main."

"The West Lot apartments?"

"Yeah," I answer.

I notice the increase in speed, but he seems to have a good command of the car so I don't mention it.

"I like that area. I grew up a few blocks from there."

"You did?" I'm surprised. It isn't a bad neighborhood, but it isn't nearly as nice as where his parents live now either.

"Yeah, we moved across town when I was in high school. My cousin Lucas lives there now. I'll take you to your apartment and if you give me your keys, I'll get your car back to you tonight."

"That's really not—"

"You need your car before tonight?"

I shake my head.

"You want to be on time or not?" He smirks.

"You're going to get me there in three minutes?" I check my phone. "Two minutes."

He nods. "Give or take two minutes. Anything less than five isn't late."

If my stomach weren't in knots to get to my son, I'd be impressed with his cockiness even in a time like this. He breezes through the side streets toward my neighborhood with a sureness and ease that further proves his knowledge of the area.

Despite the amazing time I had today, it's relief and happiness I feel when Joel pulls up to the curb in front of my apartment building. I open the door before he's come to a full stop.

"Thank you so much." I jump out of the car and then pause before shutting the door. "Today was really great. Your family is fantastic. Thank you for all of it. And for getting me home impressively fast."

With his cocky grin imprinted on my brain, I close the door and rush to my son.

12

JOEL

*A*fter an early evening practice, I shower and then head down to the theater room. Sunday night is movie night with the roommates and I'm looking forward to a night of Tom Cruise and chilling.

"Which Cruise feature film are we watching tonight?" I ask Z as I plop down in the front row with my phone and take the soda he passes my way.

"*The Mummy.*"

I give him a head bob. Don't really care about the movie tonight. Tired as shit and just want to relax.

Bless enters the room. Bless is Blair and Wes. It's their couple name and it's way cooler a name than they deserve, but I came up with it, so no one should be surprised it's baller.

Makes me think of what kind of couple name Katrina and I could have.

Katel. No.

Jina. Fuck no.

Man, based on possible couple names we're not looking good. Scratch that, based on everything we're not looking good. I don't do relationships. And a kid? That really threw me. Was not expecting that. Makes sense now, though, her hesitation, why I haven't seen her around at parties.

> ME
>
> Everything turn out okay?

> KITTY
>
> Yes. Thanks for getting my car to my apartment. You didn't have to do that.

> ME
>
> Sure I did. I needed to further impress you with my chivalry.

> KITTY
>
> Two points.

> ME
>
> Shit. I don't even get three for that? That seems three-point worthy.

Once Nathan joins, we start the movie, but I'm not paying any attention to Tom. I'll have to google the synopsis and quotes later so I can be prepared should Z quiz me on it. Guy is serious about his Tom Cruise.

KITTY

Fine. Three points.

ME

Any particular reason you didn't tell me
you had a kid?

KITTY

You didn't ask?

I chuckle quietly, not because it's funny, but because I
can almost hear the way she says it all sweet and innocent
like. Nathan glares at me, but I just flip him off.

ME

Well let's just cover the basics right now
then, shall we?

ME

Got any other kids?

ME

Ever been arrested?

ME

Favorite movie? This one is the most
important, obviously.

My fingers itch to ask about the father of her son, but
it's none of my business and it doesn't even matter. As long
as she's single, that's the only thing I should care about.

KITTY

No, just the one. His name is Christian and he's three. No arrests or criminal record. And I can't possibly pick just one favorite. What's yours?

ME

Bond – the new ones. Casino Royale is my favorite.

KITTY

I guess if I have to pick, I'll say The Fault in Our Stars.

ME

So, really, why not tell me about him before when you were making excuses to wash your hair and binge watch Saved by the Bell.

KITTY

Both worthy excuses if you ask me.

ME

...

KITTY

I guess I figured once you had a real reason you'd stop coming by and asking me out.

ME

So let me get this straight. You were willing to keep turning down awesome dates with me because you thought I'd ghost once I found out you had a kid?

KITTY

Something like that.

ME

Oh Kitty, you've wildly underestimated me.

13

KATRINA

*C*hristian is getting out of the bathtub when the doorbell rings.

"Dry off and get in your pajamas," I say as I walk to the front door. I'm counting down the minutes until bedtime and simultaneously feeling guilty about wanting my kid to be asleep already. Mondays are the longest days. Three classes, critique group, and Christian has soccer practice. I've been going nonstop all day and I'm so close to blissful silence and handfuls of Goldfish crackers (Those things are addictive!) while I mindlessly watch TV.

I open the door, expecting my neighbor to need sugar or flour or whatever it is neighbors ask for. For reference, none of my neighbors have ever done this, but it's always what I expect/hope for when the doorbell rings. I'm not awesome at very many things, but I've got sugar and flour on the ready.

A FedEx delivery woman stands on the other side of my door holding a box and one of those electronic scanners. "Hi. Are you Katrina Phillips?"

"Yes."

She pushes the electronic scanner toward me. "Sign here."

Once I've scribbled some semblance of my signature on the screen, she shoves the box in my hands and wishes me a good night.

I don't recognize the return address, but it was sent same day shipping, so it has to be something amazing. I take the box inside and set it on the counter, delaying the excitement of finding out what's inside.

I walk around the apartment picking up toys, grabbing the giant carton of Goldfish and a can of Diet Coke and placing it on the coffee table for later, all while keeping an eye on the box as if staring at it will somehow give me some clue what it is.

"Christian, are you ready for bed?"

On cue, he races out to the living room still sopping wet with a towel thrown over his head. "You're supposed to dry off before you leave the bathroom," I remind him as I take the towel and wrap it around him and then hug him tightly. "Did you brush your teeth?"

Instead of answering he smiles big showing off his little teeth and giving me a whiff of the minty toothpaste.

"Go get your pajamas on I'm right behind you."

I steal another glance at the box and follow Christian into his room.

The apartment is small, but Christian has his own room on the other side of the apartment from mine. Per our lease agreement, we can't do anything about the boring white walls, but his room is decorated with artwork from preschool, pictures we've colored together, and a few Hobby Lobby-esque pictures that my mom bought to help decorate his room when he was little.

I help him pull on pajamas and get under the covers, and I lie down beside him on the small toddler sized bed.

"What was your favorite thing that happened today?"

His little face beams and I know he's already thought of his answer. "Soccer practice."

"You did a great job. I'm very proud of you."

"Do you think Dad will come watch me?"

"I'm not sure, but we can call him tomorrow and invite him."

He nods vigorously. "What was your favorite thing?"

"I had the most delicious lemon muffin today." I close my eyes and rub my stomach dramatically which makes Christian giggle.

"That's silly."

"Alright, buddy. I love you. Get some sleep."

"Night, Mom."

As I close his bedroom door, I let out a real sigh, feeling content for the first time all day. I did it. I survived another day. Maybe that seems melodramatic, but motherhood is rough. Going it alone doesn't make me feel all independent woman and tough. It makes me feel tired and older than I am.

I grab the mystery box and bring it to the couch. I turn on the TV and pull up an old *Saved by the Bell* episode for background noise before I finally tear into the package.

The first thing that hits me is the fragrance. Peppermint, cedar, and leather. I've had months to pick apart the smells of Joel and as I pull away the tissue paper, it's his scent that floats out with the thin white sheets. I reach in eagerly and pull out two large blue bottles. Shampoo and conditioner?

I hold the bottles in front of my face completely stumped. Why the heck would he send me... Oh my God. When it hits me, I can't help but swoon a little. One of the first excuses I ever gave him was that I needed to wash my hair. Two points for originality. Flipping the top on the shampoo, I inhale. It smells amazing. This didn't come from a department store. It looks and smells too expensive. Okay, fine, three points.

ME

> Thank you for the shampoo and conditioner this will come in handy the next time I need to blow you off.

JOEL

> You're welcome. Also, just a thought, another plan could be you wash your hair, get dressed up and let me take you to dinner? Araceli's Thursday seven o'clock?

ME

> I can't.

JOEL

You really can't or you're blowing me off again?

ME

Really can't. I don't have a sitter.

JOEL

I am sure I could find someone for that.

ME

I'm sort of picky about who I let watch him. He's only stayed with family at night.

JOEL

And family can't watch him Thursday?

ME

No.

Two long minutes pass and I assume he's given up.

JOEL

Alright then we're doing this another way. Tomorrow night seven o'clock. Virtual date. You don't even have to leave your apartment.

ME

Virtual date?

JOEL

Details to come. See ya at seven, Kitty.

And just like that, I have a date for tomorrow and a new favorite thing of the day.

"MOM, YOU LOOK PRETTY." Christian stares at me like I have three heads as I walk into the living room where he's watching *The Incredibles*. His smile falls. "Are we going somewhere?"

"Nope."

With a shrug, he goes back to the movie and I'm thankful I don't have to try and explain why I'm dressed up. If I can't wrap my own brain around it, I definitely can't explain it to a three-year-old. What the heck is a virtual date anyway?

It's twenty minutes until seven. Christian doesn't typically go to bed until closer to seven thirty, but I pushed everything up tonight to get him into bed before my date.

"Alright, buddy, bedtime."

When he looks like he's going to protest, I add, "Three books tonight so go pick them out and I'll be right there."

As he runs off, I run a shaky hand through my hair – washed with my new shampoo and conditioner, curled and I even used an old bottle of hair spray that hasn't been touched since... well, I'm not even sure. I opted for leggings and a shirt that shows off my midriff and hangs off one shoulder. It's comfortable but sexy.

I gotta be honest I don't know if a virtual date includes the ability to see the other person. Maybe we're going to text. I'm torn between the hope that it includes video chat and nervous that if we do, something will go wrong. I can just picture Christian busting into the living room in the middle of my date – that would be awkward.

I grab my phone and take it with me to Christian's room. He sits on his bed with a stack of books next to him. Way more than three, but honestly it might be better to give in tonight and hope reading in mass quantities puts him to sleep.

Christian is sitting on my lap, head leaned back on my chest when I feel my phone vibrate with a text. We're on book four, so I do the fast version, skipping unnecessary words and sentences, and then tuck him in. By some miracle, he seems tired and I cross my fingers as I grab my phone, give him a kiss, tell him my favorite thing of the day – him, and head out to the living room.

JOEL

> Picking you up in five. And by picking you up, I mean I'm going to call you.

ME

> Do people still do that? Talk on the phone?

JOEL

> Only when there's no other option.

Guilt gnaws and panic sets in. Crap, this is going to be the worst date in all of Joel Moreno's dating history. That's a long list to be at the bottom of. At least it'll be memorable for being the worst. Ugh.

JOEL

Can't wait, Kitty

I press the phone to my chest and smile. He always knows just what to say.

At exactly seven, my phone rings. I take two deep breaths and then answer, "Hello?"

"Hi, Kitty. You look beautiful."

I giggle into the phone. "How do you know?"

"You always look beautiful."

Feeling the blush creep up my neck, I divert the conversation. "So, what exactly are we doing on this virtual date?"

"Check your email."

"My email?"

"Yep, I sent you something."

I walk to the dining room table where my laptop sits and open my email. There's something really exciting about seeing his name in my inbox. Seems silly since I'm talking to him on the phone, but as I click on the email, subject Best Date of Your Life, I feel more special than I ever could have imagined.

There's a link and I click it, praying it's not porn, and am pleasantly surprised when it takes me to a website to claim my free movie. I attempt to read the Spanish title aloud, "*La Val...*" My words trail off and I decide to just go for the synopsis which is thankfully in English.

"Now, full disclosure, I've never seen it, but my mom

said it was super popular when she was young, and it takes place just a little later than your Hector and Imelda story."

I finish reading the synopsis, smiling ear to ear. "This is amazing." I can practically hear his grin. Cocky bastard. "We're going to watch this together?"

"Yep. I've got it all fired up and ready to go so just let me know when you're ready."

I unplug my laptop and carry it with me to the couch.

"Where are you? At your place?"

"Yep, in my room. Want a visual?"

Heck yes, I do. "Sure."

A moment later the text arrives. Joel sprawled out on a bed, propped up on the headboard with a laptop on his legs. He's naked from the waist up and I follow his bare torso down past the chiseled abs and V-cut. I'm mentally undressing him and I'm not the least bit embarrassed until I hear his voice through the speakerphone. "Put it in your spank bank for later, Kitty."

I close out of the picture. "Spank bank, really?"

"Are you suggesting I'm not hot enough to be used as spank bank material or that you don't spank the bank. I'm calling bullshit either way."

"You're too much." I shake my head and press play on the movie. "Okay, I'm ready."

For the next ninety minutes, we watch the movie. There's commentary on the wardrobes and how the quality of filmmaking has changed, but for the last half of the movie we're both so glued to the screen, not a word is uttered. Or at least I assume that's why he's quiet. Maybe he's fallen asleep.

I press a hand over my heart and bask in the feeling of awe that few films can pull off. "That was amazing."

"I can't believe I'm going to admit this, but that wasn't terrible."

"You picked a movie that you thought might be terrible?" I laugh into the phone.

"Well, I was confident you'd like it."

That's oddly sweet. "I did. Thank you. This is the best virtual date I've ever had. Also, it's the only one."

It's given me some ideas for my play, and I itch to write, but I'm not about to end our virtual date prematurely.

"And it's not over yet."

Butterflies dance in my stomach at the prospect of what's next. "There's more?"

"Well, just like a regular date, after the movie you're more relaxed and open so it's a good time to talk and get to know each other."

He continues to impress me with his insight. And he's right, I do feel more comfortable now.

"If we were on a real date, I'd reach for your hand and we'd walk from the theater down to that ice cream store at the corner of Fourth and University. Ever been?"

"No, but I've seen it."

Joel Moreno is good at romance. I didn't expect that. I expected charm and smooth moves, but this feels so much more intimate. Personal. A small voice in my head whispers that this is probably how he makes every girl feel.

"What's the most romantic thing you've ever done for a girl?" I ask, needing to know if this is just who he is. Wine and dine, make girls feel like they're the most important thing in the universe, and then never call again.

I hear him expel a breath. "I don't know."

"But you've taken girls to the movies before?"

"Sure."

"And to the ice cream shop after?"

He hesitates, but I know him well enough to know he won't lie. "Yeah, I have."

Obviously, I expected this answer. I know all about Joel's reputation, so it shouldn't sting to hear tonight isn't exactly something special. He's just treating me like he would any other date – well, the virtual aspect aside.

"What about you? What's the most romantic date you've ever been on?"

No way am I telling him it's this date. Especially now that I know it's his go-to move.

"Prom night. My father lost his job right before so I couldn't afford a dress and decided not to go. Anyway, the guy I liked skipped out too, showed up at my house unannounced the night of the prom and we danced under the stars."

"Why didn't you just wear a dress you already owned or better yet why didn't he buy you a dress?"

"Oh my God. That would be your answer. It's moot. That didn't happen to me, it was a *Saved by the Bell* reference." I groan when he doesn't respond. God, my life is boring. "Never mind. I guess the most romantic thing someone has done for me is buy me roses. They were a surprise and he sent them to school, so it was like he was publicly declaring his love."

"Lame. Flowers are cliché."

"Every guy thinks that, and every guy is wrong."

"And prom – yours wasn't romantic?"

"I didn't go. That part was true."

"How come?"

I pause and consider how to phrase my answer. "They don't make prom dresses in maternity size."

"Ah."

We're quiet and I cradle the phone between my shoulder and ear as I pick at a piece of lint on my leggings. Images of Joel in a tux, some beautiful girl on his arm, pulling up to his prom in some ridiculous car, probably a Hummer limo, makes me feel resentful and jaded.

"Practice in the morning?" I ask, checking the time and realizing it's later than I thought.

"Yeah, guess I should let you get to bed and do the same."

"I had fun tonight. Thank you for this."

"It was my pleasure, Kitty. Just one big disadvantage to a virtual date."

My heart hammers in my chest and I feel like I'm back at my parents' house talking to a boy and not wanting to be the first one to hang up. "What's that?"

"I can't kiss you before I say goodnight."

"Kissing on the first date." I make a tsk sound. "I thought the rule was no kissing until the third date."

"Think we already broke that rule."

"Didn't count. It was a non-date."

He laughs, and I enjoy the warm, rich sound.

"Night, Joel."

"Night, Kitty."

14

JOEL

"Where were you last night?" Nathan lights a cigarette as we walk from the gym back to the house.

"Home."

"You were?" He cocks a brow and then his face shifts in understanding. "Oooh, I see. Nice. Shelly?"

"Hell no." I shake my head as if it'll rid me of the memory.

"Tara?"

Another shake of my head.

"Who was it? If you holed up in your room with her all night, she must be a doozy."

"Actually, I was alone. Well, sort of." I clear my throat. "I had a virtual date."

He blows out a long puff of smoke. "That some sort of online hookup thing?"

Nervous as shit, an anxious laugh rumbles in my chest.

"Nah, man. Old school style, talking on the phone."

"I don't understand. You just talked to some girl on the phone? Seems like taking her out on an actual date would be a whole lot easier."

"It's complicated," I admit.

"Since when do you do complicated?" He side eyes me as he takes another drag.

"I..." I consider my words. "I don't. I'm not. I made a deal with a girl, she owed me a date, but couldn't leave her house. I improvised."

"That sounds like the opposite of uncomplicated. Tell me, what does one do on a 'virtual date'?" He air quotes.

"Fuck off." I shove his shoulder. "What's going on tonight?"

We make plans to have people over and as we get back to the house, Nathan and I split to shower and make calls.

I haven't heard from Katrina today, not that I expected to, but I'm wondering what she's up to and if she's thought of me. I can't seem to get enough of her and I'm about to drop all pretenses of even trying.

As I towel off, I grab my phone. Instead of sending out the group message that we're having people over, I pull up her number. My finger hovers over her name and I decide to call instead of text. Hearing her voice last night, soft and unassuming, was nice.

"Hello?" she answers sounding rushed and agitated and I immediately feel like an ass for calling. Who calls unannounced these days?

"Uh, hi. Sorry, did I catch you at a bad time?"

There's a pause. "Joel?"

"Yeah. Did I not come up on caller ID?"

"Sh– crap," she exclaims quietly away from the phone. "I didn't check before I answered. I assumed it was one of the other moms calling to get an ETA."

I'm completely thrown off my game. She sounds busy and uninterested and now I feel like a chump. I decide to go with short and concise. "We're having people over tonight and I wanted to invite you."

"Oh. That's nice, but I can't. I've got twenty hungry kids and their moms pissed that I forgot it was my turn to get snacks for soccer practice and if I don't find something gluten, nut, and dairy free and get it back to Russell Field in the next hour I'm going to get blacklisted."

I feel her exasperation through the phone and can perfectly picture her standing in the grocery store pacing the aisles. "I gotta go. Thanks for the invite though."

She hangs up leaving me holding my phone up to my ear and feeling like an idiot. She's done nothing but tell me how unavailable she is, and I just keep pushing. I don't know what it is about this girl that I can't just accept we're not at similar points in our life to have anything beyond flirting over coffee. It's been a long time since I cared enough to pursue someone like this and the knowledge of how that ended alone should have me running the other way.

I dress quickly and then shoot off a few texts to invite more people over. The guys are already downstairs when I head to the kitchen. Grabbing my keys and an apple from the counter, I do a quick survey of the liquor laid out. "I'm gonna go get supplies. Any preferences?"

Z and Wes shake their heads. Nathan speaks up. "I think we're good, man. We can probably get by on what we have."

"Never hurts to have too much," I throw back as I head out the door.

It isn't until I'm pulling up to Russell Field that I start to re-think my decision to interfere. I stare out to the kids running around, moms huddled together watching the kids intently. I sit in my car and wonder if this is possibly the worst idea I've ever had. I've all but convinced myself to turn the car around when I spot her. Standing off on her own looking out of place and even from my car I can tell anxiety rolls off her in waves.

I move to action, grabbing the bags from the backseat and crossing the field like a man on a mission.

The other moms spot me first. Kids suddenly forgotten, their stares rake over me like I'm Superman. I think it must be the groceries or maybe the fact I'm even here. The only other guy on the field is the coach. Don't dads show up for this kind of shit?

I ignore their curious glances – focused only on getting to Katrina. I can tell the moment she notices me. Before her gaze even meets mine, she stills, and her eyes widen while she scans the field. Like she can feel my presence before she sees me. A myriad of emotions crosses her face as she takes me in. Confusion, happiness, surprise. She steps forward slowly. All eyes are on us.

"Wha—"

"Sorry I'm late," I say loud enough that the nosey moms hanging on my every word can hear me crystal clear. I lift the groceries at my side. "Where you want them?"

She opens her mouth and closes it, glances over to our captive audience and back before she answers, "Right over there."

I follow her to a folding table with a bag of individually boxed raisins and a gallon of orange juice with paper cups sitting next to it. I can't help the smirk at her last-minute snack selection. "I had to improvise," she grits out quietly.

I shoot her a wink as I set the bags down. We unpack the items in silence, but I feel her watching my every movement.

Her eyes aren't the only ones I feel on me. The group of women that'd been ignoring her when I pulled up, now walks toward us. Their leader is wearing yoga pants and a tank top with a zip up hoodie left open at the top so her cleavage is on display. When she speaks, her tone is Splenda- sweet, which is to say, fake as fuck. "Katrina, I don't think I've met Christian's father."

"Oh, no, he's..." Katrina's face reddens and it's clear she's uncomfortable, but I don't know if it's because I'm here or because Christian's father isn't. Either way, I want to erase that look.

Stepping forward, I extend a hand. "Joel. Nice to meet you."

"Samantha. Bryson's mom."

A whistle blows and the kids race toward the sidelines at top speed.

I look to Katrina. "I should probably go."

But my goodbye is interrupted as a little blonde head throws himself around Katrina's legs. "Mom, did you see it? I kicked it in the goal."

"Good job, buddy." She offers him her hand and he slaps a low five.

I gawk. I can't even help it. Knowing she had a son was one thing. Seeing him, watching them interact, knocks the breath out of me.

Brown eyes meet mine. He looks so much like Katrina that I can't help but smile. Button nose, big eyes, dark lashes, and a mess of blonde hair.

"Uh, Christian this is my friend Joel."

He tilts his head up to really take me in.

"What's up, little man?" I put my fist out and he studies it warily before bumping his little fist to mine.

"What's for snacks?" One of the kids calls out and that gets all their attention. Eager hands reach out and push past us.

I follow Katrina's lead and we move to the other side of the table and help kids fill plates with snacks. For ten minutes we work in silence helping kids, filling plates, cleaning messes, re-filling plates after half the kids spill their food on the ground. I'm damn near breaking a sweat when the coach blows the whistle and the kids take off back to the field.

We toss the trash and Katrina finally breaks the silence. "You didn't need to do this."

"I was on my way to the store anyway." I glance over at the other women who are back to scrutinizing our every move. "They always like that?"

She shrugs. "I don't really fit in with the other moms."

I can tell by her tone that she thinks this is somehow her fault.

"Christian looks just like you." I turn to watch the action on the field. What a hot mess. There's no way to tell who is on offense or defense, it's just a mass of small bodies running around the ball. "Those your mad soccer skills on display out there too?"

Christian breaks out in front of the pack and kicks the ball toward the net. It doesn't quite make it, but he's undeterred and keeps rushing forward, into the goalie box to kick the ball again. He raises his arms in victory and looks to his mom. The smile on her face is proud and she jumps and claps like he just won gold at the Olympics.

"I should go."

After she's done cheering, she turns to me. "You really didn't have to do this. Practice is only an hour long it's not like they were going to starve," she says in annoyance and I admire that she's not bending to fit with the other mom's expectations.

"Kitty?"

"Hmmm?"

I lean down, my lips brush her ear. "Just say thank you."

15

KATRINA

I've got his coffee ready and two cinnamon muffins in a to-go bag when Joel walks up to the café.

"Morning, Kitty."

I slide the bag and coffee in his direction. "Thank you."

A smile pulls at his lips. "You're welcome. How's our soccer star?"

My heart flutters at the way he says *our*, but he seems completely unaware that he's done it and I'm not about to make a big deal out of it. I know he didn't mean it in the way it sounded, but it feels good to talk about Christian with someone like he belongs to both of us. I've gone it alone so much that I'd forgotten how great it is to be part of a team. Having Joel show up for me reminded me that I need to let more people in. Not everyone is going to let me down.

When it comes to parenting the responsibility has always fallen on my shoulders. Victor spends time with

Christian, but he doesn't make decisions and he isn't here every day. And I'm still frustrated that after his big speech on Sunday, he couldn't bother to show up to Christian's soccer practice.

"I'd hold off on Olympic dreams, he spent most of the last half of practice spinning in circles until he got so dizzy, he fell down." His low chuckle sends goosebumps over my skin. "Anyway, coffee and pastries on the house this morning."

He nods, the smile never leaving his lips. "You free tomorrow night for another virtual date? Team's travelling, so I probably won't be able to talk on the phone during the ride, but thought we could watch a movie and text?"

The way my heart beats against my chest, you'd think he just asked me to fly to Paris. "You already got your *one* date. Besides, don't you have to, I don't know, study plays or mentally prepare or something?" I wave my hands in the air.

"Nah. I usually watch Netflix or sleep. We're going up tomorrow night, but the game isn't until Saturday afternoon. Good to see you're worried about me though, Kitty. I'll text you at seven. I'll even let you pick the movie this time." He knocks on the counter twice with his knuckles and then steps away.

———

"EARTH TO KATRINA." Willa waves in front of my face.

I glance around the table, each member of our critique

group stares at me questioningly. "Sorry. I was daydreaming. What was the question?"

"In my story the heroine's mom is struggling to accept the choices she's making – moving away from home, her choice of boyfriend, the college she's picked. We were discussing how this would impact the heroine's relationship with her mom, her actions, her inner thoughts. It's such an important time in her life – time to grow up and grab independence by the balls – at least that's the heroine's thinking. What do you think?"

I blush, the situation feeling all too familiar and personal.

"Oh, um, I'm not sure. I guess the heroine would pull away, distance herself from her mom." I bring my pen up to my lips like I'm deep in thought, considering it from the heroine's point of view. I don't need to. I've lived it. "She'd find herself telling her mom less, not sharing the details of her life in order to avoid fighting with her. I think we are all probably guilty of doing that, right?" I look around nervously but continue when they all look like they're considering my words carefully. "We know our parents don't want us drinking all night or skipping classes, but this is the time where we finally get to make those decisions. Plus, we all have to learn things on our own. Every generation repeats the mistakes of our parents not because we don't know better, but because we need to face the consequences on our own."

Willa flashes me a big smile. "Yes! I love that. That's so true," she says as her fingers fly over the keys of her laptop.

The rest of the group weighs in and we break until next week. With my mom fresh on my mind, I call her while I walk to my next class.

"Hello?" she answers like she doesn't know it's me when I know caller ID announced me.

"Hi, Mom."

"Katrina!" she exclaims. "It's so good to hear from you."

"I know. I'm sorry I haven't called in a couple weeks. Classes and work have been keeping me busy and then of course Christian. Thank you for the cleats you sent him. He's loving soccer."

I take a deep breath. When I told my parents I was moving to Valley and going to college just as I'd planned before I'd gotten pregnant, they'd been less than enthusiastic. They're great and I'm positive that if I'd stayed, they'd have helped me any way they could, but my parents were counting down the days until they could start traveling and do all the things they weren't able to because they were also teen parents.

My mom was only sixteen when she had my sister and then, surprise, I came along fifteen years later. That's a lot of years to parent, I get it, I'd be ready for a vacay too.

And part of me had wanted to stay and take all the help I could get, but having Christian so young changed so much, I decided I didn't want to be like my parents waiting thirty years to do the things I wanted because I had a kid. I want Christian to see me working toward my goals – graduating and eventually being a screenwriter.

"Of course, send me his game schedule when you have

it and your dad and I will try and make the trip to see him play." The reminder that we're too far away for them to just pop by unplanned makes me stay silent for too long. "Katrina? Are you still there?"

"Yeah, I'm still here. I'm sorry that we're not closer. I miss you guys," I say. "Things are going great for us, though." Before she can get a word in, I continue. "And Christian is doing great in preschool. We're doing great, Mom."

One more great and I'm officially overcompensating. I slow my pace as I get close to my next class.

"Oh, honey." I hear her sigh. "Of course, you are. Your father and I are so proud of you, but we just worry. I don't want to see you make things harder on yourself than is necessary. I remember what it was like trying to be young and raise a child and your grandma was only five minutes away. She saved me more times than I can count. I just think you need to let people help you more. You don't have to always go it alone."

"I know." My voice is small. Guilt washes over me and I wonder if I'm being selfish. It's not the first time I've questioned if my actions are what's best for Christian. Would he be happier if we were closer to family, had Sunday lunches like Joel's family, and grandparents on the sidelines at his soccer games?

"I know too," she says with a hint of agitation as if she's expected my stubbornness but not quite accepted it.

"I've got a class. Tell Dad I said hello and Christian and I will video call this weekend so you can chat."

"Okay. Give him our love."

I lean against the wall outside of my composition class and let out a long breath.

ME

Okay. Let's talk tonight about Christian staying with you for the week.

I hear the professor start class and I tuck my phone into my backpack and enter the classroom without waiting for Victor's reply.

16

JOEL

I drop the tray table and prop my iPad on it before texting Katrina.

ME

Ready for our second date?

KITTY

New phone – who is this?

I balk.

KITTY

Kidding. Yes, I'm emailing you the movie now.

I pull up my email and laugh earning a side eye from Wes who sits next to me.

ME

I don't think Saved by the Bell counts as a movie.

KITTY

Each episode is just over twenty minutes so we can watch a few so it's the same amount of time. Season five is my favorite, but I think we should start at season three because it has the infamous prom episode I was telling you about.

I angle my iPad toward the window and plug in my headphones. If the guys catch me watching *Saved by the Bell,* they're gonna give me all kinds of shit.

ME

Alright, Kitty, I'm pressing play. What's your fascination with SBTB anyway?

KITTY

I have a sister that is fifteen years older than me. As you can imagine, we didn't have a lot of things to bond over growing up, but when I got older and wanted to escape my parents, she'd let me come over to her place and we'd have movie nights where she'd introduce me to all her old favorites. The Princess Bride, Titanic, Clueless, Friends, Family Matters, and Saved by the Bell.

ME

That's cool. Only the one sister?

KITTY

Yep.

We watch three episodes, mostly texting about funny things from the nineties – the hair, clothes, dancing, dear God the dancing. But I learn more about Katrina, too. Like for instance, she's deep. I guess I should have known this since she's a writer. Aren't artists all good with their emotions and feelings and shit? Well anyway, she is. I like hearing what she thinks about things, even stupid things like how Mr. Belding is more of a father figure to Zack than his own dad.

ME

We're pulling into the hotel.

KITTY

Oh, okay. Well good luck tomorrow.

ME

Trying to get rid of me?

KITTY

I assumed that meant you needed to go.

ME

Nah. Give me fifteen and I'll call you before we turn in for the night?

KITTY

Sure.

I follow Nathan through the lobby and up to the third

floor of the hotel where we're staying. In the room, we toss our stuff on the beds.

"I'm gonna shower," I tell him. I've got Kitty on the brain and I need a release before bed.

Nathan nods and digs out his cigarettes from his bag. "I'm going for a smoke."

He leaves the room and I sit on the bed, taking out my phone and iPad. Wes and Z ride Nathan for his smoking habit and excessive partying, but it's his life. As long as it doesn't affect his performance or the team, it doesn't bother me.

I turn Saved by the Bell back on. There are only a couple minutes left in the episode we'd been watching and dammit she's got me wanting to know how the gang is going to tell Slater he's a terrible deejay and... fuck my life.

I smile as I watch the cheesy ending and then undress ready to hit the shower before I call Kitty. I pick up my phone and decide to send her a pic while she waits. I don't send girls dick pics, just my friends when we're messing around. I admit that's probably messed up, but whatever. I crop the picture so she can tell I'm naked, but she can't see the goods and press send.

Before I can take the two steps to the bathroom, I get a text back. I'm grinning before I even pick the phone up anticipating her response. I expect a cheeky reply. Instead, she sends me a pic back and heat courses through my body and shoots to my dick.

She wears black leggings and a white tank top that doesn't quite cover her stomach and dips down low enough up top that her tits perk up and beg to be noticed. My hand travels to my cock and fists it. I'm so painfully hard.

It's a pleasant turn to my night. I'd thought I was going to have to use my imagination and the memories of her hot mouth, but now I've got new material.

I stroke myself slow, letting my gaze fall on her heart-shaped face and playful smirk. She's taunting me with those full lips and mesmerizing eyes. Tightening my hold and quickening the pace, I rake over her body imagining what's beyond the clothes but somehow loving that she's not naked. I want to undress her myself, piece by piece, exploring new territory and laying claim.

My balls draw up and I'm so close.

"Woah. Fuck. Sorry man." Nathan's voice registers slowly only seconds before my release can take hold and I'm equal parts annoyed and pissed.

"I thought you were going for a cigarette," I grit out, walking into the bathroom and covering myself with a towel.

"Sorry, man, just forgot a lighter." He's quiet for a minute and all I can hear is the soft sound of voices coming from my iPad. "Dude, were you jerking it to *Saved by the Bell*?"

I step out of the bathroom and grab my phone then turn off my iPad. "No. I just left it on."

"Why were you watching it to start with? Kelly was hot. No judgment."

"It sounds like fucking judgment."

He chuckles, grabs a lighter from his bag and heads back to the door. "I will be back in thirty minutes. That enough time?"

Instead of answering, I flip him off, walk in the bathroom, and slam the door behind me.

———

Z NODS his head in approval and claps his hands as he takes his place at the block and I walk toward the free-throw line. "Nice work. Let's get that extra point."

I take my shot and Arizona State calls a time out. We're destroying them. Up twenty points at the half, in large part to me. Everything I throw up tonight finds net. Some nights are like that. Most aren't.

I make the shot and the other team calls a timeout. Nathan and I bump fists as we take a seat on the sidelines.

"It's alright cause I'm saved by the... it's alright cause I'm saved by the bell," he sings quietly with a fucking grin.

"Fuck off," I say, but I'm smiling.

After Coach gives us a weak pep talk about running through the plays and tightening defense – there's only so much inspiration you can muster when you're blowing the other team out of the water – I head back out to the court seeing the cameras and announcers and wondering if Katrina is watching. She said she was, but I don't know if that was just her feeding my ego.

The idea of her watching may have something to do with my stellar performance. I'm in a zone like I've never felt before. I'm always confident and ready to play, but a different sort of calm has settled over me tonight and the only difference I can pinpoint is her which doesn't really make any sense, but I take my good luck charms very seriously.

Looks like my before game ritual has changed. From now on I need a little dose of Katrina before each game.

―――――――

Katrina

"You're my good luck charm," Joel says and points a cocky smile at the screen.

He's wearing headphones and leaning against the bus window. It's still light out, but just barely, and the soft glow of his phone casts a shadow around him making it hard to see anything else.

"I doubt that very much, but I'm willing to take credit. Is there some sort of payment for my services?" I toss the snark at him before I've thought through my words and I can tell by the huge grin that breaks out on his face that I've played right into his hand.

"Actually, there is. A date with me. A real one – no phone required. I mean don't get me wrong I'm loving using my phone for something besides texting and memes, but I think it's hindering my charm. I'm best appreciated in person."

I laugh against my better judgment. God, he's ridiculous.

"I don't have a sitter until next weekend." I stop and wait for him to connect the dots – I've already checked and next weekend is no good – he has a game. "You have a game, so..."

"Let me take care of the details."

Unease settles in the pit of my stomach. I'm sure he thinks he can just ask some random person to watch Christian, but that's not going to work. I can count on one hand the people I'd trust with Christian and most of them live too far to pop over for a date night.

"Don't worry," he says as if reading my thoughts. "I have someone in mind that I think you will approve of, but I don't want to say until I check. In the meantime, show me what you're wearing?"

He moves his head like he's trying to see past the bottom of my screen. I laugh but angle it out and down so he can see the leggings and Valley basketball t-shirt I'm wearing.

"I've got team spirit," I say and wave my hand around with an imaginary pom.

"Screw team spirit as long as you've got Joel Moreno spirit."

God, the way he says it sounds so hot and dirty my sex clenches.

"What'd you do tonight?" he asks, leaning his head back on the headrest, his black hair still wet from showering.

"Christian and I watched the game and ate pizza. He crashed early because he missed his nap two days in a row, so I was working on stuff for the play."

"How's that coming along?"

"Good. I think the script is just about finalized. They're letting me sit in on rehearsals which is amazing."

He stifles a yawn.

"I think you're tired."

He shakes his head in protest.

"I should go anyway. Christian doesn't understand weekends are for sleeping in."

We hang up and I lie in bed watching thirty minutes pass, then an hour. Then two. I'm tossing and turning and just about to give up on sleep altogether when a text lights up my phone.

JOEL

Open your front door.

My heart pounds quickly and I sit up and fling back the covers. He can't be.

I move through the house quietly without turning on any lights. When I reach the front door, I look through the peephole and inhale sharply.

"Open the door, Kitty."

I step back quickly and hear him chuckle. Taking a deep breath, I open the door and stare at him, certain the surprise is written all over my face. My eyes scan up and down taking in the way his athletic pants and long-sleeved t-shirt make him look like an athletic god. "What are you doing here?"

"I realized something, and I had to come see you."

Wrapping my arms around myself, I stay firmly on my side of the doorway and don't offer to let him in. I haven't really thought this through, but I know I don't want Christian to wake up to someone he doesn't know in the apartment. "What's that?"

He steps forward and grips my hip, pulls me to him and leans down until I can feel his breath on my cheek. He smells of mint and leather and cold and the combination makes me shiver into his touch. Instead of answering my question, he brushes his lips over mine softly. So much softer than I ever would have thought Joel Moreno capable of. I can feel him smile on my lips and then he presses harder, beckoning me to open. His tongue sweeps in and I melt into him, thankful he's got a tight grip on me because I feel ridiculously shaky.

He pulls back and leans his forehead against mine only loosening his hold on my hip slightly. "Tonight was our third date."

"Got a favor."

Blair narrows her gaze. "I'm not setting you up with any of my sorority sisters."

"I don't need your help getting a date, but thanks for thinking so highly of me." I roll my eyes and grab one of the donuts from the two boxes she brought over. "Can you babysit Thursday night?"

"Can you repeat that?"

"You heard me, weirdo."

"Who would I be babysitting?"

"Uh." I rub my jaw. I haven't mentioned to Blair that I'm talking to Katrina partly because she's the only one that seems to know her, and I already know how highly Blair thinks of me by her constant reminder that I'm not good enough for her friends. "Katrina's son, Christian."

"Why?" She crosses her arms and damn, I feel like I'm

about to get Blair's wrath. All five foot nothing of her is making me more nervous than I care to admit.

"Katrina and I have been talking, and—"

"Oh no. Jooeeel," she whines, and I grind my teeth because I can tell by her tone that she doesn't approve. "Katrina is not someone you can screw around with."

"Again, thanks a lot for the vote of confidence. Can you watch him or not?"

"She's agreed to go out with you?"

I sigh. "She's worried about a sitter. From what I gather, she doesn't have a lot of people here she trusts, but I think she'd trust you."

She bites at her bottom lip studying me carefully.

"Please?"

"I have stipulations."

Of-fucking-course she does. "Such as?"

"I want to talk to her first."

I roll my eyes again. "She's very well aware of my reputation. You don't need to warn her off."

"Yet, it appears she's still willing to go out with you." She shakes her head. "That's non-negotiable. I'll stop by the café and talk to her."

"Anything else?"

"Yes, actually. Gabby is moving down next month."

I smile. "Yeah? That's awesome." I've only met her a couple times, but from what I know of Blair's best friend Gabby, it's no small miracle that she's finally moving to Valley. "She gonna take classes this semester?"

"She's going to finish out the semester with her online

classes and then take a couple summer classes to help get settled before next year."

"That's awesome," I repeat.

She smiles. "It is, and I want to throw a party in her honor."

"Sure, that's no problem."

"A big party. Think prom meets foam party. Gabby missed senior prom and she's got it in her head that we have foam parties every weekend." Blair scrunches her face up. "I don't know where she got that from, but it doesn't matter, those are my terms."

A prom slash foam party? Both of those sound super lame. Combining them doesn't help. The things a guy will do for a good lay. Shit, that's not even true. I could get laid right now if that's all this was.

"Fine. We can work out the party details, but it has to be after the season."

She nods firmly like she's CEO of the party planning committee.

"You'll talk to Katrina today?"

"Oh yeah." She laughs. "I have so many questions for her."

***

Katrina

"Hey, Blair, it's so good to see you," I say as I untie my apron and step out from behind the counter.

"You too," she says with a tone that tells me she knows about Joel.

It's not completely surprising considering Joel and Wes are roommates, not to mention my run-in with Vanessa.

"You have time to chat for a few minutes?"

"Of course," I chirp cheerily despite the sweat now beading up between my cleavage.

She holds up a finger. "I just need to get some muffins for the guys first."

After she orders two dozen muffins, we settle into a table in University Hall.

"So, how's the new job?" I ask of her new job working at the tutoring center.

She smiles. "It's going really well, I miss the café some days though."

"We miss you too. It's not the same without your quotes. Garrett tried to take over the quotes on the evening shift but quickly gave up when people started correcting his spelling and grammar."

She laughs. "And you, anything *new* with you?"

"I'm assuming you're referring to Joel by that look in your eye."

Her eyes get large and her smile larger. "How and when? And how?!"

"He came in the café last semester and asked me out."

"You've been seeing him since last semester?!"

"No." I shake my head. "I turned him down, but he kept coming back every week."

"Seriously? That sounds... so unlike him."

"I'm pretty sure his ego wouldn't rest until I said yes."

"Well, obviously you finally did because he's asked me to babysit Christian for you on Thursday."

"Oh, you don't have to—"

She places a hand over mine. "I'd love to watch him. Honestly, that's no problem. I just wanted to make sure you hadn't lost your mind. Joel's great, don't get me wrong, but..."

As her words trail off, I can only nod.

Her fingers squeeze mine. "You must like him a lot."

"I do. I mean everyone likes Joel – he's easy to like, but he's different than I expected, too." I meet Blair's eyes and she's grinning so big I feel like I need to backtrack so she doesn't get the wrong idea. "It's just one date."

"One date that he's going to a lot of trouble to get. Something tells me he might have met his match in you."

"No, I don't think so. I'm really not his type."

"Joel's type is beautiful women. You're definitely his type."

"Thank you."

"So, let's talk details, you want me to come to your place? A sorority house probably isn't the best spot to babysit."

We make plans for Thursday and I finally let myself feel the thing I've been putting off – excitement.

18

KATRINA

*J*oel takes it all in. His long legs stretch out in front of him and he props his head on one large palm. I should have just written a story about Joel Moreno. He'd look hella good on stage with a spotlight on his ridiculously chiseled face.

I hear Brody and Tabitha, but it's Joel I watch as they embrace and recite the words I've written. It's surreal to have written something in the silence of your apartment and then *poof!* watch two people make it come alive.

When the scene ends, I leave him to chat with Brody. The expression he wears tells me he's not quite feeling it yet and I want to make sure I capture any insights he has.

"Do you think the scene needs more dialogue?" I ask when I approach him.

"Nah, I don't think that's it. It's missing something. The connection isn't there. Why is Imelda so drawn to me? And vice versa? I'm not saying we necessarily need to tell the audience the backstory, but I want to know, so I feel it in my bones. Ya know?"

Nodding, I swallow a lump in my throat. I let my shoulders slump feeling inadequate and like a total fraud. Why did I think I could do this? I don't know anything about all-consuming love.

Brody walks off, the rest of the cast and crew already packing up, and I return to Joel.

"It's a killer story," he says.

I check his expression but only find sincerity. "Thank you. Brody wants me to help him understand the connection between Hector and Imelda. That first scene is critical."

It's the only intimate scene with both Imelda and Hector in the entire play. We breeze past the happy courtship and then the entire second act is told through a split stage. Imelda living her life taking care of Coco while missing Hector and then Hector touring the world writing songs. It's a unique way to show their life together and powerful, I hope too, but it means this scene where they meet has to be amazing.

"Hey." He leans down to catch my line of vision. "You'll figure it out."

"It needs more angst and passion. It sets the tone for the entire play. If the audience doesn't buy it here, they won't feel the pain and anguish later."

"Pain and anguish, huh?" His lips twitch. "I thought this was a love story."

"It is... but uhh... it doesn't have a happy ending."

"Don't love stories typically require a feel-good ending?"

"No, not in every case. *Phantom of the Opera, The Fault in Our Stars, Me Before You,* and basically everything Nicholas Sparks has ever written."

The stage clears off leaving Joel and me alone. We walk to the front and I rest a hand on it. A tactile reminder of what is at stake. My words, my vision will be brought to life. It's a once in a lifetime opportunity.

"Close your eyes," he says, linking our fingers on one hand and reaching for my other on the stage.

"Why?"

"No questions. Just do."

I snort. "Okay."

"You asked for my help. This is me helping."

I let my eyelids flutter shut. Sensations overwhelm me – *he* overwhelms me.

My skin pricks and I feel his warm breath on my cheek before he speaks.

"Tell me how you see it. Don't try and make the words pretty just tell me everything. What do you see?"

It takes a moment for me to focus on the scene and not the way it feels to be this close to Joel. What do I see?

"They're standing away from the crowd, the festival is in the background – lights, laughter, music – but they're oblivious to all of it."

"What does Hector see?"

I shift my focus, imagine myself staring down at Imelda from Hector's point of view. "He sees a young woman that is fiery and determined. He's drawn to her beauty and spirit, wants to write music about her and the way she makes him feel."

"And how does she make him feel?"

"Alive," I whisper. "Like life never really mattered until now."

"And Imelda?"

My mouth pulls into a smile as I picture the lovable Hector. "That's easy. Imelda is drawn to his charm. He makes her lighter and reminds her to stop and smell the roses."

I open my eyes, feeling the magic of the extraordinary world I've created colliding with real life. Joel's smile is exactly how I picture Hector's in this first scene and if my insides match the outside, then I'm looking at him just like Imelda looked at her man.

The lights on the stage dim breaking the magic. "Looks like they're closing up for the night."

He drops my hands and steps back. "It's gonna be great, Kitty."

We gather our things and he leads me through the theater and outside.

"Thank your mom for me. The questions she answered were really helpful."

He waves me off. "She was happy to do it."

We're quiet for a moment as I struggle to stop thinking about the play. I want it to be perfect. Something that I did all on my own and against all odds.

"I know you said you got the idea from your son, but

what was it that inspired you to write a tragic love story? Aren't chicks into happily ever after?"

I smile. "The scene in Coco where Imelda sings. Their story is tragic, but it's also so beautiful to think that love can conquer anything. Even death."

"That's beautiful."

I shrug. "Well it's just a story, but it's nice to dream about."

"You don't believe love can conquer anything?"

"Let's say I'm skeptical. What about you?"

"Love conquering death? No." He shakes his head. "But I try and live my life in a way that makes conquering death unnecessary."

Such a Joel answer. Yolo. Except that expression only works when you're brave and cocky enough to go after everything you want.

"Is Christian excited about the play?"

"He doesn't totally understand, but he's excited that I've allowed him to watch Coco a handful more times this month while I was trying to get the script just right."

Talking about Christian, even in passing, feels so strange. I can't remember the last time a guy my age made any effort to ask about him. And I never bring him up because that scares guys off faster than I can get his name out.

"And Christian's father, is he the reason you kept turning me down?"

A laugh filters out into the night as we reach our cars, parked side by side in the lot. Mine reliable and practical and Joel's Tesla flash and arrogance. Tonight I get to ditch practicality and pretend I belong in his world.

"No." I tilt my head up and watch the way his face reacts to the news. Is it delight or surprise that I see? "We aren't together. Never really were."

"I see." He runs his tongue over the front of his teeth and looks out over the deserted parking lot.

"Well—"

"So why then?"

I know exactly what he's asking, but I play dumb. "Why what?"

"Why did you turn me down thirteen times?"

My insides warm. I don't know if his tally is accurate, but the idea he's tracked the number of times he asked me out makes me giddy.

"Because you're Joel Moreno."

He smirks. "That's usually a point in the pro column."

"Don't act like you tried all that hard to convince me to change my mind."

His mouth drops open. "Hell if I didn't. I asked you out every week for nearly five months. I've combed through more pickup lines than a fourteen-year-old boy. I had to resort to helping you with your play, which I'm enjoying, don't get me wrong, but just know I'm doing it to get in your pants."

"Oh my God." My outrage is unconvincing as I laugh at his earnest statement.

He shrugs one shoulder. "Just being honest. This is going to end with us naked."

I want to jump him. Tell him I've wanted to sleep with him since the first moment he flashed me the Joel Moreno smile, but I chicken out.

"So, what's next?"

He leads me to the passenger side of his car and opens the door. "Next, I feed you."

When we pull up to Araceli's, the parking lot is packed and there's a line out the door.

"I really don't mind if we go somewhere else," I insist as he opens my door and takes my hand.

"Nonsense. This place is the best."

He holds my hand loosely and I follow behind as he walks to the hostess stand.

"Joel Moreno," he tells the girl behind the podium. His hold tightens on my hand. "I have a standing Thursday reservation."

Her voice quivers. "I'm so sorry, Mr. Moreno but we gave your table away." She shifts uncomfortably. "A gentleman came in and said you wouldn't be needing it tonight and that you'd given him your okay."

"I see. We'll wait at the bar for a table," he says, not waiting for the hostess to respond, he walks past the podium toward the bar.

The girl looks nervous or maybe embarrassed as Joel tugs me past her. I give her an apologetic smile, hoping to ease some of her nerves. I'm also still reeling in the information I've just gained. Joel has a standing reservation every Thursday?

It shouldn't upset me. I know that this is what he does

– takes girls out, lots of girls, but I guess I'd hoped I was different in some way. Or that at least he'd take me somewhere else. But of course he wouldn't – it's his play for a reason.

Instead of stopping at the bar, he pulls me outside and wraps an arm around my waist. I hear him chuckle softly as we walk toward a table in the back corner.

"Coach Daniels, I thought that was you."

I wouldn't have recognized the Valley basketball head coach apart from the team, but as we approach the table, Coach Daniels stands, and he and Joel face off awkwardly.

"Joel, I'm surprised to see you here."

Joel smirks. "Coach this is Katrina, we were just stopping in for dinner, spotted you, and I wanted to say hi." Joel's gaze turns to the woman sitting at the table and mine follows. She's young, overly done up, and looks more excited about my date than hers. Her eyes dart between all of us trying to grasp the situation.

"Ah, Mindy this is one of my players Joel."

"Nice to meet you."

I offer her a smile which she doesn't return. Instead, she stands. "I need to go to the ladies' room. Please excuse me." Her gaze rakes over Joel one more time as she tosses her hair over her shoulder and walks away.

Coach Daniel's face softens as we all watch her walk away from the table. When she disappears from sight, he looks to Joel, a guilty expression on his face. "Thank you for that. We're almost done if you'd like your table."

Joel shakes his head. "Nonsense. Enjoy. We'll wait for another table."

Coach nods and his gaze slides to me and he smiles before looking back to Joel. "Finally needed that standing reservation, I see."

Joel pulls me to him, and I lean against his hard side all too happily. "See ya tomorrow morning, Coach."

"What was that about?" I ask as he leads me to the bar. There's only one seat and he ushers me into it and then slips one leg between mine as he crowds between the high top bar chairs.

"What was what about?" he asks, not quite looking me in the eye.

"That." I point toward where we just left his coach and date. "Does the team have a table or something?"

"Uhh, no." He looks embarrassed and I can't wait to hear this. Ought to be good. "My—"

"Joel Dax Moreno," a woman's voice interrupts and I turn to find a stunning brunette approach from behind the bar with a smirk that can only be described as the Joel Moreno effect. "You nearly had my hostess in tears."

She leans over the bar and they meet cheek to cheek and exchange a peck. When she pulls back her eyes meet mine and Joel follows her eyes to me. *Yeah, buddy, I'm still here.* I'm annoyed and annoyed that I'm annoyed. He hasn't done anything, and I already knew he'd slept his way through Valley so it's not like I can hold that against him.

"Maria, this is Katrina."

Maria extends a hand. "Pleasure."

I plaster on a smile and shake her hand. "Nice to meet you."

She grabs a glass and begins filling it like she's done it a million times. She's comfortable behind the bar, but she's not dressed for the job in a blouse and pencil skirt. "It's been months. What have you been up to?"

"Practice, school," he answers with a lift and fall of one shoulder. Interesting. I hadn't noticed it before, but Joel doesn't seem to like to talk about himself. As Maria and he catch up, I think back to all our conversations and realize this is true. For as cocky as he is, he's perfectly content to keep the conversation off himself.

Maria slides the glass in front of Joel. He doesn't question it which stabs me in the heart a little more. She knows his drink of choice.

"What can I get you, Katrina?"

I flush as they both look to me. A drink. Shit. I don't have a drink of choice. I barely drink at all. I'm quiet too long and finally Joel speaks. "Let her try the Reisling." He looks to me for confirmation.

I nod, and Maria grabs a wine bottle and glass and fills it before sliding it to me. I sip hesitantly, hell-bent on hating anything in this moment, but the cold and sweet wine dances on my tongue.

The sound of glass shattering somewhere in the restaurant makes Maria stand straight and take a step back. "It was good to see you. Don't be such a stranger." She turns her big brown eyes to me. "Good to meet you."

Joel's attention snaps back to me with a playful smile. "How's the wine?"

His ability to turn the charm from one woman to the next irks me. I swivel in my chair, forcing him back. "I need to check on Christian. I'll be right back."

I don't wait for an answer as I weave back out of the restaurant. The sun has set, but a hint of pink and orange still streaks through the sky as I walk to the side of the restaurant out of the traffic coming in and out. I wrap my arms around my waist and force myself to breathe. God this was a mistake. This whole thing was a mistake. I'd been right to want to keep Joel as fantasy. The reality hurts too much. Every time I turn around there will be someone he's slept with and then we'll be over before I can even enjoy it. I'd been wrong convincing myself that I could have fun Joel Moreno style. Pretending to be okay with it and expecting him to treat me differently because I made him work for it a little more is just laughable.

Pulling out my phone I see I've already got a text from Blair.

> BLAIR
>
> Christian ran circles around us. You're my hero.

She's attached a photo and I laugh as I see her and Wes looking exhausted and disheveled and a sweet, sleeping Christian passed out on the bed. I run my finger over the screen wanting that. I want to be with Christian and I want someone that will be by my side exhausted every night but able to laugh and love every second of it because it's all worth it.

"Hey." Joel's voice grabs my attention. He walks hesitantly toward me, hands in his pockets. "Everything okay?"

I hold the phone out. "He's asleep."

He smiles down at the photo and then steps to me and rests a hand at my hip. His phone beeps and he pulls it out, not letting go of me. His grin gets bigger and he turns his phone toward me. I read the text exchange from Joel's phone.

JOEL

All good?

WES

Yep.

So much more concise than the novel of questions I was about to shoot off to Blair. Everything is fine.

"You checked up on him?" I'm touched he thought to do it.

He shrugs it off. "I knew it was important that you know he's okay."

I let out a long breath and hopefully some of my anxiety. Christian is fine. I'm a mess, but that's of my own doing.

"Want to tell me why you really ran out here?"

My eyes widen in surprise and he chuckles lightly.

"Come on, Kitty. I know you better than you think I do."

Inhaling through my nose and letting out another deep, cleansing breath, I decide to go for honesty. "I think this was a mistake."

His grip on my hip tightens possessively.

"I thought I could be okay with this and we could have fun and I could live in the moment and all that." I sneak a glance up at him. "Yolo, like you said." I chuckle softly. "But I can't be one of those girls that you take out for dinner and drinks to make her feel special and wanted right before you move on to the next."

"What girls?" His tone is hard.

I motion toward the restaurant behind us. "Like Maria."

He steps closer until we're chest to chest which is how I feel his shake before his laugh cuts through the silence.

I stiffen.

"Maria is my cousin Lucas's wife. They own the restaurant and are very, *very* happily married."

I feel like the wind has been knocked out of me. Well, sh– crap.

His fingers lift my chin and I meet his eyes with a sheepish grin. "I like this jealous side of you, though."

"I'm not jealous," I say, realizing I am and knowing the tone in my voice is proof of that.

He laughs again. "You totally are. Don't worry, though, I like it. It's the first time I've gotten a glimpse at how you're really feeling. You do a good job of keeping everything locked up in here." His hand moves to my chest and he taps it lightly.

"I hadn't realized," I say honestly.

"Look, I know what kind of woman you are. I dig it. I respect it."

I hear the conviction in his words, but I can't help but be disappointed he doesn't try and defend himself either. At least he's honest.

"You want to go back in?"

One last deep breath before I chuck the calming exercises and probably my sanity. You only live once.

"Yes."

19

JOEL

I didn't plan this very well. We left her car on campus so I don't have any reason to drop her off at home so I can get inside and we can take this thing to the next level. The next level is sex in case that wasn't crystal clear.

"Oh my God, that was amazing. No wonder you bring all your dates here," Katrina says as we walk out of the restaurant. She no longer sounds put off by the idea I've brought other girls here and I'm hesitant to clarify.

"Never brought anyone else here, Kitty."

"But you have a standing reservation?" She studies me carefully. "And you never did tell me why your coach was at your table."

"I've had a standing reservation every Thursday since October." I wait for her to make the connection feeling all sorts of exposed by that statement.

"You've had a standing reservation every..." Her words

trail off and her smile spreads slowly as if she's weighing the truth in ounces.

"I wanted to have somewhere to bring you when you finally said yes."

"And you never brought anyone else even after I turned you down every week?"

I glance up at her and then down, open the car door and close her in before I shake my head in response.

I groan as I walk around the car. I should have lied. I sound like a fool. What's honesty if it keeps me from getting laid? Damn morals.

I slide into the car and we head back toward campus in a heavy silence.

"So." She clears her throat. "You went to a lot of trouble for me."

"It wasn't any trouble."

I shoot her what I hope is a playful smile, but I find her face serious and considering.

Dammit. This is what comes from trying too hard. I look like a total chump.

"Thank you." She turns in her seat as much as the seatbelt will allow. "I've been second guessing your every move because I had all these preconceived notions about you, but that's not fair. I'm sorry for that and I really appreciate tonight and all the help with the play."

Great, now she thinks I'm some sort of good guy. "You're welcome, Kitty. Can I talk you into hanging out a bit longer?"

"I should get home. I know he's sleeping and it's irrational, but I don't want to be gone too long."

"No explanation necessary. I figured you'd say that, but I was thinking maybe some ice cream and *Saved by the Bell*?"

"I don't have any ice cream, but I've got some popsicles."

"Sounds perfect."

I call Wes after I drop Katrina at her car. I let her lead the way to her apartment even though I know the way probably better than she does.

"Hey," Wes answers sounding groggy as he whispers into the phone.

"We're on our way to the apartment now. Everything okay?"

"Yeah, we all passed out early. Kid is great, but man he's full of energy."

I hear Blair in the background. "Ask him about the date."

"You hear that?" Wes asks.

"Yeah, I heard her. Went well. I'm following her back to the apartment for popsicles."

He chuckles. "I bet you are."

I don't correct his assumption. Grumpy fucker.

"Be there in five."

Pulling up at the apartment, I shut off the car and pop the console where I stash my condoms. I pull out one. Then grab five more. A tad overzealous perhaps but I've got big plans to screw Kitty until it's physically impossible to go again. I don't exactly want to work her out of my system, but I'm hoping that after tonight the heavy feeling I get in my chest every time I see or talk to her goes away.

Wes and Blair are already out the door as I jog up the stairs to Katrina's second-floor apartment. They look like they've been through the wringer.

"You two look like shit."

"Feel like it, too," Wes says, rubbing a hand over his jaw and looking down adoringly at Blair. "You should hold out for much more next time he ropes you into babysitting."

"Yeah, yeah. I appreciate it."

I hustle past them, but Blair calls out behind me. "Treat her well, Moreno."

Blair only uses my last name when I'm in trouble. Like she wants to remind me of who I am, and my last name somehow represents that.

I tap on the door quietly and hear Katrina shuffling inside. The door opens a moment later and she's the picture of comfort. Changed out of her dress, she's wearing leggings and a baggy t-shirt hanging off one shoulder, hair pulled up on top of her head. Normally I'd be bummed a chick put on loungewear, signaling that there will be no getting into her panties, but my dick twitches in appreciation confused because those leggings just show off how rocking her body is. A girl that can pull off Spandex is a true gem.

"I changed," she says, pulling on the hem of her shirt.

"Wanted to slip into something more comfortable for me?"

She snorts, ignores my comment and walks over to the TV stand to grab the remote. "Want to pick up where we left off? We didn't quite finish the episode where they're trying to save The Max."

I did and then beat off to the theme song, but sure as shit not saying that. "Sounds good."

She hesitates as I move toward the couch as if she's not sure where to sit or what to do. She takes a seat on one end and curls her feet up under her taking up as little space as possible. She's folded herself up to pocket size like that's gonna keep me from touching her. Fat chance, Kitty.

I sit down in the middle and pull her legs on to my lap. She giggles nervously as I take her dainty feet in my hand. A piece of blonde hair has come loose and hangs at the corner of her eye. Reaching forward, I brush the pad of my thumb over her smooth skin and tuck the hair behind her ear without thinking.

The simple movement takes me back to a million years ago and I freeze with panic.

October, Senior Year of High School

"Are you in this or not?" Polly asks as she pulls her hair up, twisting it and placing a clip to hold it back. She's missed a strand and I tuck it back, shuffling my feet in front of my locker. I stare at the clump of hair, now behind one ear, because I know damn well if I look her in the eyes I'm done. Those big green eyes are the reason I started chasing her and the reason I asked her to be my girlfriend. I thought I was going to be one of those guys that played the field and sowed my oats as Mr. Walter called it in sixth grade when we got the sex education talk.

I'd seen what true love was like. My parents were crazy about each other, even after seventeen years of marriage their love was obvious. Love like that was beautiful and special, I assumed, but I also saw how much work it was.

Every Monday my father brought home white roses, my mother's favorites. On Tuesdays, they had a date night – every week, no matter what. On Wednesdays, they played tennis together at the country club in some couple's league. I could go on and on... every day was spent showing their affection. Sounded fucking exhausting.

Sure, I wanted all of that eventually, but I was content to let love take a backseat until I looked into those mossy green eyes. Now I'm fucked, but I get it.

"'Course I'm in this. What does my buying you a phone have to do with this?"

"Consider it my early birthday gift," she says.

"I thought we were going to hang out Saturday, celebrate the big one-eight then." My gift depends on that being true.

"Didn't I tell you? I'm going to visit my sister this weekend in Phoenix. She wants me to meet her friends and they're having a party so it's sort of perfect. I can celebrate my birthday with my sister this year."

Well, shit. Polly's sister is just a year older and they're close. It's been hard for Polly since her sister went to college. I wait for her to invite me, put a silver lining on my ruined weekend, but she doesn't.

She holds up her busted iPhone and then stands on her tiptoes to catch my eye and stick out her full, pouty lips. "My screen is cracked. Don't you want me to be able to text you while I'm gone?"

"Of course I do, but—"

"Then what's the problem? You can afford it."

An unpleasant weight settles on my chest. Well technically I can't, but she knows I could get the money from my parents. I'm not even sure what the big deal is. Add it to the list of expensive shit I've bought her in the six months we've been dating. But those had been gifts I'd wanted to give her. She's never come right out and asked for something before and I don't like the way it makes me feel used.

I turn and open my locker to pull out the gift I got her. Two front row tickets for Katy Perry this Saturday. Even got backstage passes because I know it's my girl's favorite singer.

Polly slides in front of me, blocking my access. "Come on, if you really loved me, you'd do this for me."

She looks up at me with big eyes. The tickets are worth way more, plus I thought it was something cool we could do together. I don't really like Katy Perry but figured her excitement would make it worth it.

I nod and close my locker shut behind her. "I'll get it for you after school."

She places a kiss on my cheek and rushes off. The bell rings and I let out a sigh as I re-open my locker and grab my biology book.

"Yo, Timmie."

The guy two lockers down looks up at me like he's surprised I know his name. "Got a girlfriend or boyfriend? Significant other?"

He's still staring at me confused. "Yeah, I'm dating Cheri."

"Really?" I can't hide my surprise. Cheri's head cheerleader and this guy... well, he doesn't look like he could keep up with Cheri but guess I've misjudged him.

I pull out the tickets and toss them at him. He fumbles them, dropping his books in the process and making me embarrassed for him and also hopeful that maybe he can score some cool points with Cheri. Shit, maybe he doesn't need them, he somehow already got her. Doesn't matter, I don't need them.

"Woah, thanks man," he says as he looks them over and then tucks them into his pocket.

"No problem."

21

KATRINA

*H*e's quiet through two episodes. Other than holding my feet in his lap, he's made no move to touch me since he tucked my hair behind my ear. I know he's got practice in the morning so I thought he'd be anxious to get in and get out... so to speak. In and out of me.

"You want to watch another?" I ask, looking down at the remote and not meeting his eyes.

"I should probably go."

I'm surprised by his answer, although I'm not sure why. It's late. I guess I figured sex was higher on the priority list than sleep. Did I lose him with the leggings? Crap, I knew I should have kept the sexy dress on.

"Right. You've got early practice tomorrow."

His thumb caresses my foot. "Yeah. We've got a big game on Saturday. Speaking of, how would you and Christian like to come to the game? I can leave tickets for you at will call."

"Oh wow. That's really nice of you, but you don't need to do that. We usually watch the games here."

"So, you really do watch? You weren't just putting me on?"

I laugh. Of all the things to lie about that one never entered my mind. "Yes, we really watch."

"Come to the game. There's nothing like being at Ray Fieldhouse on game day and it's the last home game of the season."

"Okay."

He grins, looking more relaxed and like himself, and sits forward. "I should go so you can get some sleep before the little man wakes up."

Is that why he's leaving or is it just an excuse? I can't get a read on him. If he's suddenly not into me then why would he invite me to the game? Good God, this can't be him trying to be a decent guy and going slow for my benefit. Can it?

I move my feet so he can stand and then follow him to the front door weighing my options and trying to decide what it is *I* really want from him. I've been so caught up in what he wants or doesn't want that, I've barely entertained my own wants.

He turns at the door and reaches out for my hand. I let him weave our fingers together and I peer up at him trying to read every thought or emotion that might be there. He's given me no real reason to hesitate or second guess and that's the most surprising thing of all. Joel Moreno has a heart. Or at least a conscience.

In for a penny, in for a pound.

"You could stay," I offer and then wince at the totally forward words. "I mean, tomorrow is Friday and I don't work or have any classes so being tired isn't the end of the world."

He smirks but doesn't say anything arrogant to make me instantly regret my decision. Instead, he threads a hand through my hair and brings his lips to mine.

"Do you *want* me to stay?" His question vibrates against my lips. He sounds earnest and hopeful as if my answer changes his.

"Yes, but—"

My answer is cut short as he slams his lips to mine in a kiss that takes my breath and makes my head swim. I pull back. I need to tell him my conditions before I'm swept away by his touch.

"Wait."

He captures my face with both of his massive hands and stares down at me. "Does the but change anything that could possibly happen in the next two hours?"

"No, but—"

"Tell me later then."

His hands go to my hips and he leans down and scoops me up. His intent is clear, and I jump into his arms all too happily.

"Which way?" he asks, breaking the kiss only long enough to get out the words.

I respond by motioning with my head and Joel moves in the direction of my bedroom. I've never been more thankful that Christian's room is on the opposite side of our apartment. It provides a buffer to noise, which has never been an issue before, but I'm thinking might be tonight.

No sweet nothings. No cocky jabs about how I'm finally giving in to him. None of what I expected as he lays me down on the bed. He's heavy as he settles on top of me. A reassuring weight that this is real. He's here and this is happening.

Kisses that turn my body to flames and light my soul on fire, touches and caresses that are hard and rough yet soft and caring. The dizzying emotions that spiral through me make me break the kiss and bury my face in his neck.

"Are you okay?"

I dip my head, not trusting my voice. I'm nervous. So nervous. I want this, but I don't want it to be the end either. If I sleep with him, that will be it. I know this. Have known it. And I want it more than my next breath, but I'm so not ready to give him up.

He rolls to the side and pulls me next to him so that my back is at his chest. He presses kisses to my neck and brushes my hair behind my ear.

"*Estás asustada,*" he whispers.

My body molds to his and I can feel every hard inch of him. I can't help it, nerves or not, I wriggle my butt against his crotch. He groans and that makes me feel braver. I reach around and cup him through his jeans and he groans so desperately right before he takes my hand and wraps it, with his, on my stomach. I move our connected hands down and the heat of his palm and the contact, so close to where I want it, makes me squirm.

"You're killing me, Kitty," he practically growls as he moves his hand higher and wraps it protectively around my waist.

"But I thought—"

"You're not ready and as much as I want this, I want there to be no doubts when I ravage your pretty little body."

He's right and I hate that I can't shrug my inhibitions to be the girl that Joel has hot, dirty sex with, without having to stop before he's even copped a feel.

Oh, and I can feel how very much he wants to do just that.

"Hey, Joel?"

"Yeah?"

"Christian wakes up at five. If he sees you here, he'll ask questions and..." My voice trails off because, ugh, this is hard.

"I'll be gone before he wakes up."

"Joel?"

He sighs. "Yeah?"

"Thank you."

I know he's smiling as his hold tightens around me. "You're welcome, Kitty."

22

JOEL

My phone vibrates in my pocket and I turn on my back and pull it out only opening my eyes enough to see the screen. My daily wake up text from Nathan. Shit, that means I missed the first wake up alarm. How the hell did I sleep through Z pounding on doors?

Opening my eyes fully, my attention falls on my surroundings and I remember where I am. Shit, it's after five which means I failed to get out of Dodge before Christian woke up. I sit up in the bed and run a hand through my hair. As I'm trying to decide whether to risk a getaway, Katrina opens the door and slips inside.

"Hey," she whispers, and my eyes travel down her body and back up to the plate she carries. "I brought you breakfast."

"Sorry I overslept. I meant to get out of here before Christian woke up."

"It's fine. You were sleeping so soundly I couldn't bring myself to wake you. Besides Christian is eating cereal and watching cartoons, so you're as good as hidden back here."

"I gotta get to practice."

"I'll create a diversion." She sets the plate down on the nightstand and I reach out for her hand and tug her down. She giggles as she falls on top of me. The guarded expression she wore last night is gone.

Rolling with her, I mumble against her skin, "Can't remember the last time someone offered me breakfast in bed." Letting my hands roam to her hips and under her shirt, I'm exploring her smooth skin like I wanted to last night. Bonus, I can see now that it's light outside. Stopping at the bottom of her bra, I wait for any sign that points to no, but she nuzzles against me and I move higher to the promised land.

Cupping her over her bra, my fingers catch on something and I pull her shirt up to better investigate.

"Kitty, did you wear this for me?"

She looks a little embarrassed as I stare down at her lacy white bra that has a tiny pink bow attached to each strap. She looks like a present waiting to be unwrapped.

"I love it," I say as I run my thumbs over her nipples through the bra. She shivers into my touch and I bring my mouth to one peak and bite.

I have every intention of taking my time until my phone pings with a text. Know that's Wes without even looking. She squirms underneath me, wriggling her hips until I move beside her and trail a hand down to her pussy, cupping her through her leggings. God bless the thin material that does nothing to buffer the heat pulsing from her. Her sweet sex sounds fill the air and I can't wait to properly adore every inch of her.

I'm seriously regretting being a good guy last night because there isn't enough time to do the things I want to do to her before I gotta get to practice or before Christian comes looking for his mom.

Finding the waistband of her leggings, I slide my hand underneath and down. Christ, she's not wearing underwear. Which means she wasn't last night either.

"What no matching panties?" I joke.

She catches her bottom lip between her teeth and now I'm fucking curious.

"They have a bow on the back, but it looked like I had a bubble butt, so I took them off."

Chuckling at the image of her checking out her ass before I got here, I show her my approval by removing my hand and placing two fingers to her lips. "Suck," I urge.

She hesitates but opens slowly for me. Once I'm inside, her tongue caresses my fingers and her cheeks hollow.

"Good girl," I say, pulling them free and then guiding my hand back down, finding her clit and rubbing slowly.

Her hips rise to give me better access and I waste no time giving her what she wants. I continue in lazy strokes that become faster as she grinds into me. She fucks my hand with such abandon, I'm wondering where my tentative Kitty went. Maybe I read her all wrong.

I pull away just enough to fully appreciate the view of

Katrina sprawled out under me looking like she'll die if I don't make her come. I'm a generous guy, happy to be the one doling out orgasms as well as receiving them, but never have I so enjoyed watching someone get theirs knowing I'm gonna be going home with blue balls.

"That's it, Kitty. Come for me."

I circle her clit faster and slide a finger inside her as she cries out. Her eyes open and lock on mine. My heart hammers in my chest as I feel her completely let go and ride the pleasure.

When she goes limp, I move my hand and roll on top of her letting her feel how turned on I am. My dick twitches and fucking begs me not to move.

"That was fucking hot, Kitty. You feel so good," I tell her and mean every word. "Gonna have to request a viewing of those pretty panties you discarded when I've got more time. Call you later, Bubble Butt."

I place a kiss on her mouth and jump up, grab a piece of bacon from the plate of breakfast she brought me. As I bring it to my mouth, I breathe in the smell of her on my fingertips, pop the bacon in and then lick my fingertips. "Thanks for breakfast."

Pussy coated bacon... my new favorite.

She rights her clothes and sits up looking adorably rumpled and shy. "Give me two minutes to distract Christian and then you're clear to make a run for it."

———

"MORENO," Coach calls out from the sideline and motions me over.

Practice is basically over and all that is standing between me and a hot shower is ten more free-throws.

"What's up?" I ask, wiping my face with my practice jersey.

"Tough game this weekend. How are you feeling?"

"Good. I'm ready. Team is looking good too."

He nods. "Got a couple more calls from Sara Icoa. She's going to be here Saturday and she's got a good relationship with the Lakers."

Lakers are my top choice. Ever since I was a kid, I've bled purple and gold. There are lots of good teams in the league, but anything other than LA is going to feel like the second choice. Sara Icoa is Z's agent but has been pursuing me hard this year too. I want to finish college – even if this year is my best shot at displaying my talents. With Z and Malone graduating, next year is looking like a rebuilding year for Valley. Not the best year to try and get a spot on my dream team.

I'm silent as I consider my future against another year at Valley.

"With the new NCAA rules, you can talk with an agent without declaring for the draft. If you want me to set anything up, just let me know. I know I'm not telling you anything you don't know, but as much as I'd like to keep you here next year, it might be good to keep your options open."

I glance around my favorite spot on campus, maybe in

all of Valley, and try and picture tomorrow being my last time playing in Ray Fieldhouse. "Thanks, Coach."

"Also." He clears his throat. "I wanted to apologize for last night. I didn't mean to steal your reservation."

I smirk. "Araceli's is the best, right?"

He chuckles. "It was perfect."

"And the woman?"

"Well, I'm not sure there's going to be another date, but she was less awful than the last one. Do yourself a favor and when you find a good woman in your twenties, marry her. Dating after thirty is awful."

"Well, I'm in no rush for marriage, but the advice is noted."

"And the young woman you were with last night? She aware of that? She looked pretty smitten."

"She's aware."

Maybe too aware of my past. She seems to be constantly waiting for me to move along and maybe I should before things get too messy.

"Can I ask you a question?"

He nods, eyebrows raised. "Sure."

"Ever date a single mom?"

Understanding dawns on his face and he eyes me with something like pity as he puts the pieces together.

"Yeah, I have. Nothing serious, though. My experience with dating women with kids is there's no half ass. It's either serious or it's not and they usually go into the relationship already expecting one or the other. If your girl really is aware that you're not looking for anything serious right now, then I'd say she's already made her peace with that."

I consider that. Has Kitty put me in the nothing serious column? She should. Isn't that what I've done to her and every other girl since Polly?

But fuck, why does that annoy me so much?

23

KATRINA

I'm all smiles as I bring the box from the door to the living room. "Christian, you got mail."

His eyes light up at the box with his name written in large black letters.

"Who's it from?"

I already know, but I'm not sure exactly how to explain, so I ignore his question by distracting him. "Let's see what's inside!"

As he tries to tear into the box, failing to rip past the heavy mailing tape, I grab scissors from the kitchen and then re-join him on the floor. "Here let me help."

A few quick cuts and Joel's scent permeates the air.

Christian dives for the open box, pulling out a mini basketball and a foam finger with the Valley U branding. I can't help but laugh.

While he's busy pulling out enough Valley basketball merchandise to outfit an entire cheering crowd, I text Joel.

ME

Thank you. Christian is so excited.

JOEL

There's something in there for you too.

I look over the pile Christian has amassed, spotting one t-shirt that's clearly too large for my son.

"I think this one is for me," I tell him as I hold it up in front of me. The t-shirt is like many others I've seen, Valley U Basketball screen-printed on the front with our road-runner mascot, but the back has Moreno and number thirty-three proudly displayed.

ME

I was really hoping for a Zeke Sweets jersey. Where can I get one of those?

JOEL

If you show up today in a Sweets jersey, I'm going to spank you later. Fair warning.

My body tingles. At Joel's hand, I think I might just be okay with a little spanking.

ME

Promise?

I'm goading him, which isn't really fair because it isn't like there's going to be time for that today, but I just can't help it. Flirting with him is fun.

JOEL

Can we hang out after the game?

I'm about to remind him I'll have Christian when he sends another.

JOEL

I'd like to take you and Christian out for pizza after the game since I ruined your game day ritual.

ME

That sounds nice.

And it does. Way, way too nice.

ME

Good luck today. Break a leg or whatever the appropriate sentiment is.

JOEL

I can think of all kinds of sentiments I'd like from you.

Jesus, how does he make everything sound so dirty?

Thirty minutes before the game, Christian and I make our way to our seats in Ray Fieldhouse. I had to hand off our tickets to an usher because my hands were shaking so badly I couldn't read the seat numbers. I don't know why I'm so nervous. I'm regretting wearing his shirt though. I'm one of about fifty other girls I've already spied wearing the same one. I'd felt special as I pulled it over my head and now I just feel like one of many in the Joel Moreno fan club.

"Seats one and two." The woman hands me the tickets as she stands at the bottom row and motions toward our seats.

I take the tickets and verify she's not insane. I'd expected seats in the student section, not first row behind the team's bench. This is too much. Christian is oblivious, of course, and his excitement puts me more at ease as he jumps up and down with the ridiculous cut-out of Joel's face on a stick. Christian waves it around and points to the floor where Valley is warming up. "There he is!"

Joel waves and dribbles the ball over our direction.

"You guys made it," he says, looking from me to Christian.

"These seats are..." I shake my head. "Ridiculous."

"Wanted to make sure you got a good, up close and personal view of how amazing I am." He winks and I can't help but laugh.

"You want to come meet Ray Roadrunner?"

Christian's face lights up. "Can I, Mom?"

How can I possibly say no to that?

"Yes, but please be careful with him?" I plead with Joel, not caring in the least if I sound overprotective.

Christian rushes to the court and Joel bends down next to my son, hands him the basketball he'd just been dribbling, and they exchange a few words back and forth. My heart hammers in my chest as I watch them so easily interact. I take my seat, sitting forward so I can watch Christian as he crosses the court. Ray Roadrunner is standing on the sidelines next to the cheerleaders, and Joel leads him over and the mascot raises his hand for a high five which Christian slaps, and then Ray feigns like Christian has hurt his hand.

Next, Joel takes him around to the guys and each one gives him a fist bump. Christian's smile couldn't get any bigger. And then just when I think they're about to head back my way, Joel picks Christian up like he weighs nothing and places him on his shoulders. The team clears the way and Joel steps to the basket and encourages Christian to shoot. The ball goes up and in and the team cheers. So does the crowd. I look up to see Christian and Joel being displayed on the jumbotrons for all the fans to see.

Christian is beaming when he turns in my direction to make sure I saw. I clap from my seat and can't help but laugh at how happy he is out there. It's a universal truth that the way to a woman's heart is through her kids. My chest is rising and falling rapidly, betraying any chill feelings I might want to display as Joel brings Christian back to our seats.

"Mom, did you see that?"

"Yes!" I hug him against me. "That was amazing, buddy."

Looking up to Joel, I smile. I expect him to be regarding me with a smirk and maybe a parting jab, but the expression on his face as he watches me and Christian is soft and sincere. As I prompt Christian to tell Joel thank you, and do the same myself, Joel simply nods and steps away to rejoin his team.

Joel was right, there's nothing like being in Ray Fieldhouse on game day. Since it's the last home game, the senior players are brought out to a lot of applause. When Wes is introduced, the place gets to their feet to honor Blair's boyfriend who was injured earlier in the season. I look around for her and spot her in the student section jumping up and down wildly.

Much to my surprise and happiness, Christian stays glued to the action for the first half. He cheers especially loud for Joel and waves his foam finger and Joel cutout high in the air. When the buzzer signals halftime, we stand.

"Want to grab some popcorn?" I ask him and he answers by darting to the aisle. Grabbing on to his hand, I feel eyes on me and look up to see Isa smiling at us.

I wave and let my gaze flit over the rest of the aisle where Joel's entire family sits. Kill me now. They've been sitting within spitting distance the entire first half without my realizing it. Joel's father is talking with someone I don't recognize, but Isa moves to the end of the aisle as we approach.

"Katrina, this must be your son."

I tug on Christian's hand. "Christian this is Joel's mother, Mrs. Moreno."

"It's a pleasure to meet you," she says to him and then smiles back at me. "I was thinking about you earlier this week. How's the play coming along?"

Christian pulls on my hand, bored by the adult conversation.

"Good. Thank you again for answering my questions."

"Maybe you'll come back to the house for Sunday lunch again?" she asks, and I get the distinct feeling her motives are self-serving and that Joel would probably freak if he knew his mom was inviting girls over. "And you could bring Christian, of course."

I let Christian pull me with him. "Oh, thank you. We'll think about it."

We get in line at the concession and I text Blair as we wait.

ME

I'm at the game. I saw you jumping up and down for your man.

BLAIR

Where are you sitting? Are you coming to The White House for the after-game party? Should be a lot of people to help celebrate Zeke and Wes' last home game.

A pang of disappointment hits me that I can't go and then guilt. Did Joel know about the party before he made plans with me and Christian? I can't imagine he'd want to miss a party in honor of two of his roommates.

ME

No, Christian's with me. We're sitting behind the team.

BLAIR

Let's catch up sometime this week. I want details about whatever is going on with you and Joel!

ME

I'll text you this week.

I tuck my phone away, promising myself I will text Blair this week. I've done a shitty job of making connections with people, using Christian as an excuse. If I've learned nothing else from spending time with Joel, it's that I need to put myself out there more. I've fooled myself into thinking it was best for Christian, but as I look at the huge grin on his face today, I know that it was about protecting me and not him.

24

JOEL

*T*ypically after a game, we make our way straight to the locker room, but since it's the last home game, we linger on the court letting the seniors soak up the moment. I try and do the same just in case. I don't really think I can give up another year of this, but if the right opportunity landed in my lap... well, I don't know what I'd do.

Z and Wes hug at half court. It's a bittersweet moment for them as seniors and because of all the shit Wes has been through this year.

Nathan bumps my shoulder. "Ready to party?"

"Yeah, gotta do some stuff first." I nod toward the section my parents sit and I know he assumes I mean hang out with the family. I don't bother correcting him. "I'll see you at the house later. Try to keep things under control."

I glance over at the sidelines looking for Katrina and Christian to let them know I'm gonna shower before we head out, but they're nowhere in sight. My family hovers on the sidelines, Dad talking to the athletic director and my mom watching me.

"Hey, Ma. Seen Katrina? I was supposed to meet her after the game."

Her brow furrows. "She said goodbye and headed up the stairs. Maybe she thought—"

But I don't stick around to hear the end of that sentence.

"I'll call you later," I call over my shoulder and take the stairs up out toward the exits as fast as the crowd will allow. My back is patted, and people call out to me. I mumble my thanks and keep going with a singular focus. I run a circle around the top level, but they're nowhere in sight. I finally give up and head down to the locker room where I can grab my phone and text her, but there's one already waiting for me.

KITTY

Congratulations on the game! Christian had a blast, thank you so much! We need to take a raincheck on this afternoon, but I'll text you later.

Well fuck, I got blown off. That fucking stings.

I'm still pissy as I pull into the garage. Music is blasting and it annoys me for no good reason. My head is all messed up and I feel like an idiot for thinking I could convince Katrina to let me in with floor level tickets and some shitty Valley merchandise.

Nathan is in the kitchen when I walk through and

takes one look at me and passes me the unopened bottle of Jack.

"Thanks. Seen Z?"

I missed him after the game and want to make sure I talk to him before I get too deep into this bottle.

"No, but I've got a pretty good idea."

I nod and take the bottle with me upstairs. Z's door is shut, but I can hear the faint sound of music coming from inside. I knock. "Z?"

"Come in."

I open the door and find Z lying back on his bed, shooting a basketball in the air. "Missing the party downstairs."

He doesn't smile at my joke, which it obviously is because Z misses nearly every party.

He glances at me before he sends the ball sailing back in the air. "What are you doing up here?"

"You got Sara Icoa's number?"

He stops and sits up. "Are you thinking of entering the draft?"

I unscrew the top of the bottle and take a swig before answering. "I don't know, but Coach thinks I should keep my options open and the way next year is looking it might be best."

"I thought you wanted to finish your degree?"

I lift one shoulder. "A degree isn't really necessary for what I want to do."

Play pro ball and then be a broadcaster. The degree is important for my parents and there is something special in being a second-generation graduate from the college my dad helped build.

He grabs his phone. "I'll text you Sara's number, but I'm meeting up with her next week if you want to tag along. I'm sure she'll be more than happy to answer whatever questions you have."

"Cool. Thanks." I feel the vibration of my phone in my pocket and resist looking at it. It's been going off every few minutes. I'm sure my absence downstairs has been noticed because I'm never not in the center of a party at The White House.

I don't make any move to leave and Z lifts a brow. "Any particular reason you're up here asking me about this now instead of getting lit and making out with half of the women's tennis team?"

I chuckle. It was the women's beach volleyball team and it was one blurry night that I don't even remember.

"Ever feel like you're not the person everyone thinks you are?"

He regards me seriously. "Every day."

I don't know why Z keeps to himself the way he does. I've never pressed him on it. Guess I assumed it was his way of keeping his focus on ball and his goals, but now I wonder if it's something else entirely that keeps him up here while the rest of us are enjoying our thirty seconds of fame.

"Only a few months left, might want to consider sucking it up and enjoying what's left of college."

He shakes his head. "I'd rather stay up here."

"Suit yourself."

I leave Z to do whatever it is he does locked away in his room and I head down to the party.

Downstairs, Blair spots me from across the room and dashes away from Wes toward me. "I heard Katrina and Christian were at the game." Her voice goes up ten octaves as she talks animatedly with both hands. "Can I assume that was your doing?"

When I nod, Blair's smile is nuclear.

"I think I underestimated you, but I'm a little disappointed you're here when you know there's no way she can bring Christian to this sort of thing."

"Yeah, well it doesn't matter."

She crosses her arms as clear a sign as any that she's not budging until I fill her in.

I take another drink. Liquid courage. I've caught feelings and this sucks.

"We were supposed to go out after the game, but she canceled via text."

"And she didn't say why?"

"Nope."

"Did you ask?" Blair presses.

I shake my head and she lets out an exasperated sigh that somehow still sounds chipper and upbeat. "There are a million totally legit reasons why she might have bailed. Instead of sulking around here getting wasted, why don't you ask her? Better yet, go over there and talk to her in person."

The fact that Blair is trying to get me and Katrina

together makes me chuckle. "What happened to me not being good enough for your friends?"

"Oh, you're still not anywhere good enough for her, but I'm really enjoying watching you fall all over yourself trying."

I glare, but she just flashes a sweet smile. "If you're not willing to risk it all, then you don't want it bad enough."

Cock an eyebrow and take another generous swig from the bottle.

That doesn't deter Blair from continuing to speak her peace. "When's the last time you gave anything but basketball your A-game?"

"I don't know."

Lie. I remember. And it's exactly why I'm pissed I put myself in this position twice.

25

JOEL

December, Senior Year of High School

The pep band is playing, and my team is already out on the floor warming up.

"Listen, Polly, I gotta get out there, but we'll talk about it after the game."

It's the final night of the Valley High winter basketball tournament. Winning this tournament is all that should be on my mind, but my girlfriend has other priorities.

"But the formal is next Friday, and we *have* to get a limo."

"We can talk about it—"

Two steps toward the court and she cuts me off, crossing her arms as her green eyes take on a golden tint. "Do you not care about formal? Or me?"

Polly is beautiful and outspoken and used to getting her way. I admired those qualities in her a year ago, but lately, it feels like it's at the expense of me and my goals. Or maybe she's right and I've just stopped caring. I'm five months away from graduation and with the colleges scouting me I'm guaranteed to end up playing somewhere awesome. It's hard to care about formals and limos when I'm about to be a college ball player. One step closer to my dreams of the NBA.

But I do care about Polly.

"I love you and I will make sure it's everything you want, but right now I gotta win a championship game, babydoll." I brush a kiss on her pouty lips and haul ass to the court.

We win the game and the mood in the locker room is light. Guys joking around, dancing, and enjoying this moment with the team. Someone has turned on an old school Jock Jams playlist and I sing along to "Crazy Train," air guitaring when appropriate.

I'm walking on cloud fucking nine until I step out of the locker room. Polly waits for me and the pinched expression tells me that she's not impressed by the thirty points I racked up on the court. Still, I go for playful when I fall in beside her and drape an arm around stiff shoulders.

"Hey, beautiful. The team is heading for pizza to celebrate. You wanna ride over with me?"

"Ugh. Not pizza again. I thought we could go somewhere nice. Just the two of us. Didn't your cousins just open a nice restaurant? Let's go there."

Her sentiments aren't totally unjustified. Pizza is the

go-to after a win, but even with four years of post-victory pizza binges, there's nowhere else I'd rather be.

"Come on." I link our hands together and try to do my best to look charming. Normally an easy feat, but Polly's hard features don't soften under my puppy dog eyes. "We can make winter formal plans after we eat."

The tiniest crack of a smile pulls her full lips apart and tip upward.

Valley High basketball players, their families, and girlfriends take up most of the small pizza joint. My parents and sisters are here and that's where I lead Polly.

"Congratulations," my mother says when we approach.

I barely manage to thank her before Michelle jumps up and throws her arms around my neck. Polly drops my hand and steps aside while my youngest sister squeezes in excitement. "You were amazing!"

"Thanks, Smelly." I use her nickname and tug on the end of her ponytail. She pulls back and retreats to her seat and I turn to Polly who's vanished. I spot her with some of the other basketball guys' girlfriends, huddled around talking about who knows what.

I go ahead and take a seat with my family. The pepperoni pizza in the middle of the table is nearly gone so I know they'll be heading out soon. Grab a slice and take a huge bite while simultaneously listening to my sister fill me in on the game like I wasn't there. She's almost as big a ball fan as I am. Though, she prefers the sidelines to playing. Something about too much running and sweat for her liking.

My phone buzzes in my pocket and when I pull it out and read the screen I stand, still chewing.

POLLY

> I thought we were going to talk about winter formal. I saved you a seat.

She's made no attempt to get to know my family in the time we've been dating. I guess that's normal, but my family is so much a part of me and my life it feels weird to keep the two separate. But I did promise her we'd talk about formal.

"See you guys at home later. Gonna celebrate with the guys."

My family doesn't put up a fight. I know my parents understand, but Michelle's smile dims and I hate that.

"Smelly, wanna binge watch *Teen Wolf* tomorrow? I'm like five episodes behind." Because I only watch it when she forces me. She knows that, but it doesn't stop her eyes from lighting up and she can't nod fast enough. That's one woman in my life appeased.

————

THE FOLLOWING Tuesday morning I'm sitting in first period willing the bell to ring. When it does, I take one last look around the room, verifying I'm not crazy. All the girls are looking at me, whispering. Except it's not *that* kind of look. Discretely, I run a hand under my nose to check for boogers. Run both palms over my face and hair. Four long strides and I'm in the bathroom and staring at my reflection.

"What gives?" I ask to the empty room.

I turn to leave when Timmie enters. It's a general rule that dudes aren't allowed to chit chat in the bathroom, but since neither of us has our dicks out, I don't blow him off when he says, "Hey, Joel."

"What's up?" I ask, completely rhetorical and head to leave him to do his thing in peace.

I've got one hand on the door to leave when he continues talking, "Sorry to hear about Polly. Or maybe I should say congratulations? Sorry, I don't know what the appropriate thing to say is, but whatever it is let's just pretend I said it."

He starts to unzip, and I push out of the bathroom and replay his words in my head. I head to Polly's locker. She was out sick yesterday and other than a few texts, I haven't talked to her since the weekend. A crowd of girls are standing off to the side giving her the same look I got all through first period.

"Hey," I ask, concern and confusion lacing my tone.

Those green eyes pierce through me and she looks nervous. "Hi."

Polly is a lot of things. Timid ain't one of them. "What's going on?"

The one-minute warning bell for second period rings and she shuts her locker and glances around before speaking.

"Listen, Joel, we need to chat."

I bob my head for her to continue.

"Not here. How about after school?"

I've got practice until five thirty and there's no way I can wait that long to know what the hell is going on. "Tell me now."

She swallows and turns her gaze to the floor. My heart is galloping in my chest and I clench my jaw in anticipation because this does not feel like good news.

"I'm pregnant." Her voice is barely a whisper and I'm so shocked that it takes a few seconds for her words to register.

I'm stunned and utterly speechless. I know I should say something. Literally anything would be better than what comes out of my mouth, which is fucks all for nothing.

Her eyes fill with tears and she shakes her head. "I've gotta go to class."

———

SOBS SHAKE her shoulders and Polly looks up at me with such agony I want to make it all disappear. I was an ass earlier. She needed me to tell her it would be okay and instead I froze. She avoided me all afternoon, but I've finally cornered her before practice to make sure she knows we're in this together.

"Hey, it's not the end of the world." I wrap my arms around her and squeeze. "Our families will help. My mom had me young."

Sure, my parents are going to be pissed I wasn't more

careful not to knock up my high school girlfriend, but family is everything in the Moreno household. They'll be upset, but they'll still love and support me. I can already picture the big smile on my mother's face at the sight of her first grandchild. I can't believe it, but I'm a little excited. Scared shitless, but excited.

"No, you don't understand." She turns her head and pushes at my chest until my hold breaks.

I still. Hidden in the corner between the locker rooms and my high school gym, I watch Polly square her shoulders and swipe at the tears on her face.

"What is it?" I ask tentatively.

Her expression morphs from fear to timid smile. "Nothing. I'm sorry. I'm just scared."

I close the space again. "Me too. We'll be scared together, babydoll."

26

KATRINA

"*T*his pizza tastes funny." Christian pushes his plate away. The pizza is fine, but he's still upset that we're missing one person. Apparently, unbeknownst to me, Joel had told Christian that he was taking us to pizza.

I would have done what I did either way, but if I'd known Joel had already told Christian about our after-game plans, I would have taken Christian for tacos or something else instead of our usual pizza.

"I'm sorry, buddy. Joel had a lot of people wanting to help him celebrate tonight and it wouldn't be fair if we made him miss that."

Christian considers me for a moment. "But he said he was excited about having pizza with us. He was gonna eat an entire pizza on his own." Christian's eyes widen like this is a feat worth seeing firsthand.

Sighing, I pull out my phone. Joel hasn't texted me

back and the game has been over for two hours, so I'm sure he's seen my text by now. Hopefully he went to the party with his friends. That's where he should be.

But flaking on him feels crappy too.

"Come on. Let's take this home and we'll watch a movie and you can sleep in my bed tonight."

I've got him. I rarely let him sleep in my room, but I think tonight it might be as comforting to me as it is to him.

On the way to the apartment, I replay the last few weeks trying to sort out my feelings for Joel. I think, no I know, there's a genuinely good guy underneath his cocky exterior, but that doesn't mean he's ready for my life. The real, ugly, exhausting parts. Swooping in and playing the fun uncle is one thing, being a father figure is another entirely. There's really no in between for me. I can't date a guy and expect Christian not to be a part of it. That wouldn't be fair to me or Christian. And it's not fair to Joel to give up the things he loves – partying and hanging with friends – because I can't.

My downstairs neighbor is standing outside her door when I carry a sleeping Christian past her while balancing the pizza box. She gives me a disapproving look.

"What's her problem?" I mumble as I walk up the stairs.

I get my answer when I see Joel sitting down and leaning against my front door.

I smile down at my neighbor who continues to stand there.

"Have a good night," I say, hoping she takes the hint.

With a grunt of annoyance, she heads into her apartment and I continue up the stairs. I can smell the alcohol on him. Great. Just what I need, another little man to babysit.

I nudge him with my foot as I unlock my apartment.

"Hey, Kitty," he says, only opening his eyes slightly.

"What are you..." I hear my neighbor's door re-open below. "Never mind, get inside and I'll make some coffee."

I leave him on the stoop and carry Christian into my room and lay him on the bed. With any luck he'll nap long enough I can get Joel a ride back to his place.

When I close the door and head back to the living area, I find Joel standing at the end of my kitchen countertop taking in the place like he's just realized where he is.

"What are you doing here?"

"You stood me up," he says and even though he tries to play off his tone as playful, I can hear the hurt.

"I didn't stand you up," I insist. "Blair told me you guys were having a party to celebrate the last home game of the season and I didn't think you should miss that."

He nods. "Why didn't you tell me that?"

I shrug and he sways.

"Go lay on the couch and I'll make you some coffee. You didn't drive here, did you?"

"Uber," he says as he flops down on my couch, his legs hanging off the end.

I put the pizza in the fridge and then pour two mugs of

coffee and cross to the living room. I sit on the coffee table and offer him a mug. "Here."

"Thanks, Kitty."

"Why are you here Joel?"

He takes a drink and then lays his head back. "I wanted to show Christian I could eat a whole pizza by myself and win you one of those stuffed animals from the crane at the pizza place."

I can't help but laugh and when I do Joel's eyes open and he grins up at me. "I'm a grown man, Kitty. I can make decisions on my own. I don't need you to make them for me based on what you think I want."

I swallow the lump in my throat because he's right. Instead of letting him decide, I took away an option and forced his hand.

"I'm sorry. You're right. I'm not used to people, especially guys, choosing us over parties or whatever. It's easier to keep people at a distance than to continue to be disappointed."

I open my eyes to find Joel watching me carefully. Too carefully. Like he can see past my guard.

"Drink your coffee and Christian and I will take you back to your place when he wakes up from his nap."

I stand and pick up his heavy legs to make room to sit next to him. With little help from him, I manage to get situated with his legs across my thighs. His breathing starts to even out and I lay my head back and close my eyes.

"Hey, Kitty?"

"Hmm?"

"I like you."

I laugh because he sounds so earnest. I don't dare meet his gaze though. I'm afraid my feelings will be written all over my face.

"Also, I really want to have sex with you."

My eyes fly open and I catch the smirk on his face at my surprise. I toss a throw pillow at him and he uses it to cover his eyes right before he falls asleep.

We're awakened to Christian's happy squeals. "Joel! Joel! You're here! Mom look, Joel's here."

"Sh– crap," I exclaim as I try and catch Christian before he hops onto Joel. I don't succeed, but Joel just laughs as my son jumps on his chest.

"Easy, Joel's not feeling very well."

Christian goes quiet for a beat and his sweet face gets serious. "Is that why you couldn't have pizza with us?"

"Uhh, no. That was my fault, buddy."

Joel shakes his head as I try and explain, the smallest movement like he doesn't want Christian to see. "I just had to do a few things first. Sorry, I missed it, little man."

"We brought the pizza home to eat in bed. Mom's letting me sleep with her tonight."

"Well aren't you a lucky guy," Joel says and grins at me over Christian's head.

"Come see my room." Christian pulls at Joel's hand and he stands and follows my son across the apartment to his room.

I stand and take the coffee mugs to the sink and rinse them. I can hear Christian pointing out every single item in his room with pride and my heart squeezes at Joel's patience. Joel makes me want things I have no business wanting from him, but I'm not doing any favors to Christian by keeping people out of his life in the off chance they'll let us down either.

"Mom, can Joel stay for pizza and a movie?"

Joel stays quiet as Christian pleads with big brown eyes.

"Sure he can. Do you feel up to it?" I ask, unable to look him in the eye.

"I'd love to."

"I'm gonna bring all my stuffies into your room, Mom," Christian says as he runs back toward his room.

Joel comes around the counter. "You sure you're okay with this?"

"Are you? An hour ago I thought you were passed out for the night."

He rubs a hand over his scruffy jaw and around to the back of his neck. "Yeah. Think I might need another cup of coffee or two, though."

"That I can do."

"Now, can you answer a very important question?" I lift the pizza box out of the fridge. "Cold or hot?"

"Cold." He takes the box and I grab plates and napkins and lead him to my bedroom.

"I'm gonna grab the coffee," I say as I place everything on the end of the bed.

"Not so fast." He grabs my hand and draws me to him. "Are we good?"

As if I could stay mad at him, but I do need him to understand that there are rules for being around Christian. "Yes, but no more showing up drunk."

"Got it." He looks embarrassed as he nods. "Anything else?"

"Just don't make Christian any promises you can't keep. He likes you."

"I like him too."

"I'm serious. He's not used to having someone show up like this and—"

He stops my sentence by bringing his lips to mine. I pull back just a little. "You didn't let me finish."

"I got it, Kitty. I'd never do anything intentionally to hurt either of you."

I believe him, but intentional or not, the chances of him hurting me or my son seem high.

At my silence, Joel captures my mouth and cups my face possessively. He tastes of coffee and alcohol and the faintest hint of peppermint. The way he kisses me reminds me of his words earlier. *I really want to have sex with you.* God, me too.

Christian's footsteps register as he runs into the room and I pull back as he jumps on the bed with his stuffed animals in tow.

"Alright." I try and clear my head as Joel and Christian take their places on my bed making the king-sized mattress look small.

The three of us eat pizza and watch *The Secret Life of Pets*. Christian starts the movie at the foot of the bed, while

Joel holds me against his chest, but eventually Christian wiggles his way between us and the only places I'm touching Joel are shoulders and legs.

"He's out," I whisper as the credits roll. Christian's snuggled against Joel's chest, mouth open and eyes closed. "I'll just move him."

"I got him." He stands, holding Christian securely as I pull back the covers. Joel sets him down and I bring the covers up around him and tuck his favorite stuffed dog next to him.

I motion toward the door and Joel follows me out to the living room where we take our spots back on the couch from earlier.

"Does he sleep through the night?"

"Yeah. He goes hard during the day, but he sleeps well."

"He's a great kid."

"Thank you."

"You don't talk about Christian's father. He around much?"

"He was visiting about once a month when he was going to school in Phoenix, but he's moved closer so I'm hopeful Christian will see him more now. It's been hard for him to see Christian regularly, but Christian looks forward to their time together just the same. It works for them."

"And does that work for you? You've got a lot to handle on your own."

"You sound like my mom." I groan. "I made my choice to go to college like I'd planned before the pregnancy knowing I'd also be raising a kid. That's on me and I don't regret it."

"Still, it's gotta be hard to juggle it all."

"My mom had my sister when she was sixteen and gave up everything. She had big plans to go to college and she never did. I didn't want that to happen to me."

He nods with a serious expression on his face.

"Anyway. It's a point of contention for her. She thinks my decision to come to Valley was selfish. She wanted me to stay at home where she could help watch Christian while I took classes at the local community college."

"Christian seeing you hustle is good for him and even from the small amount of time I've been around you two, I know you're not selfish."

"Thanks for that." I let my head fall back against the couch and peer up at him. "Tell me something about you. Something that makes you less perfect."

He chuckles softly. "There's a long list to prove that fact."

"Tell me one."

He pulls his bottom lip behind his teeth as if he's deep in thought. "I got it," he says finally. "Fifth grade I cheated off Mallory Sinclair. A whole bunch of us did and I was the only one that didn't get caught because I agreed to kiss her after school in exchange for her not telling the teacher."

"Oh my God. Using your charm and good looks started at an early age, I see."

He flashes a wry smile.

"Did you have a lot of girlfriends in high school or have

you always been..." I struggle to find the right word and Joel raises his eyebrows.

"Curious how you're gonna finish that sentence, Kitty."

I roll my eyes. "You're a player. You know you are. Were you always?"

The cocky grin disappears, and his lips form a straight line. "No, not always."

"Did someone break your heart, Joel Moreno?" My own heart beats wildly in my chest because the stoic expression on his face makes me think that's exactly what happened.

He chuckles, though, causing me to second guess my theory. *"Estas asumiendo que tengo corazón."*

"No fair with the Spanish. Maybe you're just a cynic when it comes to love?"

Shaking his head, he leans closer. "Nah, I just know what's what and I live my life accordingly. People don't see *me*, girls don't want *me* – they want what I can offer – a good time, money, a piece of the spotlight, and I give them that, nothing more. I don't break their hearts because they don't give them to me and vice versa."

I read the sincerity on his face.

"Oh my God, you really believe that, don't you?" He looks at me with a puzzled expression. "Joel, girls are willing to take whatever you give them because they're silently hoping for more. Every girl wants to be the one that changes your mind and captures your heart – the one that makes you want more."

He looks amused, his perfect lips pulled up into a smirk and brown eyes light with humor.

"I'm serious. That's what makes great love stories like *Twilight* or *Fifty Shades of Grey* so romantic. They can have any woman they want, but only one woman truly changes them. Girls want to be your Bella or Anastasia."

His eyebrows lift. "Did you just call *Twilight* a great love story?"

"I'm serious. Okay, maybe for some girls it's about money or fame or how insanely hot you are, but the vast majority are risking heartbreak in hope of being the one to capture yours."

He runs his thumb along my jaw, tilting my chin up. "What about you? Did Victor break your heart?"

I shake my head. "No, but sometimes I think he broke my ability to trust."

The words are out before I can stop them. Regret, sadness, pity, so many emotions cross his face and I feel like the world's biggest Debbie Downer. With his hands still on my face, I crawl into his lap. I'm not dumb enough to believe that I'm the one that's going to steal Joel's heart, but I stand by my theory because smiling and laughing, and just hanging out with him, feels almost as good.

"When I'm with you, I feel a little more hopeful that I can move past it," I say so quietly that I'm not sure he hears me at first.

I feel his chest rise and fall and he whispers back, "Me too, Kitty."

27

JOEL

My insides hurt and my lips are chapped. I kissed Kitty senseless for the better part of two hours and then made her come with my fingers. I've got the worst case of blue balls in the history of mankind. I'm starting to think there's something wrong with me. If she were anyone else, I would have fucked her on the couch or in the bathroom. I'm ninety-nine percent sure the kid would have slept through it, but that one percent fucked with me and I didn't feel right about it with Christian sleeping in the other room. It's a wonder parents ever have sex at all.

I slept on the couch instead of catching a ride back to my place which is where I am when Christian sneaks into the living room and climbs on to the couch with me. A peek at the clock tells me it's five o'clock on the dot. I'm tired as shit, but I don't have the heart to send him away.

"Morning, little man. Your mom still sleeping?"

He nods. "I'm hungry."

"Me too." I sit up. "What do you usually have for breakfast?"

"On Sundays we have pancakes."

"Pancakes, huh?" I rub the back of my neck. "That might be a little too advanced for me. How about some cereal?"

I open a few cabinets until I locate the cereal boxes and pull out Cheerios and Lucky Charms.

His eyes widen. "I can have Lucky Charms?"

Shit. Is it okay for him to have that much sugar at five a.m.? I don't have any clue. "Does your mom let you have Lucky Charms?"

He bites his lip and hesitates before answering. "Only once a week."

"And did you already have them this week?"

He shrugs.

"Looks like Cheerios it is." I locate two bowls, two spoons, and the milk and Christian and I sit together at the dining room table eating our cereal. It sort of reminds me of any other morning eating breakfast with the guys, except Christian watches me carefully and mimics every movement. When I lift the empty bowl to my mouth to drink the milk, he does the same and nearly spills the entire bowl on himself.

Christian wants cartoons after breakfast, so I turn on the TV for him while I do the dishes. I keep waiting for Katrina to walk out and take over, but I don't have the heart to go wake her up. I mean, when is the last time she got to sleep in?

I don't have practice until this afternoon, but I feel sluggish and slightly hungover. The cure I've become accustomed to is working out so I do what I can on the living room floor alternating sit-ups and pushups. At some point, Christian joins in and that's exactly how Kitty finds us. I meet her gaze mid-sit-up. Her eyes rake over my bare chest and the weeks of kissing and talking are not enough.

"Hi, Mom. Look at my muscles," Christian says proudly, pausing to flex a bicep.

"Impressive," Katrina says and then shakes her head. "Don't mind me. I just need coffee."

She moves to the kitchen and I hear the coffee brewing but feel her eyes on me still.

"Alright, little man, think you can help me with this next one?"

Christian jumps up and I get on my stomach. "Hop on my back."

If she's gonna watch, might as well put on a good show.

It takes a few tries to balance his weight, but eventually, he lies on top of me and wraps his arms around me while I push up and down from the floor. After ten I look over to find Katrina standing, hip resting against the side of the counter between the kitchen and living room, sipping her coffee and not even pretending she's doing anything but watching me.

"Do you like the view, Kitty?"

Her tongue darts out and she wets her lips. She doesn't

meet my stare, instead continues to look me over like a piece of meat. I'm not offended. Not even a little bit. "I'm not sure what you're talking about, I'm watching Christian," she says, but her voice is tight and we both know she's lying.

Shit, maybe this was a bad idea. Kitty wanting me and watching me like that has my body ready to give her everything and there's a three-year-old tornado on my back.

Laying on the ground, I look over my shoulder to Christian and lift my fist around to him. "Thanks for the help."

He bumps his knuckles to mine and then hops off. "Mom, can I take a bath?"

I sit back on my knees and watch Katrina try and get a hold of herself. I'm used to girls getting flustered and watching me like eye candy, but the way Kitty looks at me is so much hotter. She's not one to be so easily impressed, I should know, and it's the sign I've been waiting for that she wants me. Really wants me.

She clears her throat and finally tears her eyes away from me. "Umm, sure. Yeah, let's get you in the bath."

I stand up and adjust myself. I think that's what I need. A shower. A very, cold shower. I head back to Katrina's room and into the small bathroom attached to it and strip off my jeans and boxers.

"Oh." Katrina's voice behind me is startled and I turn to find her eyes wide in surprise but that doesn't keep her from standing there frozen as she checks out my junk.

"I'm gonna take a quick shower," I tell her and make no attempt to cover myself.

"I, uh... towel."

I spot the white towels stacked on top of a shelf over the toilet and grab one for her. She still stands there with towel in hand and I grow bigger at the hungry look in her eyes and the flashes of every dirty thing I want to do to her.

She backs out of the bathroom so slow I have to hold my breath and count to five to keep myself from reaching out and stopping her.

"Soon, Kitty." I wink at her and she flushes before turning and disappearing from sight.

———

"You disappeared early last night," Wes says as I take a seat next to him on the sideline. He's got a dry erase clipboard in hand and I'm having a hard time taking him seriously as a new assistant coach. He doesn't officially start until after graduation, but since he can't play, he's helping out with offensive strategy. Don't get me wrong, he's got the eye for it and I think the younger guys stand to learn a lot from him, but it's still weird to have one of my best friends playing coach.

"I went to Katrina's."

"You know Blair is going to strangle you when you decide to move on from playing house, right?"

"Who says I'm playing?"

His eyebrows shoot up and he studies me closely. "So you're serious about her then?"

I lift a shoulder and let it fall. "She's a cool chick."

"With a kid. I hate to be the one to be all doom and gloom on the situation, but your track record isn't exactly indicative of your being able to handle a relationship, let alone one that includes a kid."

Is that what everyone's thinking? That I can't handle it?

As if he's read my mind, Wes says, "Look, Blair would never say it because she's rooting for you and Katrina – that's what she does, but I'm not sure you've really thought about what being with Katrina means – short term or long term."

"You ever wonder what it'd be like to have a kid in high school or college?" I ask him.

The panicked look on his face is all the answer I need.

"My high school girlfriend got pregnant," I tell him before he can compose himself to answer.

"No shit?"

"Yeah, that look on your face right now is how I felt at first. I remember how fucking scared I was when she told me, but I was excited too. Being a parent is a beautiful thing. I respect the shit out of Katrina for doing it on her own." I check his expression which is disbelieving, and chuckle, but Wes and I are different. Our families are different.

Coach barks out orders for our after-practice workout and Wes and I fall silent.

I groan at the grueling conditioning I have to look

forward to when all I want to do is go home and pass out. Maybe Wes is right. I mean one night over there and I'm dog tired.

"I've thought about it – what it means to be with her short term and long term," I tell my buddy, but it feels more like I'm finally admitting it to myself. "I liked my life before I met Katrina, but when I'm with her and Christian, I dunno man, I'm just taking it one day at a time."

He nods, considering my words and letting them soak in. That's Wes, always thinking and calculating. I stand ready to get through the next hour so I can go home and make up for the sleep I lost this morning. One thing is certain, if I'm gonna stay over again, I need to teach the kid how to sleep in on weekends.

"Hey," Wes calls. "You didn't say what happened to your high school girl. Did she have the baby? There a little Joel or Joelina out there somewhere?"

It's a wound that never quite heals and pain slices through me as I shake my head. "Nah, wasn't meant to be, I guess."

28

KATRINA

I'm beyond nervous as I pull into the driveway at Nadine's house.

"Christian, we're here."

I grab his bag out of the back before I unbuckle a sleepy-eyed Christian.

Victor and I have always maintained a civil relationship, but it doesn't make seeing him any easier. I never loved him, and he never loved me. We were a short fling that had long repercussions.

"Here, I'll get him," Nadine says, and I move so she can lift Christian from his car seat.

I glance around realizing Victor's car isn't here. "Where's Victor?"

A look of guilt crosses her face before she schools her expression. "One of his friends asked him to fill in on a softball league now that he's moved home. He'll be back later."

Unbelievable. I bite my tongue, but Nadine reads my expression.

"I tried to talk to him."

I nod because I'm sure she did. She isn't perfect, but she never has trouble speaking her mind. "I think maybe it's time I talk to him about it." I let out a long breath. "Are you sure you want to keep him the whole week?"

Technically this time is Victor's, but we both know she's the one that's really going to be watching him.

"Yes, I'm sure."

"Alright, a whole week buddy. You excited?" I look down to my son who is nothing but excited. I've never been away from Christian for an entire week, and even knowing I'll see him Wednesday at soccer practice, I'm feeling all kinds of out of sorts.

"Victor is going to drive him back and forth for soccer practice on Wednesday. I'll text him to remind him of the time and place. You know you can call me any time and I'll be here as soon as I can."

She chuckles. "I know, dear."

"I'm going to miss him," I admit as I brush his hair back off his forehead.

"You're a good mother, Katrina."

My eyes prick, but before I can thank her for the nicest words she's ever spoken to me, she takes a step toward the door.

"Now get out of here and we'll call later tonight to check in."

I drive to my parents' house still upset about Victor

and trying to decide how I'm going to handle it. I've never hidden how I feel about his half-assed parenting effort, but I've never really talked to him about it either.

My mother, her best friend Lisa, and my sister sit outside on the porch when I pull up. Red wine in hand, a paperback copy of *Big Little Lies* sits between them.

"Book club?" I smirk as I walk up the stairs.

They giggle like teenagers.

"Let me guess, none of you actually finished the book?"

"Well we did try," Lisa says.

My mom stands to greet me and clutches me to her chest. "I was hoping you'd bring Christian."

"I had to drop him at Nadine's for his week-long visit with Victor."

"Here, you probably need this more than I do then." She pushes the glass toward me, and I take a gulp and then cough.

"It's an acquired taste," she says taking the glass back.

"Was Christian excited to see Victor?"

I sit down on the porch swing and wrap a hand around the chain that holds it to the ceiling. "He wasn't there."

"What?"

I shake my head. "He's here, just playing in some softball game this afternoon."

I stomp my feet and make an annoyed growl in my throat. They stare at me like I've lost my mind because I never lose my shit in front of them. Call it self-preservation, but I don't want to show them how right they might have been about me needing more help. "Sorry, I'm just so frustrated. I thought him moving back here was going to be good for Christian, but it's the same shit. I invited him to Christian's soccer practice, and he told me he was busy."

"By all means, yell, scream, just do it to him," my mom says as she flails the hand not carrying her wine.

"What?"

"You've been letting him get away with it for far too long if you ask me."

"But you've never said anything."

"Wasn't my place. Still isn't. This has been going on for three years. More than that, really, he couldn't even make it to most of the doctor appointments." Some of those I may not have told him about, but it feels unproductive to share that now. "You knew Victor wasn't the most reliable young man from the beginning. I thought at some point you'd stand up to him for Christian's sake instead of trying to be super mom. You can't be all things for everyone."

My mother huffs as if she's the one truly put out by Victor. "I'm going to get more wine."

"I think I'll help," Lisa says, leaving me alone with my sister.

I kick off the ground to put the swing in motion as the screen door slams shut.

Mary moves to sit beside me. "I know Mom doesn't come right out and say it, but she's on your side on this one."

"She has a weird way of showing it. Ever since I left for college, she's made me feel like I'm the one who messed up by running off with Christian in tow."

"Are you kidding?" She chuckles. "She is so proud of you. She and Lisa were just talking about how when they were your age, they were both straddled down with kids on each hip wishing they'd followed through on their dreams."

I roll my eyes because Lisa only has one kid and by the time my mother had enough kids to have one on each hip, Mary was fifteen. I understand the expression, though.

"She worries about you, wants the best for you. The same way you want for Christian."

My mother and Lisa reappear with another wine bottle and an extra glass. My mother hands it to me. "Are you staying?"

Two glasses of wine and the worst book club discussion in all of history later, I head off to my old room and plop down on the bed. Mary had to get home to her family and Mom and Dad went out to dinner. I opted to stay home and stew in my misery. Christian calls and tells me all about his afternoon which I'm pleased to find out includes Victor playing soccer with him. In a moment of weakness, I text Joel.

ME

Whatcha doing?

Smooth, Katrina. Great opening line.

JOEL

Just got to the hotel.

ME

What time's the game tomorrow?

JOEL

Not til 6 – won't be back until Sunday.

ME

Good luck!

He doesn't respond right away, and I toss my phone to the end of the bed wishing more than ever I could get lost in fantasies with Joel. I roll over on my stomach and pull up the covers not caring at all that I'm still fully dressed. I've got a week all to myself. God, it's been so long since I've been able to make plans with no one else to consider.

As I drift off, imagining a day at the spa or maybe declaring it sweatpants week and bingeing Netflix and ice cream, a much better idea occurs to me and I spend the rest of the night dreaming about it.

29

KATRINA

*B*lair, Gabby, and I shuffle from our seats out of the Sun Devil's stadium. Valley defeated ASU and I'm minutes from Joel knowing I came all this way to watch him play.

"So, you didn't tell him you were coming?" Gabby asks with big eyes.

We pile into a cab and give the driver the address of our hotel.

"Should I have?"

"No, it's fine. He's going to be so excited to see you," Blair insists.

God, I hope so.

"He will." Blair nudges my knee. "What are you doing on Tuesday? Gabby is moving into an apartment and we're going to make an evening of it. Unboxing, drinking, and boy talk."

"That sounds good. Christian is gone all week with his father."

"What's he like? You never mentioned him, and I was always afraid to ask."

I grimace at the thought I might have come across that closed off. "He's a good guy, a little flaky. We had a study hall together and hung out a few times, but I got pregnant after we were together only once, so I don't really know that much about him either. I mean, we've tried to be friendly and civil, but it's hard."

"Damn. One time?"

I nod to Gabby who looks horrified to know that sort of thing really happens. "Yep. First and last time I had sex."

"What?!" Blair shrieks earning us a look from the cab driver in the rearview mirror

My cheeks blaze with heat. "Yeah, been a bit of a dry spell."

"Holy shit. You haven't slept with Joel yet?"

"Umm..."

Blair laughs and Gabby joins in.

"What?"

"This is too precious. Joel gave Wes the worst time about how long it took us to have sex after we started hanging out and that was only a few weeks."

"It hasn't been that long and with Christian around there hasn't really been an opportunity."

Until now.

Gabby opens the clutch on her lap and hands over a sleeve of condoms. "Plenty of opportunity tonight."

The cab pulls up to the hotel and I shove the condoms into my purse before filing out behind Blair.

"Wait, why are *you* carrying condoms?" Blair asks Gabby as the three of us catch the elevator up to our room.

Gabby has this habit of letting her long blonde hair fall over the scars on the left side of her face when she's nervous or unsure, which she does now. "I just wanted to be prepared for anything. What if I meet some hot guy tonight?" Her eyes light up. "Or maybe I can convince Coach Daniels to let me into his room," she says and smiles deviously.

"The coach, really?" I ask. "I mean, he's hot don't get me wrong, but he's like forty."

"I'm not looking to get married and have babies, just jump his bones."

Blair shakes her head and looks to me. "This is what happens when you go too long without sex. Take this as a warning, go forth and have sex or else you'll end up like Gabby."

Gabby punches her playfully.

"Longer than four years?" I ask.

"Try twenty-one," she whispers even though we're alone in the elevator.

We arrive to our floor and I gape as the doors open. "You're a virgin?!"

A group of young guys enters the elevator and Gabby's face turns crimson at their knowing smirks.

We rush out past them, but one of the guys yells out, "Happy to help later in room three fifteen."

Gabby practically sprints down the hall. Blair and I follow, laughter echoing throughout the floor as we enter our room.

"I'm sorry," I say when I can force the laughter back. "I just had no idea." I wave a hand in front of her. "You're gorgeous. I don't know how you've managed to keep your V-card."

"After the accident, I didn't leave the house much," she admits.

Blair takes her hand and threads their fingers together. I don't know a lot about the car accident that left Gabby with the scars marring her beautiful face, but I get glimpses of her insecurities and I hope her moving to Valley will be good for her.

Blair's phone beeps and she drops Gabby's hand to pick up her phone. "The guys are getting on the bus now to head to the hotel. We've got about fifteen minutes to get ready."

My stomach twists into knots. "Should I text Joel?"

"I say, you put on the sexiest outfit you packed, and we'll wait downstairs for them. Shock attack." Blair claps her hands. "Go get ready."

––––––––

Joel

"Wanna grab a drink at the bar?" Wes asks, looking too damn happy for him. His usual preference after an away game is to go to his room and chill with Z.

I shrug, deciding not to question his sudden interest in hanging out. "Sure, let me just drop my stuff in my room first."

"And maybe you should shower, too."

"Dude, what's with you?"

He's all smiles as he exits the bus ahead of me. I text Kitty on my way to the room.

ME

Did you see the game?

KITTY

I did. Congratulations on another win.

ME

Thanks. What are you up to tonight?

Inside the room, I drop my bag on the bed. I don't really care if Wes has to smell me or not, but I want to hear from Kitty before I head down, so I jump in the shower while I wait for her to respond. Once I'm out and re-dressed, I still haven't heard from her, so I pocket my phone and head down to the bar.

When I see Blair sitting next to Wes, I bristle. Why invite me to tag along? Glancing at the rest of the table, I see Gabby and Nathan are with them. And someone at the far end of the table I can't see, hidden by Nathan's big head. One drink and then I'm out.

My phone vibrates, and I reach for it, reading the text as I walk across the bar.

KITTY

Hanging out with you.

I start to type a response, but something pulls my attention to the table and as Nathan leans forward, I've got a perfect view. She fidgets nervously watching me with wide eyes. My chest aches. Actually fucking aches. She's here. Kitty's here.

I ignore the rest of the table, walk up to her, and pick her up enjoying the squeals of delight as she wraps her arms around my neck.

"You're here." I clutch her to me, start to put her back down, but instead hold her against me and crash my mouth down over hers.

I hear the guys laughing at me and I flip them off with one hand, not breaking the kiss until I've shown her just how glad I am she's here.

When I finally pull back, she's breathless and her cheeks flushed. "I guess that means you're okay with me being here?"

"More than okay with it." I take the seat she was sitting in and pull her on my lap.

There's conversation. I think I even take part in it. Laugh at the appropriate times, answer when asked a direct question, but damn all I can focus on is Kitty. She's here. For *me*. My mind is kinda blown. And not just that she was willing to give up a night, drive all this way to watch me play, but at how glad I am.

The hotel bar shuts down early, so we only have time for one drink, which is perfectly fine with me.

"Uhh, where am I sleeping?" Nathan asks as we all stand.

Wes hands him his key card. "You can stay with Z. Gabby can stay in the girl's room. Blair and I will get another room."

"That's ridiculous," Gabby protests. "I'll just stay with the guys."

There's some back and forth, but Gabby is insistent. "It's fine. I'll sleep on the floor or couch. Whatever."

Nathan places an arm around her shoulders. "You can have the bed. I'll sleep on the floor."

With that settled, Katrina looks up to me like she's unsure. I pull her to me. "Wanna go to my lair?"

She giggles as I pick her up and throw her over my shoulder like a rag doll, placing a palm on her ass to cover what the fabric doesn't. I've gone caveman and it feels fantastic.

I'm ready to ravage my Kitty. Fucking finally.

———

Katrina

He doesn't put me down until we're in the room. He's a man on a mission. Kicks his shoes off, pulls his shirt over his head. I giggle as I watch him undress like he's being timed.

"Gonna leave any of that for me to take off?"

His hands still at his jeans. He pops the button but doesn't push them down. "You want to undress me?"

I nod and step forward. Whatever nerves I had about this moment dissipate as his eyes darken and his chest rises and falls as I let my hands trail over his stomach. His abs are cut and a trail of dark hair disappears into his boxers.

His hands ball into fists at his sides as if he's holding back from touching me. Letting me have this moment. Hooking my fingers under the denim, I push down taking his boxers with them. I move lower with his clothes shimming them off his legs. I've already seen him naked, but he's as impressive as I remembered and my core throbs.

I peek up at him, finding him watching me with such desire it makes me uncharacteristically bold. His length twitches as I bring my mouth to him and I place a soft kiss to the head. A groan escapes his lips and I continue kissing and adoring every glorious inch.

His hands don't move from his sides until I take him into my mouth. Gently, his fingers thread through my hair and he applies the slightest pressure guiding me as I suck and lick.

I know he's holding back, but screw that I want everything he's willing to give. I take him deeper until he hits the back of my throat and I peer up to meet his tortured gaze. I try to smile around him, telling him with the look of pure bliss I know must be on my face that it's okay to let go.

He answers by pulling my hair tighter until the slightest prick of my scalp sends pulsing waves of pleasure through my body. He takes my mouth until tears leak from my eyes and I fight my gag reflex, but it's the hottest moment of my life.

A rumble leaves his chest and when I think he's going to come, he surprises me by stepping back and pulling me to my feet. I'm uncoordinated and a bit dizzy as he holds me upright and wipes a thumb across my lips cleaning up the saliva gathered around them. "Your mouth is perfection, Kitty, but when I come, I want to be buried balls deep inside you."

My body hums in anticipation and I sit on the end of the bed, so ready for that and more.

He steps to me with a wicked grin and dips low, taking my legs and throwing them over his shoulders. My panties are gone in a flash, dress now bunched up around my hips, and his mouth meets my sex.

Holy sh– crap.

The vibration of his laugh against my sensitive flesh earns another moan. Guess I said that out loud. "You're fucking adorable censoring your curse words when I've got my tongue on your pussy."

"Force of habit." I just barely get the words out before his teeth join the action and I scream – not in pain but in pure ecstasy.

He guides me on to my stomach and lifts my ass into

the air, continuing the sweet torture on my clit and bringing a finger to the party. "Christ, you're so wet."

His finger glides smoothly in and out as he drops open mouth kisses on my thighs and ass. My face goes hot as he spreads my cheeks and keeps right on kissing me. Oh my God, he's going to lick my ass. The realization hits me too late and I have no time to be bashful, or flip over before his tongue pushes inside my hole in sync with his fingers below.

"Fuuuck." There's no use censoring my words as I get my first rim job. Is that what the kids are calling it these days? Or ever? I wouldn't know since I've never discussed it. Let alone had it performed.

"Relax," Joel says in a hushed tone. "You trust me?"

"Yes," I say. And I do. God help me, I really do.

"Good." He slaps my ass playfully. "We should have the condom talk."

I laugh at his openness. Probably should have had it ten minutes ago, but better now than tomorrow. "I'm on the pill, but I think we should still use a condom just in case."

"I'm clean. We get blood work drawn every couple months, and it just so happened to fall last month," he says all this, my, well, my everything, still up in the air on display.

"Okay, but since then you could have come in contact with something." I'm not sure if it's more humiliating that we're having this conversation or that he's basically having it with my lady parts. I walk on all fours up the bed and to the nightstand to get my purse. I pull out the condoms Gabby gave me earlier, set them on the bed still refusing to look up as I sit back on my knees. Wow, adulting is hard. But then again, the other option is an STD or child and well I learned my lesson on safe sex the hard way.

"Haven't come in contact with anything, but if you want me to wear one, of course I will." He follows me onto the bed and pulls my dress up and over my head. I'm not wearing a bra and he cups my breasts in his big palms. "Damn, Kitty. Your tits are fantastic. Add motorboating to my new list of hobbies."

"It's not like you can tell by looking with every STD," I tell him before I lose this moment and my last opportunity to voice all my concerns.

He removes his stare from my breasts and shakes his head slowly, side to side. A broad smile overtakes his handsome face and his eyes bore into mine. "No, you misunderstand. It's not possible. I haven't been with anyone since then. Been focused solely on you, babydoll."

"Come on. You can't expect me to believe that." I roll my eyes and push playfully at his bare chest.

"It's true."

"Why?" The question is out before I can stop it. I don't want him to lie or pretend we're something we're not, but I need to know.

"Same reason I had a standing reservation at Araceli's. I knew eventually you were going to say yes."

"Wow. You're good."

He takes me down onto the bed with him, rolls on top

of me, cradling my head with his hands as he stares down at me. "Kitty, you have no idea."

The attention and love he gives my body is so very Joel. Thorough, dedicated, and hot as fuck.

He's rough but somehow still gentle. Not one single inch of my body is missed. He gives me everything except the one thing I'm dying for. I'm grinding beneath him, pleading with my hips, for him to put me out of my misery. "You ready, Katrina?"

No mocking or playfulness in his tone. He's making certain of my consent. I'm so ready. Four years too long ready, but I can't imagine it any other way. Here with Joel, just like this is perfect.

"So ready."

He kisses the top of my nose and shifts, grabs a condom and covers himself before lining up at my entrance. I watch in fascination as he glides inside of me so painfully slow I try and slide down to help. He pins me in place by holding my hips still. "You're so fucking tight."

My body climbs and my heart beats so fast I know it's as much my feelings for the man as it is this moment. He fills me up so full, but it's not just his huge ego or even huger (totally the right word for this moment) dick, it's my heart remembering what it's like to let someone in mind and soul.

Completely at his mercy, I let him finally have me. All of me.

30

JOEL

*K*itty is naked in my bed. Well, not my bed, but I'm not about to get hung up on the details. She's here and naked and she's fucking mine.

"What time does the bus leave tomorrow?" she asks, tracing circles on my chest as she lies beside me.

"Early, but I can sleep on the bus."

"Can we hang out when you get back?" Her voice is cautious and unsure.

I pull her on top of me. "Yep. I plan to steal as much of your time as you'll let me this week."

She presses her smile to mine. "Do I finally get to see your lair?"

"Oh yeah. There's lots more ravaging to be done." I'm already picturing a week filled with Katrina naked and in every place and position I can dream up when I remember I have a meeting with Sara Icoa tomorrow. "I've got a few things to do with the team and Sunday is movie night with the roommates but come over. Blair crashes more often than not so you can be my plus one."

"I thought you promised ravaging. Sounds suspiciously like hanging out fully clothed."

She says it in a teasing manner but shit she's right. We had sex and instead of moving on, I want to pencil her in to every free minute I have. And hell yeah I plan on ravaging her as often as possible, but that's not all I want to do with her.

I guess I'm quiet for too long because she shifts. "You okay? Sorry, I was just kidding. I'd love to hang out."

Plant a kiss to her temple and tuck her in close beside me. "Just tired, I guess. Been a long day."

She yawns in agreement.

"Night Kitty."

————

Katrina

"This place is insane," I say to Blair as she leads me around The White House. The guys are getting movie night set up while I get the grand tour. It's the coolest place I've ever seen, and I was so not prepared after seeing the shit hole the baseball guys live in.

"Joel's family bought it and turned it into a mini version of the basketball dorms of some of the larger universities. I heard Kansas has a barber shop in theirs."

"Seems a little like overkill."

"Right? But the guys love it. They even have custom bedding, not that they care about that, but I think it's awesome. Wes is sad about moving out next year. I guess Z will too so who knows who will move in and take their place."

"What happens when Joel graduates?" I ask.

She shrugs. "I'm not sure. If he ends up going pro next year instead of playing his senior year, Nathan would be the only one left."

My heart drops. If Joel goes pro next year? I didn't even know that was a possibility. To be fair, I hadn't asked. I've carefully avoided any conversations around the future. I haven't even allowed myself to ask him what his plans are next weekend because I don't want to come across as clingy. But the way my hands shake I know my heart has started wishing and hoping for more regardless.

We stop in front of the last doorway. "And this is Joel's room. I've never –"

"Not so fast." Joel runs from the top of the stairwell and jumps in front of her. "Access denied. Only girls allowed here are the ones who put out." The smile on his face falls as if he's realized the bad joke.

It stings to think about how many girls he's let in past these doors, not gonna lie, but I force a laugh and eye roll and place a hand to my chest dramatically. "So charming."

"I, uh, got us out of movie night," he says.

"Lucky dogs. Wes is pumped about the new *Mission Impossible*. See ya later."

"Thanks for the tour," I call after her.

She disappears down the hall and Joel pulls me to him. "Sorry about that. We don't have to stay here if you don't want to."

"Don't be ridiculous." At the thought of being denied the full Joel Moreno experience, I realize this is exactly what I signed up for. Hot sex and fun, no strings attached. "I will most definitely put out."

He nips at my top lip. "Before you put out, I have a surprise." He opens the door and pulls me in after him. "Come on."

He doesn't flip on the lights, but he doesn't need to. The whole back wall of the room is floor to ceiling windows that let in the Arizona sun and give a view of the backyard. French doors lead out to a small balcony and there's a single chair where I try and picture Joel sitting by himself. Why not two chairs? I know the answer to that without asking, but it makes me a little sad.

His bed is huge, and I see the custom bedding Blair was talking about – white with blue stripes and the Road-runner mascot.

"Wow. My apartment could fit in your room."

He looks around like he's never noticed how big it is and shrugs.

Grabbing a laptop from a desk, he takes it to the bed and opens it. "I thought we could have our own movie night."

Intrigued, I move to sit next to him on the bed and laugh when I see what he's selected for this intimate moment. "James Bond, really?"

"You said you'd never seen it. Consider it a critical part of your screenwriting education."

I think I'd rather him ravage me again, but I'm completely helpless to say no to what he obviously planned out as a romantic gesture. All those months of restraint and now I'm practically offering myself up on a platter and the tiniest bit disappointed that we're not going to get naked again immediately but also touched he wants to share something as simple as his favorite movie.

Gah, I'm conflicted. Leading with my heart is too risky. Letting my body do all the feeling seems a safer and more enjoyable mission.

He stands quickly. "I forgot the snacks. Be right back."

"Bathroom?"

He points to a door behind me and then leans down and brushes a kiss on my lips before leaving.

I go through an impressive walk-in closet, my eyes landing on enough shoes to make any woman jealous. And the bathroom. Good God. Inhaling, I can smell and feel him everywhere. It's cleaner than I expected, dark wood cabinets and white countertops. I pee, wash my hands, and then wander into the shower.

Which is where he finds me.

Arms wrap around me and I startle. "You scared me. What if I was peeing?"

"You really think that would have stopped me?"

"Boundaries."

"Not necessary," he says, and I swat at him. "What are you doing in my shower?"

"I'm wondering what would have happened if I'd said yes the very first time you asked me out."

I turn to watch his expression, which is pensive, and I assume he doesn't remember.

"You told me you'd let me use your shower."

"Oh, I remember." He presses a button and all the lights go out in the bathroom except a light in the middle of the shower, which doubles as a showerhead. Water rains down in front of us and about a dozen water jets spray from every direction. There's even music playing. "Regretting your answer about now?"

Yes.

"No."

He presses the button again and the shower turns off. My shirt and leggings aren't soaked, but I'm uncomfortably wet.

"Let's get you out of these wet clothes," he murmurs.

"You've been waiting your whole life to use that line, haven't you?"

He doesn't answer as he pulls my shirt over my head.

"What about Bond?"

"I think he would very much approve of my priorities."

I point to the shower controls. "Bond is nothing without his gadgets."

"Not true. That's the coolest thing about James Bond – he doesn't need money or flash." He presses the button and the shower turns back on. "But he likes them just the same."

31

KATRINA

"Oh my God. She really died?" I'm crying, and Joel is laughing.

"Well, yeah. Her death is what makes Bond, Bond."

I cry harder, cover my face, but can't drown out his laughter.

"I thought you'd like it. Tragic love story and all."

"I did." Another sob breaks free.

He shuts the laptop and pulls me to him. I'm not usually such a sap. I mean, okay I totally am, but I wasn't planning on crying in front of him of all people. I was not prepared for the depth of the movie. Or the man next to me.

"What makes Joel, Joel?"

After the shower, I put on one of his t-shirts forgoing my bra and he's got one hand underneath cradling my left boob. He did it the first time during the movie and it resulted in more making out that also required re-starting the movie, but now I'm not even sure he's aware he's doing it. His palm just rests there like my left breast is his personal stress ball.

He doesn't respond so I ask again. "Vesper dying makes Bond, Bond. What made you, you?"

I feel his body tense and I lean up on one elbow so I can see him.

"Nothing nearly as tragic as that. My life has been easy." His words would be convincing if it weren't for the gruff tone. He shrugs and continues. "My parents were strict but loving and they set a good example for working hard to achieve my dreams."

"Playing in the NBA?" I ask, remembering Blair's comment about him playing professionally.

He nods and laces our fingers together. His big palm makes mine look so dainty by comparison. "Yeah, since I was a kid. Don't really know how or when it started, but I've always wanted to be the next Kobe Bryant and play for the Lakers."

"Blair said you might drop out to go early."

I hold my breath as he answers.

"I met with an agent earlier today. There are pros and cons either way. My parents really want me to get my degree, but I don't need it to be a ball player."

"What about after?"

"The plan is to use my ball career to get into sports broadcasting. A good portion of the broadcasters these days are old pros." He pulls back and places a hand under his chin. "I mean with this handsome mug, I figure I belong on TV one way or another."

"That's why you're majoring in communications," I say.

"What about you? What do you want to do after school?"

"I don't know anymore. When I was younger, I imagined myself moving to LA and trying to get a job as a screenwriter, but with Christian and our families being here, I don't really see that happening. It's hard enough being an hour away."

"LA is only six hours by car."

"That's a long way to shuttle a kid back and forth every week."

The awareness of how having a kid makes my life different finally dawns on his face. I can't just pick up and leave. Christian has a father who, even though he may not be the most reliable, deserves to be able to see his son. Not to mention has a legal right.

"When do you have to decide about next year?"

He blows out a breath. "End of April, officially, but I need to decide soon so I can get my parents used to the idea if I do skip my senior year."

He's quiet and lost in thought for a moment before he looks to me and smiles. I feel the mood go with that smile, but I stay silent hoping he'll share more about his hopes and dreams. What he wants for his life. Literally anything. He gives so freely and yet holds back so strongly, too. I wait, holding my breath for more words that I'm not even sure matter, but I want all the same.

Joel

"What's your schedule like today?"

Katrina's eyes dart around us as we walk through campus toward the English building. "Sorry what?"

I take her backpack that she insisted on carrying herself, from her shoulder and place it on the ground in front of us. Taking her hands, I stop and force her to look at me. "I asked what your schedule was like today? What's going on with you? You've been acting weird since I parked the car. You embarrassed to be seen with me, Kitty?"

Her gaze previously focused past me, snaps to mine. "What? That's ridiculous. No."

"Then what is it? You're practically running to class and looking around like you're afraid someone is going to see you."

"People are staring at us," she says and motions with her head to a group of girls who are indeed looking our way. One of the baseball guys, Clark, passes by and juts his chin up in greeting. "Correction. *Everyone* is staring at us."

"They're not staring at us. They're staring at me." I shrug. I'm used to it. I mean, when you're as tall as I am, you can't walk around without people staring. Plus, I'm a social guy so most of them I've hung out with or talked to – the others just know who I am.

She glances around as if verifying my claim. "God, what a life you live," she says with a smirk.

Letting go of her hands, I wrap mine around her back and pull her closer. "Not gonna lie, it's a good life, Kitty. Better when you stay the night and I get to walk you to class."

I have to bend down to place my lips on hers. She hesitates and the idea that she might not be into PDA crosses my mind until I hear her sigh and she presses her body to mine. I have zero problem with public displays of anything, so I let my hands travel down to her ass and I pull her hard against me while I sweep my tongue into her mouth.

When she finally breaks contact, she's heavy-lidded and breathless. "I'm gonna be late."

She doesn't move and I chuckle as she stares at my lips. Her tongue darts out to wet her lips and instead of doing what I want to do – continue to kiss her senseless – I pick up her bag.

"Come on, Kitty."

After my morning class, I head home. Katrina picked up an extra shift at the café and I don't have to be back at the gym until later, so I'm bored. I find Z shooting hoops in our home gym. Shocker.

I grab a ball from the rack and join him. It's only a half court so it isn't like he doesn't see me, but the only acknowledgment I get is his movement to the left side of the basket giving me the other side.

I don't usually push Z into talking, but today I need someone to bounce my thoughts off of.

"You think I'm hurting my chances of being drafted if I stay and finish college?"

He doesn't stop shooting as he answers. "Of being drafted? No. If you stay healthy and your numbers are anywhere close to as good as they are now, someone will pick you up. When we win the tournament this year, there will be a lot of press and that might help you get a better deal, but..."

His words trail off and I mull them over. Z always talks in certainties about us winning. It's like he's got God's ear or maybe he's just that fucking sure of himself and his ability to carry us to victory. Do I need a better deal? I mean obviously I want a sweet contract, but the dream was always to play in the NBA not sign a multi-million contract.

"Still undecided?"

I nod and take a shot that bounces around the rim and out.

"It'd be pretty sweet if we were both starting our rookie seasons next year."

"You gonna actually get out next year, maybe date or at least strike up a conversation with a chick?"

He grunts.

"It's not going to get easier to tell the good ones from the jersey chasers. Might want to consider settling down before you're a millionaire."

I'm not even sure that's why he's avoided chicks thus far and his face gives nothing away.

He stops shooting and looks me dead on. "That what

you're doing with Katrina?"

Cock my head to the side. "I'd hardly call a couple dates settling down."

He raises both eyebrows and stares me down with a look that calls bullshit.

"Part of me is ready to give all this up and move on, but the other part feels like I'm taking the shortcut." Like I've always done. Easy, uncomplicated, whatever got me the most satisfaction in the moment. That pretty much sums up my life. Especially my relationships. I've worked hard at ball and school, but never with women. Not since Polly. Thinking about Katrina and how much harder everything is for her haunts me. I look for the path of least resistance because of one bend in the road. Okay, it was more like a fucking sinkhole, but the way I let it change me... I let it change me like Polly was my Vesper. And fuck that.

Yes, I'm comparing myself to James Bond. Cars, money, women. I'm not an assassin, but I'm deadly from the three-point line so we'll call that basically the same thing.

From the moment I pushed into Katrina's life, I've done things that surprise me. I've taken the hard road. Okay, harder than usual but to be fair, I've enjoyed every moment of it so not exactly a burden. I've changed since I've met her and it may have started out as a game to win her over, but it stopped being about that a long time ago.

"Think I'm gonna stick around another year," I say, and the words feel right. Finish my degree, keep putting in the work, and go pro when it's my time.

"Doesn't Katrina have another year too?" he asks, smiling so big his teeth make an appearance.

It's not about her, though, at least not entirely. He's got my defenses up and I reach for the first response that comes to me. "That gives me another year before I gotta worry about the serious jersey chasers. Then again, I've never discriminated against the girls that are only interested in me because of ball."

He grins, and I laugh, but it feels all wrong as it shakes my chest. The words are true. I've never cared if a girl was only after me because of who I am and what it means for their sexual bucket list. It didn't matter because I was using them the same way. Easy, uncomplicated, and meaningless. But now... it doesn't have the same appeal as it did before.

32

KATRINA

Gabby's place is close to campus in a cute new townhome development. Blair and Vanessa are planning on moving in with her at the end of the semester, so the three-bedroom home looks empty with only Gabby's odds and ends.

The guys are moving the heavy stuff and the four of us are pretending to put away kitchen goods.

Vanessa pours wine into four plastic Valley cups. "We need wine glasses."

"Nope." Blair shakes her head. "I've got those and some margarita glasses. They're at my parents' house, but I'll bring them up next time I visit them."

I look up in time to see Joel and Z coming through the door with a large round chair that is big enough to curl up in and sleep. The strain of the weight forces Joel's muscles to bulge around the sleeve of his bicep.

"Gotta little drool." Vanessa nudges me and wipes at the corner of her mouth.

"Shut up."

When the moving truck is empty, we push the guys out the door. Wes gives Blair big puppy dog eyes when she tells him she's staying with Gabby tonight.

"What about you? Can I convince you to sneak away later?" Joel whispers in my ear.

"I'll text you in a bit."

He brushes his lips over mine. "Mmm. You taste like wine and bad decisions."

"Someone once told me wine makes people emotional," I tease and try to calm the banging of my heart. My emotions were already in overdrive before I took a sip.

With a slow nod and smile, he pulls back. "Sweet. I'll be expecting you to spill all your deepest secrets later than."

I know he's joking, but I'm tempted to hold him captive and force the wine down his throat.

"I'll show you mine if you show me yours."

His gaze rakes over me and my body tingles. "Later, Kitty."

Turns out it only takes one hour for the wine to have its desired effect. I'm tipsy and suddenly all I want to do is talk to Joel and tell him I'm falling for him so hard.

Gabby pulls her hair into a messy bun on top of her head as we listen to Vanessa tell stories about Mario and his giant dick. Blair's expression is one of shock so I'm confident this hasn't been something Vanessa has shared before tonight. Damn, wine really is good at drawing out secrets.

"Seriously, he has to have athletic cups custom made to protect all that." She motions toward her crotch and then moves her hand down her thigh and stops a good foot down as if to give us a visual of how low her boyfriend's penis hangs.

"I can't hear anymore," Blair says and covers her ears. "I'll never be able to look him in the eye again."

I'm listening but still caught up watching Gabby. All that blonde hair piled up above her small face makes her look younger. She catches me staring and dips her head like she thinks I'm staring at her scars.

"Your hair is gorgeous," I say. "You should wear it up more though. You look like Tinkerbell."

She scoffs. "More like Two-Face from Batman but thank you."

"Your scars are not that bad. In fact, I think they've lightened a lot the past few months," Blair insists and pulls her into a hug. "You're a badass Tinkerbell."

We burst into laughter. Crying from laughing so hard.

"Why are we laughing, it's not even that funny?" Vanessa asks between giggles.

Another hour and the conversation is back to boys. My fingers hover over Joel's number in my phone. I write the texts out in my head alternating between funny, sexy, or just casual.

"Take my phone," I plead with Blair and shove it in her direction. "I never understood drunk texting until now and I'm pretty sure I'm close to making a total ass of myself."

Vanessa snatches it from Blair and her thumbs tap on the screen. "I've got this."

"What are you saying?"

She giggles and turns the phone toward me.

ME

I want your P in my V.

"Oh my God, Vanessa."

My phone beeps.

JOEL

Be there in five.

My face warms and I press my palms to my cheeks.

"I'm effective, what can I say?" Vanessa boasts.

"Aww, I'm jealous," Gabby says. "I want a boyfriend."

"He's not my boyfriend."

Blair laughs. "I think I said that exact same thing when Wes and I started hanging out."

"I can confirm that," Vanessa offers.

Gabby flings her arm up, wine cup in hand, splashing the sticky sweet liquid into the air. "I ship you. All of you."

"What does that mean?" I ask as I dab at the wine on my leggings.

"It means I support your relationships. I love how happy all of you are and I want you to go to your sexy boyfriends and get it on."

"I thought we were having a slumber party?" Blair asks, but I can tell she's all for the idea of going to Wes.

"I'm exhausted and tomorrow I need to go try and find a job." She scrunches up her face but then smiles. "Besides now that I'm here we can hang out all the time."

"I ship you," I tell her, wrap my arms around her waist and squeeze hard. I haven't had real girlfriends in a long time, and it feels so good.

She laughs. "That's not how the saying works."

———

Joel

Kitty is drunk. I assumed she was tipsy by the text message, but by the time I drop Vanessa off at Mario's and get back to The White House with her and Blair, she's alternating between fits of laughter and eye fucking me.

Blair pushes out of the backseat before I've even killed the engine. "Thanks for the ride, Joel. Night, Katrina."

"Does your car have a name?" she asks as she runs a hand over the dash seductively.

I'm fixated on her movements, curious as hell what drunk Kitty will do next.

I unbuckle. "Nope."

"Say something in Spanish." She claps her hands and I laugh at the random topic jump and her excitement.

Eres linda cuando estás borracha.

"What did you say?"

"I said you're cute when you're drunk."

Unbuckling, she turns to me. We're still sitting in the car parked in the garage, but I'm afraid to move because once I get her to my room it's likely she's going to pass out on me. And this is way more entertaining.

"Have you ever had sex in here?"

"Uhh." Is this a trick question? I've never lied to a girl, but I feel like being truthful here could put a serious damper on the mood.

"You totally have," she says, but she's smiling so I don't bother denying it. "I've never had sex in a car before." She sighs like that's disappointing to her.

"*¿Quieres tener sexo en mi carro?*"

"I don't know what you said, but it sounded hot."

"*Estás caliente, Katrina.*"

She bites her lip looking all unsure but somehow still seductive and I can't fucking take it. "Come here, Kitty."

"Ask me in Spanish," she says coyly.

"*Trae tu trasero aquí.*"

The seat's already as far back as it'll go so when she climbs onto my lap, straddling me, there's not a lot of room. Not that I'm gonna need it. Just the feel of her on top of me has me ready to lose it. Her eyes flutter closed as my dick pushes against her pussy. God bless leggings. The thin material she wears on nearly a daily basis not only provides a view that keeps me from having to use my imagination, it allows me to feel the heat of her pussy and the soft curves of her legs and ass.

"I probably should have taken my pants off first," she says. "Not enough room over here to shimmy them down."

I capture her mouth and she rubs against me as I lift my hips to offer her more friction. Moving my hands to her hips and taking control, I slide her over the bulge in my pants. Slow and hard until her moans fill my car.

Last time I dry humped someone I was probably in junior high, but damn it's the hottest thing that's ever happened in my car. In my... anything.

Katrina arches her back and her blonde hair falls down her back. She palms both breasts, head thrown back, and she looks so fucking happy and sexy as she fucks me through our clothes.

"Oh my God, I'm coming," she says, eyes pop open and she looks stunned as the orgasm shudders through her.

It's on the tip of my tongue to say something immature like *You can just call me Joel,* but I think better of it. Probably got enough seventh grade mojo up in here with the dry humping alone. I'm giving myself a mental high five for my maturity when Kitty's orgasm sets me off and I come in my damn pants.

33

KATRINA

*T*he better part of four days I've been holed up in Joel's room. School, work, rehearsals, and Joel. If I weren't missing Christian so much, it'd be bliss.

I pull up to the soccer field, scan the cars, and then wave when I see Christian and Victor standing in front of Victor's car.

Christian's smile tells me he wants to dart to me, but Victor restrains him by holding his hand.

I hurry toward him and he pulls free from Victor and runs to meet me halfway.

"Mommy!"

Reaching down to him, I hug him fiercely feeling complete for the first time since I left him. "I missed you."

Victor approaches, hands in his pockets and looking like he feels like the third wheel.

"Thank you for bringing him," I say. "Practice is just an

hour and I have rehearsal right after. Are you staying or do you want me to meet you somewhere before my rehearsal?"

"About that."

The coach blows the whistle and Christian and the other kids run onto the field.

I cross my arms, skin already bristling.

"I got a job working nights loading trucks. I start tonight."

"You couldn't have given me a heads up?"

"Sorry. I didn't think it'd be a big deal. What do you usually do with him when you have night classes?"

"It's not a class, it's..." I count to three before I respond. "It's fine. I'll figure it out."

"You're still bringing him this weekend though, right?"

I grind my teeth. "Yeah, it's your weekend."

"Maybe we can sit down and talk, come up with a new schedule once I get my work schedule?"

I can only nod. Speaking will result in me saying something I regret later. Or screaming in front of children and their perfect mothers.

"Sorry, Katrina."

I hear the gravel crunch under his shoes signaling his departure. Pull out my phone and hover over the contacts. We're less than a month away from opening night of the play and this is the last rehearsal where I can make any big dialogue or script changes.

I could take him with me. Images of Christian tearing

through the theater like a tornado make me cringe. That's not an option.

> **ME**
>
> I know it's impossibly last minute but can one of you watch Christian tonight while I have play rehearsal.

BLAIR

Shoot. I'm sorry, I'm working at the tutor center tonight.

GABBY

I start my new job at The Hideout tonight. <nervous smiley>

VANESSA

Class. Sorry!

BLAIR

The guys just got out of practice, ask Joel <winky smiley face>

Ugh. That sounds worse than letting Christian swing from the rafters. I pocket my phone and walk closer to the field. I'd planned on reading through the script during the practice, but instead, I allow myself to just watch Christian. The big smile on his face, his carefree demeanor, the determination, and energy. In the worst of moments my son always reminds me that it's all worth it. Juggling school and parenting and anything else life throws our way – we can do it. My phone vibrates in my pocket and I retrieve it quickly hoping one of the girls had a change of plans or heart.

JOEL

> My dick is hard and confused because you're not here, but my room smells like sex and Kitty. What time are you done with rehearsal?

If I'd known I wasn't going to be spending another night at his place, I would have entertained the morning sex he attempted at five. After only a few nights I'm already dreading sleeping without him.

ME

> Change of plans. Victor had a conflict and I've got Christian tonight and tomorrow.

JOEL

> What about rehearsal?

ME

> I'm going to take him with me.

Once I type the words, I feel better about my decision. Something about declaring it makes me accept it. It's not the perfect scenario, but it is what it is. Joel doesn't text back, and I return my focus to the practice and watching Christian race from one side of the field to the next. The hour flies by and when the coach dismisses them, I scoop up a dirty and sweaty little boy.

"I've got a surprise for you," I tell him. "But first you

have to come with me to my play rehearsal and sit super still and be super quiet. Can you do that?"

It's more a plea to God than a real question for my son. But hey, ice cream is a small price to pay.

I park the car in the lot next to the theater and hold on to Christian as he skips toward the front entrance. Inside he pulls free. My backpack slips off my shoulder and I stop and adjust before chasing after him.

My mouth opens to call after him, but when I follow the path my son has taken, my eyes move up to the man he's standing in front of. Christian bounces on the balls of his feet and Joel offers his fist, which Christian bumps with his own.

"Mom, I found the surprise! Joel is here."

"This isn't the surprise I had planned," I tell him once I've closed the distance between us and look up to meet Joel's smiling dark eyes. "But this is a nice surprise. What are you doing here?"

"Thought little man could use some company while you do your thing."

I mouth thank you and he gives me a devious grin. One that tells me he's going to take his thanks in sexual favors. Fine by me.

Tabitha and Brody are already on stage, scripts in hand.

"I gotta get up there. Christian, listen to Joel." I use my sternest voice that falls on deaf ears. Though, I think Christian is so enamored by Joel he'd do just about anything he said. "I'll be up front if you guys need me."

"Actually, I was thinking I could take him to the house, play a little ball until you finish up."

Christian's eyes light up giving me very little room to say no.

"Are you sure?"

"Yeah, it'll be fun."

"Please, Mom?"

"Yeah, okay."

Christian jumps and Joel catches him and tucks his little body under his arm, carrying him like a football.

"Break a leg." He starts toward the door taking my son and my heart all in one swift swoop.

———

Joel

Christian talks a mile a minute as I carry him to my car. Chattering on about the basketball game he and his mom attended, asking if Ray Roadrunner will be at my house, and telling me how he hopes he grows up to be as tall as me. I'm opening the door for him when Kitty's voice calls out, "Hey, wait up."

I turn to watch her jogging across the parking lot. Tits bouncing and hair swaying from side to side. I'm straight up addicted to this chick. I can't get enough, which is the only explanation for me showing up here to babysit her kid.

"He needs a car seat," she says out of breath when she's in front of us.

"Oh. Right."

"I can give you the one from my car or..." The mischievous look on her face has my eyebrows shooting up.

"You want to swap cars?"

"It's easier and faster than unhooking it from mine, dragging it over to yours..." She waves her hands around like moving the car seat is an all-day affair. I see past her thinly veiled logic. She bites her lip in an attempt to keep her hope and excitement from showing.

I let out a breath, watching my sanity float away with it. "Fine. I'll take your car."

"Yes!"

She passes over her keys and I already regret this decision.

"Be careful," I warn.

"Aww, worried about me?"

"Worried about my car," I mutter as Christian and I head to her car.

When we get to The White House, I pull around back in the parking lot, spotting the guys shooting outside on the old hoop. Wes has a hard-on for the old rusted backboard and rim that was attached to an old telephone pole about a million years ago from the looks of it.

They eye the car and me with amusement. It's Christian's excitement that forces me out of the car.

"Nice ride," Nathan calls.

Z nudges him in the ribs. "You brought a ringer."

Christian grabs my hand. Such a simple thing that completely catches me off guard. I squeeze his hand gently. "You remember the guys?"

He nods, but still holds back. Strange place, people he's only seen once – yeah perhaps this wasn't my most well thought out plan. Kneeling down, I meet his scared but curious expression. "Nervous?"

Another nod.

"I know these guys are kind of big and ugly," I say loud enough the guys can hear. They scoff in mock outrage and Christian cracks a smile. "But they're cool."

He looks them over and takes a tiny step forward.

"What do you say we show these guys your mad ball skills again?" I pick him up and set him on my shoulders.

Wes hands the ball up to Christian. "Go easy on us."

The guys are all good sports, rebounding the ball over and over for Christian and cheering him on shot after shot. At some point, Z takes Christian from me and shocks the crap out of all of us with how good he is with him. Christian beams, so much happiness radiating from the little guy. He and the big man team up against the rest of us, trash talking all the while, G-rated of course.

This is fun. Feels good and right. Makes me picture a life with them. She handles it all so effortlessly and when I'm with them, I'm not wishing I were anywhere else. What would it be like if Katrina and Christian were a permanent part of my life? Shake my head and push the idea away. I can't even entertain that. She deserves someone who can give everything and I just... can't. I won't. Not again.

My thoughts are cut short when tires squeal and Katrina pulls into the driveway. Driving my car like she stole it.

The guys chuckle.

"*Daaaamn.* Can't believe you let her drive your car," Nathan says. "You've got it bad."

34

KATRINA

*D*riving Joel's car makes me feel powerful.

Or maybe it's a combination of events. Joel showing up for me, an amazing rehearsal, Joel letting me drive his car – which was almost as hot as actually driving it, and I just pulled up to the most amazing scene.

Watching through the windshield, Zeke has Christian up on his shoulders and the rest of the guys appear to be trying to stop them, halfheartedly, from scoring. Honestly, I had no idea what Joel was going to do with Christian when he offered to bring him here. I hadn't even thought it through, I was just so glad that he'd shown up at all.

I'm in love with him. I don't know when it happened exactly, but I finally admitted it to myself the minute I saw him tuck my son under his arm and stride away like it was the most natural thing.

Zeke lifts Christian off his shoulders and sets him on

the ground as I climb out of the car. He runs to me, hugs my legs, and then says *damn* like he's trying out a new word and wants to hear his own voice say something he's heard. I arch a brow at Joel whose face goes panic-stricken. The guys laugh which only eggs Christian on.

"Damn," he says again.

"Real nice, guys."

"My bad," Nathan says as Joel punches him in the arm.

I squat down to eye level. "That's a grown-up word."

"Oh." His eyes go big and round.

I feel Joel next to me before he leans down. "Sorry, buddy. Nathan said a bad word, but he's sorry. *Right*, Nathan?"

I glance up to see Nathan standing there, rubbing the back of his neck and looking sheepish. "Sorry about that, Katrina." He looks to Christian. "Only dumb guys like me use that word. You're too smart for that, right?" He offers his fist and Christian bumps it.

Satisfied, Nathan walks away leaving me with Joel and Christian.

"Sorry," he says quietly, leaning in and kissing me softly on the lips.

"I can't even pretend to be mad. I'm still too amped up from driving your car. I may never give it back."

"Don't even think about it, babydoll."

Christian pulls on both our arms and we swing him between us.

"I should get him home. Thank you for this."

We shuffle awkwardly, neither of us walking away.

"Are you coming over?" Christian asks, finally saying the thing I was too chicken shit to ask.

One side of his mouth pulls up and he nods. "Yeah, if that's cool with your mom." Both turn to me like there's any real question.

"Yeah, of course."

A full-blown smile stretches out on his face. "I got practice in the morning and an away game this weekend so probably the last chance to hang for a few days. I just need to grab my stuff. I'll be over in a few."

I bite down on my tongue to keep from voicing my excitement that he's talking in future terms. Okay, it's not exactly a lifelong commitment, but the fact he thinks we'll still be hanging out next week is good enough for me. Baby steps.

I smile and turn to leave, feeling the best I have in so long. It strikes me how easy this feels. There really is something to the Joel Moreno life, I guess.

Joel clears his throat behind me, and I swivel my head to find him smirking with his hand held out.

"Oh fine," I say and hand him his keys. "Come on Christian."

I'm still floating around wondering when life got so damn good when Joel walks into my apartment. Christian runs to him and hugs his legs like it's all just part of our routine before running back to his pizza.

Trying not to over think it, I do the same. Catching me but laughing in surprise as I jump into his arms, Joel lifts me like I weigh nothing. "I could get used to this sort of welcome."

"I ship us," I blurt out.

I feel his arms tense as he places me on the ground.

I scramble, trying to put what I feel into the right words. "I just mean that spending time with you, and spending time the three of us – you, me, and Christian – I like it and I want to keep doing it. I'm totally for whatever this is. I admit I was not expecting to feel this way but being with you makes me happy. It makes Christian happy. I know it's all happened sort of fast and we haven't talked about, well anything really, but I think I'm falling in lo—"

"Stop."

I meet his gaze. In my rambling, I'd avoided eye contact in order to get it all out, but now I'm thinking I should have looked up sooner. I see the panic and remorse in those deep brown eyes.

I shake my head, feeling foolish. "I'm sorry. I thought—"

"Mom put your plate next to mine," Christian yells out from the dining room, interrupting my humiliation.

Joel looks torn between bolting and joining Christian. I turn and move to the kitchen trying to regain some semblance of composure. Placing a hand to my trembling lips, I close my eyes and will the tears not to fall.

I can hear Joel move across the apartment and take a seat next to Christian, but I physically cannot make myself join them. I can't sit across from him and pretend like he didn't just crush the heart I offered on a silver platter. Or almost offered. I'm not sure if it's more or less humiliating that I didn't actually say the words. What sort of guy stops a girl from telling him that she's falling in love with him?

I always knew what this was. I knew who he was, but one date turned into another and another, and somewhere along the way my heart stopped getting the memo that this was casual. Being with Joel is easy – too easy. That alone should have had me on guard. My life isn't easy, and I've prided myself on making the most in spite of that.

I stay in the kitchen, cleaning dishes until I can see my reflection, wiping down counters, scrubbing at dirty cabinet doors – basically anything that keeps me busy.

"All done?" I hear Joel ask Christian.

He comes into the kitchen carrying his and Christian's plates, washes and rinses them, before turning to me. Christian's already moved on to the next thing, pushing cars around the track set up in the living room.

"I'm sorry," he says. No attempt to smooth things over. No false promises. Just his apologies for not loving me back.

"No, I'm sorry. I got swept up in everything. You make me happy, my son happy. The way you show up for us, it's, well, it's hard not to fall for you."

"I think you and Christian are great and I'd love to spend more time with you, but love and relationships are just... they're just not something I do. You two deserve so much more than I can give you. Guess I was being selfish by forcing myself into your life when I can't be what you need. It's just..." He runs a hand through his hair and mumbles to the ground. *"No estoy listo para rendirme."*

A tear slips out and I swipe at it furiously.

He places a finger at my chin and brings his lips to mine in the softest kiss that says the goodbye I know is coming. "Don't cry for me, Kitty." He steps back, eyes tormented but jaw set. "I should go."

I nod, not trusting my voice. Further crushing my heart, he goes to Christian, squats down and speaks so I can't hear him. Christian smiles and then bumps Joel's fists with his own. My son is completely oblivious that this man is walking out of our lives for good and I try to be happy about that. Better now than in six months or a year when Christian is more attached.

I follow Joel to the door. He wraps me into a hug, pressing our bodies together and threading a hand through my hair. I want to stay just like this forever. Turn back time and keep my feelings stuffed down inside where they belong.

"Lo siento. Lo siento mucho."

35

JOEL

July, One Month Before College

Baby Minka Suzanne is born the last week of July. She is everything. So soft and adorable and, I inhale the top of her head and my heart feels so full, absolutely perfect. Life is perfect.

College starts next month. I got a full ride to play basketball at Valley University. Polly is taking a semester off and then she wants to go to beauty school so she can do make up for a living. She's good at that. Even two days after having Minka, she looks flawless.

"You sure you don't want to just move in with me? There's an empty bedroom right next to mine, we can set up her nursery there. Plus, we'll have more help."

Polly finishes packing up her bag, carefully folding the tiny little pink outfits. "No, I don't think so. That would be too weird – us living with your parents. What about if we get a place just the two of us?"

"I can't afford that. My basketball scholarship states that I can't work. And, I'd rather spend my free time hanging with my best girls," I coo into sweet Minka's chubby cheeks and then place her in the car carrier.

"Hey, did you get that baby swing I sent you the link for?"

"Nah, we already got a swing."

Her face falls. "This one was so much better. It glides and swings. Plus, you can upload your own music to it and the seat doubles as a sleeper. We have to have it."

"Yeah, sure, whatever you want." This baby is already the most spoiled human in Valley.

I reach for the hospital forms, my eyes snagging on the paper lying on top. "Don't we need to fill this out before we leave?"

"I did." She swipes it from my hands. "That's a copy."

"You didn't fill in the father section."

"Of course, I did." She shoves the papers inside the bag, zips it, and hands it to me. "Ready to go?"

Her too cheerful voice makes every nerve in my body stand at alert. "Are you not going to list me as her dad? I know we're not married, and I'm cool with Minka having your last name until then, but I'm her father."

The fear in Polly's eyes knocks the wind out of me. "I *am* her father, right?"

"I –" Her voice cracks.

I glance down at my beautiful daughter, fair skin, dark

blue eyes with flecks of gold that I'm certain are going to turn green. She'll be a beautiful mini version of her mother, but she's mine. I feel it in my bones.

"Polly?" Throat thick. "She is mine, right?" It sounds ridiculous even to my own ears.

"I don't know for sure."

My knees give, and I brace myself on the wall behind me.

I have no idea how much time goes by while I stand and wait for the bombshell to finish exploding in my chest.

"I'm sorry. I love you. I'm so, so sorry." Polly's voice breaks the silence. Tears stream down her face leaving a trail of black from her makeup. "It was just one time."

"You slept with someone else while we were together?"

I process the words as I say them. How did I not see this coming? Polly and I have been careful every time we've had sex. I always use protection, but, fuck, her cheating on me was the last thing I thought when she got pregnant.

How could she be so deceiving, and I never even considered that a possibility? Were there no signs or did I just ignore them? Blinded by love. Fucking love.

She steps forward and reaches for my hand. "I love you."

I flinch at both the words and her touch. "You don't love me." I pull away. She inhales sharply, but I'm too pissed to care that I might be upsetting the woman that may or may not have just had my baby. I'll add that to my list of regrets later. "You couldn't possibly love me and keep this from me for nine months. What if –." I can't force myself to say the words. What if she isn't mine?

This, whatever it is Polly feels for me, definitely isn't love. Or if it is, it isn't enough for me.

"It was only one time," she repeats like that matters. One time that she screwed somebody else while claiming to love me. I'm not into gambling, but if I were, I'd say the odds aren't good that she's telling the truth. She might as well have boned the whole town, though, because I'm done. Not with Minka, but with Polly. Didn't plan on raising a kid on my own, but there's no chance I can raise one with Polly. I can't even look at her.

"You and I can still be together," she insists and pushes against me. "It was a guy my sister knows from college. I had too much to drink at my birthday party and one thing led to another. It meant nothing. Even if he's the father, it's you I want to be with. Minka can be ours regardless."

Grind my teeth in frustration and ball my hands into fists because I straight up want to strangle this girl with every new detail she offers.

How could I be so stupid? How could she be so conniving? "No. You fucking destroyed whatever love I had for you when you spread your legs for someone else."

Minka's mine. She has to be.

She gasps at my harsh words. I regret them immediately, but I don't apologize. I've never slut-shamed anyone in my life, but I'm seeing red and I need to hurt her as much as she hurt me. I can feel my heart harden and I walk away before I say anything else I might regret. If this is love, fuck it. Love is an exchange of power. And the person who loves the most – they trade all their power. And for what?

Never again. I'll take control of my life over love any day.

Love is bullshit.

36

JOEL

"*M*oreno, what the hell is going on with you today?"

I shake my head and wipe the sweat from my brow.

Coach's mouth sets in a firm line and he points to the sideline. "Take a seat. Johnson, you're up."

Wes looks like he might speak as I pass him standing at the top of the key with his fucking dry erase clipboard in hand, but I head him off. "Save it."

I'm angry. No, fuck it, I'm enraged. At myself. At life. At every goddamn thing.

Katrina loves me or is falling in love with me. I'm pretty sure those are synonymous. How did I not see this coming? It's the exact reason I stopped letting girls in beyond my bed. From the day Polly shattered my belief in love and trust, I'd changed. I made sure my intentions were clear – just sex, just fun, leave your emotions at the door. It had been easier than I thought until I'd walked into that damn café.

I'd been fooling myself into thinking I could dance around the lines with her and Christian, but the second the words left her mouth I didn't feel happy – I felt fucking panicked. If I gave her my love and she treated it as recklessly as Polly had, it would destroy me. It would change me beyond repair.

Fuck.

Tossing the ball to Johnson, I take another step toward the bench and still. Frozen in place as the weight of the realization hits me.

Polly wasn't my Vesper. Katrina is. Katrina's my Vesper.

My chest is already tight at the thought of not seeing her or Christian. That kid has gotten under my skin as much as she has. What if she changed her mind in a month or a year? No, not what – when. Just like before I'd have no control – they'd be gone, and I'd be wrecked. Losing Polly changed me, but if I give my heart to Katrina, it will fucking ruin me when she eventually walks away.

Knowing that I can't be what they need, that they're better off without me, fucking stings. Knowing I'm not willing to risk trying makes me feel like a coward.

Hang my head and drape a towel over me, shrouding myself in darkness. My own personal sweaty hell.

Someone approaches, and I glance at the floor in front of me, spotting Coach's old school Jordan's. Man's got good taste in shoes, I'll give him that.

"Get out of here. Go to class, go home, I don't care what you do, but get your head on."

"I'm fine," I grit out, annoyed at being sent home like a child.

"It wasn't a question, son. I don't want to see you until tomorrow morning. We've got seven days until the tournament and I need you to work your shit out."

With a sigh, I stand and start toward the locker room.

"And Moreno," Coach calls and I pause. "Tomorrow I expect your shit to be straight or you won't leave here until it is."

———

THURSDAY'S COME to be my favorite day of the week. A communications class that I actually like, followed by economics where I usually spend the fifty minutes of class time working out what I'll say to Kitty. Today I just stare straight ahead totally numb until class is dismissed. I'm at the door of University Hall before I realize my body has gone on autopilot.

I stand out front unable to go in but incapable of leaving without a glimpse. A group of people walk in, the last one holding the door out to me and I step through.

Holding my breath, I scan the café counter, exhaling when it's not Kitty I see but some dude. I get in line and wait, keeping my eyes peeled the whole time. Maybe she got held up and is running late. Fuck, I don't know. She's always just here.

"Can I help you?" dude that's not Katrina asks when it's my turn.

"Looking for Katrina."

"She's not here."

Captain Obvious.

"This is her shift." I hold my ground. It'd be easier if I just outright asked, but I don't.

"She called out sick. Coffee?"

Shake my head and turn away.

It takes ten minutes to get to her apartment from campus.

I make it in six.

"Kitty, open up." I knock on the door and am met with silence. Pace, knock some more, pull out my phone. I'm just about to call her when the door cracks open.

"Joel? What are you doing here?"

Instead of answering I push the door wide and step in. I'm well aware that I may not be welcome, but I need to explain or apologize, or fuuuuck, I dunno, something.

I open my mouth to speak, and then take in her appearance. Messy hair, dark circles under her eyes. "You're sick?"

"No, it's Christian. He was up all night."

Which means she was up all night. The thought, *I should have been here*, slams through me, but that's not right either. Still, I hate that she was by herself. She shouldn't have to do it alone.

I glance over to the couch where Christian lays, blanket pulled up around him, trashcan next to him.

"How is he?"

The look she gives me tells me I have no right to ask, but she answers anyway. "He's got a fever and can't hold anything down."

His little head pops up an inch and the smallest smile tips his tiny lips.

"Hey, little man." I cross to him, taking a seat at the end of the couch. "Heard you weren't feeling well."

"My tummy hurts," he admits. "Are you gonna stay and watch *Bolt* with me?"

"We don't want Joel to get sick, buddy," she says and Christian's face falls.

It would be bad if I get sick this close to the tournament, but it's the farthest thing from my mind.

"I've had my flu shot. Plus, I never get sick."

That much is true. Can't remember the last time I had the flu. Fingers crossed.

"Your dad should be here in a little bit," she says. I'm sure it's meant to scare me off, but I don't budge.

"Cool. I'll just stay until he gets here."

I glance back at Katrina, can't read the expression on her face, but she shrugs a shoulder giving me permission that I know is purely for Christian's benefit.

Little man crawls over to me, rests his head on my lap, and my heart hammers in my chest possessively. We watch the movie in silence. Katrina stays away, except to check Christian's temperature and instruct him to drink more water.

She checks her phone no less than twenty times and I have to wonder if Victor's blowing her off.

"He's out," I whisper quietly when Christian finally falls asleep.

"Oh good." They're the first words that have left her mouth without attitude. She stands in front of me angling like she wants to reach out for him but equally wants to refrain from touching me.

"You want him in his bed?"

"Yeah, maybe he'll sleep for a few hours. He was up all night," she says for the second time.

I stand with him, careful not to wake him, and take him to his room, place him on the bed, push back his hair from his forehead that's still warm to the touch. I feel Katrina watching me, but I don't let her rush me. I pull the comforter up to cover him and sing quietly the song my mother sang to me at night.

"Buenas noches, Hasta mañana, que Juan Pestañas ya va a llegar. El viejito de los sueños bonitos cuentos te contará. Buenas noches, Hasta mañana, que Juan Pestañas ya va a venir. ¡Ponte tu pijama y métete a la cama¡, porque ya es la hora de dormir."

I stare at him a moment longer before I force myself up.

Katrina is sitting on the couch, legs crossed under her, staring hard at me, phone in hand.

"Victor on his way?"

Her jaw tenses. "He'll be here."

I try not to let her intimidate me as I take a seat next to her. She's so angry, or maybe hurt, and I know my being here is probably making things harder, but I'm having a real hard time walking away.

"I'm sorry about last night."

"It's fine. You can't help how you feel. Or *don't* feel," she adds.

"I'd do anything for you or Christian. It kills me that I wasn't here last night when you needed me, but I don't do love and relationships so we're just delaying the inevitable. I care about you too much to do that to you or him."

"Why is that?"

Determined and angry isn't a side of Katrina I've seen before. She's fucking scary.

"I just don't. Why does it matter?"

"No, that's not good enough. I want to know why?"

"The last time I was in a relationship it ended horribly. It's not a path I want to go down again."

"In high school? How bad could it have ended?" The way she says it I know she's picturing my high school days differently than hers. Easy – the way my life is now. Easy comes at a cost. The price, deep and meaningful connections.

"My high school girlfriend got pregnant."

Her mouth forms an O and I can practically see her trying to guess what might have happened.

"For months she let me believe we were going to be a family. I was all in. I would have done anything for them. Which is why I was so shocked when the baby was born, and my girlfriend told me she wasn't sure it was mine. She'd slept with someone else while we were together and couldn't be sure. Would have been helpful knowledge before I held that baby girl in my arms. She wasn't mine, of course, but for those months leading up to it and those two days after she was born when I thought she was... I loved her so damn much." Fuck, if I concentrate hard enough, I swear I can still smell the top of her newborn head. Voice like gravel, I force myself to continue. If Katrina deserves nothing else, she deserves the truth. "I never saw it coming."

Katrina stays quiet, her lips pulled into a sad frown.

"I admire you, Kitty. I know how brave you were to have Christian and raise him basically on your own. I just..." My voice cracks and I screw my eyes shut as I say the words. "I vowed never to get that close to someone again. Not to put myself in a position where I don't have control over the situation. And with Christian in the picture, it just makes it that much harder for me. What if things end badly for us? Losing both of you, I just..."

"I'm sorry she did that to you. That's really shitty."

A rough chuckle rumbles in my chest. "Yeah."

"It's what makes Joel, Joel."

I grind down on my back molars. Polly's actions making me who I am is bullshit. I've moved on. Except, just the thought of her makes me so angry I can't see straight. I'm pissed at a girl I haven't seen in almost four years and at myself for falling for her in the first place. And doubly pissed it's fucking with what's probably the best thing to ever happen to me.

"But, Joel, there are no guarantees. Not for you. Not for

me. What she did was unfathomable, but do you really want to spend the rest of your life not trusting anyone enough to let them close? You deserve so much more. And I do too."

A knock at the door breaks the moment and Katrina goes to answer it while I stand and try to erase all the emotions Kitty has brought out in me. I gotta get out of here. I move to the door and the man walking inside eyes me carefully. Katrina looks between us.

"Victor, this is Joel. Joel, this is Christian's father, Victor."

Christian cries out and Katrina steps toward his room. "I'll be right back."

I offer my hand to Victor. "It's good to meet you. You've got a great son."

"Yeah, I do," he says, not letting go of my hand past the point of polite. I release, letting him have the upper hand.

"Well, I should get going." I motion in the direction Katrina went. "Tell them I said goodbye."

"Sure, man."

I step toward the door and then turn back. "Take care of them. And, uh, I know it's not my place, but Katrina is the type of girl who won't ask for help even when she needs it. And she needs it – they need you. You should have been here already, but you know that."

Knowing I've overstepped my boundaries, I give him a curt nod and leave.

37

KATRINA

*A*ll of campus is talking about the game tonight. Blue and yellow floods University Hall. The café has been busy, students and professors alike getting their caffeine in anticipation to a late night watching the first round of the tournament.

One week. Seven days. Long, excruciatingly empty days without Joel. He hasn't texted, not that I expected him to. The fantasy is officially over.

It's the first Thursday, outside of holidays and school breaks, that Joel has missed, and I can't help but wonder if he'd have come even if he weren't in Salt Lake City.

Gabby appears at the back of the line and waves. I'm so happy to see her I focus and get the four orders in front of her done quickly.

"Hey!" I say when she's finally at the counter. "What are you doing here?"

She's not taking classes on campus, so her presence means she's come to see me.

"I wanted to invite you to The Hideout tonight. It's my first night working all on my own and Blair, Vanessa, and some of the baseball guys are coming to watch the game." She looks at me hopefully. "And for moral support. Please? I need at least one table that I know won't yell at me."

Gabby has a way of pulling smiles from people without even meaning to and I feel the first crack of a real honest to God smile since Joel broke my heart.

"Of course, I'll be there. Christian is with Victor this weekend."

And I could use the distraction. I know I won't be able to not watch the game and watching the game can only lead to thinking of Joel. As if I've done anything but that this past week.

"Great. Thank you." She leans over the counter and hugs my neck. "My shift starts at six."

The rest of the day goes by without too much dwelling on my shitty week, and when the game starts and I'm sitting between Blair and Clark, a friend of Mario's from the baseball team, I almost feel good.

Almost.

Part of me is even excited to see Joel on the flat screens plastered on every wall. Except it's not the real Joel. It's some solemn, defeated looking impersonator. As the half-time buzzer sounds and the announcers begin to discuss the first half of the game, I realize he's just as miserable as me and it shows in his less than stellar performance.

Maybe it's stupid of me to not be jumping up and down at this knowledge, but if Joel isn't going to be with me, I want him to go back to the charming easy-going guy I longed for. I don't want or need his pain. It certainly doesn't make my own misery feel better to have company.

"This was supposed to be an easy game," Mario says as Gabby brings a new pitcher to our table.

I'm still shocked that Gabby took a job at the most popular college hangout. Half the time she's hiding behind her hair hoping no one will notice her, but there is no hiding her gorgeous blonde hair and "remarkable ass." That from Clark who, bless his heart, tried to say it as a compliment but sent Gabby running back behind the bar.

The rest of the table weighs in on the game, but I stop listening and pull out my phone.

I know there is very little chance that the guys spend halftime checking their phones, but I do know someone that may just be able to get a message to him.

Joel

Coach's suit jacket is tossed over a chair and he's currently pulling at his tie. What a shitty first half. Florida Gulf is playing the half of their lives, but even so, we should be destroying them. Shaw, our rookie point man, is overwhelmed in his first tournament game and I'm tossing up bricks.

Letting go of distractions and focusing on the present is something athletes learn to do when they get to a competitive level. It's necessity. For some players, they switch gears and are able to leave it all off the court, some use bad days to fuel their motivation. To be honest, I've never really needed to develop a coping mechanism. After Polly, I turned off that part of my brain, not just when I was playing ball but all the time. Until Katrina.

"Moreno," Coach's voice pulls me out of my own thoughts. "Gonna let you start the second half, but I've got Johnson on standby if you can't pull it together."

Spectacular.

Z nudges me, giving me a silent pep talk with his serious gaze.

Coach gives us our final marching orders for the plan of attack, and we stand to head back onto the court.

"Hey," Wes motions with his head and I hang back.

"Dude, I swear to God if you give me another pep talk about heart, I'm gonna lose my shit."

He chuckles. "Damn, I need new material." He passes me his phone. "I think this is better than whatever I could have come up with."

Confused, but intrigued, I take his phone and see a text from Katrina.

Wes pats me on the back. "See you out there, man."

I sit back on the bench in front of the lockers and run a towel over my forehead. Let out a breath and read.

KITTY

> If you're reading this after the game and you lost, well, just stop reading. But in the off chance, Wes is able to get this to you at halftime, here goes…

> You said once that I was your lucky charm. I don't know if you were telling the truth or not, but there is a whole bar of people at The Hideout about to riot so here's hoping.

> I gave this careful consideration and I've decided to go with wisdom from someone I know you'll listen to, yourself. Ready? Winners want the ball. Yep, that's it. And if that doesn't work, then just know, for whatever it's worth, I believe in you.

Read it three times before I stand, knowing I need to get out there but wanting to let her words motivate me. A lot of questions and thoughts of Kitty pull at my focus, but there'll be time later to decipher the way it makes me feel to know she has my back even when I've given her every reason not to.

Wes is waiting for me outside the locker room. Should have guessed. He looks me up and down carefully. "You good?"

I hand him the phone. "Yeah, all good."

The sound of the band playing "Tequila," the echo of basketballs hitting the wooden floor, I let it soothe something inside of me that I wasn't able to before Katrina's message.

Fifteen thousand fans are here. This is what I live for –
doing what I love in front of thousands of people. Giving
them something to hope for, to cheer for. For two hours,
they get to leave everything else behind. It's more than a
game. It's a chance to be part of something bigger than
myself.

Wes pulls out the dry erase clipboard he held under
one arm and glances down at what looks like a list. A long
list.

"Got a few notes for me, Coach Dubya?"

He grins. "Thinking you should attack the basket this
half."

I play my best ball on the outside – long shots,
jumpers, and fadeaways – that's my clutch move. I'm real
good at the fadeaway. The best. On the court and off. You
can't guard someone who shoots and moves backward. You
just can't. I've staked my future and my personal life on
that one move.

"But they've got Louis down low. Man's a brick wall."

"Yeah, which is why they aren't expecting it. I think you
can get two or three good drives off him before they adjust
and then start looking to Z and Malone. Don't need it to
work all night, just to rattle them and gain some
momentum."

Florida Gulf is a fifteen seed - nobody expected them
to give us trouble tonight. Wes is right, if we get some
momentum and throw them off, they'll likely crumble.

"Alright. Far be it for me to go against your years of
coaching experience."

Relief smooths out his features. "Alright then. Let's have a game."

Yeah, let's have a game.

38

JOEL

*T*he bus to the airport is quiet. We pulled out the win, but it was a wakeup call to how quickly the season could end. Even if by some miracle we make it back here next year, I know it won't be the same without Z. He's made me work smarter and push harder. Playing with a guy of his talent makes us all look better because we strive to be better.

Wes nudges me as I'm about to close my eyes. "Nice job out there."

"Yeah, you too. I know I give you shit about coaching, but you've yet to lead us wrong. And you didn't even have to give the heart pep talk."

"Didn't have to, someone else beat me to it."

Katrina.

Wes and I almost always sit next to each other on bus rides. Wes would never admit it, but I think he likes how I don't sit and brood like him or Z. I've never had a problem speaking my mind, getting things off my chest. But tonight, I'm lost in my head and he seems to sense that.

"So, she's your lucky charm, huh?"

Fucker read the text.

As if reading my thoughts, he says, "Had to make sure it wasn't going to mess with your head. I like the chick, but not enough to gamble a national championship on her words of wisdom."

"Yeah, I guess she is."

"You know what your problem is?" Wes angles his body toward me, and I groan. Just what I was hoping for, a critical review of my shitty performance.

"What's that?" I ask dryly, only humoring him because I know the fastest way forward is not resisting.

"You think the fadeaway is your only move. It's not."

"Fine, I'll bite. What the hell does that mean?"

"It means you're one of the best all-around ball players I know. You don't have to stick with your signature moves. Try new things, take risks. You were amazing tonight."

"Thanks, man."

"While I'm doling out the advice, I feel compelled to say that I think you could do the same off the court."

Ah, there it is. I knew this pep talk was going to lend itself to a personal intervention.

"You've seemed happy this past month. I didn't really realize it until you weren't. I mean you've always been care-free and the life of the party, but since Katrina, you've just seemed... happy. Fuck, I don't know how to explain it. I'm sorry if I wasn't supportive in the beginning. I was wrong."

I have been happy. A deeper kind of happiness that I'd forgotten existed, if I'm honest. But that doesn't mean I want to sign up for the inevitable wrecking ball in a month or six when things crash and burn.

"Whatever shit you're working out, I don't think banging the entire Valley female population is gonna help. Especially not now."

I resist rolling my eyes. Just barely. "It's not sex therapy. I just like women."

"Let me ask you, how many women have you hooked up with in the last month?"

I grind my molars.

"Doesn't mean anything."

"Fine. But you're free now, right? Obviously, you and Katrina are on the outs judging by your shitty mood. So, can I assume you've texted a hand full of girls to see who's available when we get back for a little victory high five with your penis? Since you two aren't a thing, shouldn't be an issue."

It's true that's what I would have done in the past and the asshole knows I haven't texted anyone. I've barely touched my phone the past few days because every time I do, I want to text Katrina and I know I can't. And the texts from jersey chasers come in steady succession, but I haven't read a single one. God, I hate when he's right.

"Are you done?" I ask and pull out my headphones so I can block any further attempts to chat.

He smiles way too sweetly like he knows he's made his point.

39

KATRINA

Joel and the team have been gone more than they've been at school since the tournament started. I haven't seen him, and we've only exchanged a few texts, all of them about the games. This weekend is the Final Four. It's Victor's weekend with Christian, but Christian really wanted us all to watch the game together, so I'm at Nadine's house sandwiched between my son and his father on the downstairs couch – never thought I'd see the day honestly.

As the camera zooms in on Joel, Christian jumps up and cheers. The announcers talk about how his performance tonight is going to be key for a Valley win and my stomach is in knots.

Victor offers me the bowl of chips and I shake my head. "No thanks, I'm not much of a potato chip kind of gal."

"Really? I didn't know that."

There's a lot we don't know about each other but pointing that out hardly seems productive. Victor has been trying harder. He hasn't been late or a missed a meetup and he actually came to one of Christian's soccer games. Ever since Christian was sick and I called him for help, he's been different. Maybe seeing his son that vulnerable finally got through to him.

"I have an idea," I say, watching Joel on the TV.

When I glance at him, Victor eyes me suspiciously. Fair since I've not been the easiest person to co-parent with. My anger and bitterness about his absenteeism isn't without merit, but I've certainly not helped matters by holding it over his head and acting like an ice queen around him.

"Let's play seven questions. You ask me any seven questions you want, and I'll do the same."

Pulling a Joel Moreno move. It worked for us, maybe it'll help with Victor – minus the kissing and fondling. There is absolutely zero chemistry between Victor and me now. He's still attractive, blonde hair and blue eyes with long, dark lashes women would kill for. But he's not really my type. Back then I didn't realize I had a type. Victor had been nice and comfortable.

"Alright. Yeah, that's a good idea."

We stare at each other for a minute, neither making a move to go first.

"I'm gonna get some alcohol for this. You like beer?"

"Beer's good."

Victor disappears up the stairs and I pull a squirming Christian into my lap. "How's the team doing?"

"Good." He grins ear to ear. "Maybe if they win, we can have pizza with Joel again?"

He looks so into the idea I can't bring myself to do anything but nod as he jumps off my lap to stand in front of the TV.

"Alright," Victor says, coming down the stairs with four beers, two in each hand. "Ready?"

We settle onto the old leather couch, facing each other. Me leaning back against the armrest and Victor on the other side foot propped over a knee.

"Favorite food?" I ask and take a sip of the Bud Light.

"Pizza."

"Christian's too."

He glances to our son and smiles. "Yours?"

"Cheeseburgers. Favorite band?"

"Tupac forever." He flashes a W with his left hand in the west side symbol and I laugh. I hadn't pegged him for an old school rap guy.

We fire questions back and forth, neither of us counting and only stopping occasionally to track the game. Valley is leading and Joel looks good. No, he looks great. Christian bounces between standing a foot in front of the TV cheering and bouncing on the couch between us.

"I've got a question," Victor says, pulling my attention from the TV. "What's going on with you and the basketball guy?" He points toward the TV.

"Oh. Nothing."

"Come on, we're sharing."

"He was helping me with my play, and we went on a

few dates. That's it. We're just at different places. He's not looking for a relationship, and I am. It was stupid to get involved." I shrug. "What about you? Are you dating?"

He shakes his head. "No. I mean a little at school, but nothing serious."

We fall into a comfortable silence, staring at the TV even though it's halftime and there isn't really anything to see. Valley is up by ten and the announcers seem pretty confident that they can win as long as they don't lose their minds in the second half.

The camera zooms in on Joel and Z walking back onto the court.

"I think you're wrong about him," Victor says. "Guy all but told me I needed to step up. He wouldn't do that if he didn't have a vested interest."

"Wait, what? When?" That doesn't sound like Joel. Or well, it does, actually, but I'm still surprised.

"That day at your apartment. Before he left, he told me to tell you goodbye and that you wouldn't ask for help, but you needed it."

I cringe because Victor and I are finally talking, and I don't want this to stir things up before we've barely made progress.

"He was right. I mean I was pissed at first which is why I didn't mention it before, but I thought about it, then got the same talk from my mom, so I figured he probably wasn't talking out his ass."

I laugh awkwardly, and he joins in.

"I'm sorry," I say, though I'm not sure exactly what I'm

apologizing for – for letting it get to a point where other people needed to step in? I should have been the one to talk to him about it.

"No, I am." He plays with the tab of his beer can, pushing it to one side and then the other. "I'm sorry I left. When Christian was born, it felt like you guys didn't need me. Even when he was here, Mom mostly doted on him. She took over and I let her. Then as he got older, I barely knew him. Didn't know what he liked or needed, and he sensed that."

We're quiet and I can't think of what to say. I didn't know any of this. Hadn't asked – always assumed it was purely selfishness that kept him away.

"Christian is a good kid," I say and we both look to our son who has lost interest in the game and is rolling the small Valley basketball Joel got him around the basement. "You both just need more time together. He's getting that now and I think it's been good for him."

"Yeah, he is a good kid. I can't take any credit for that. It was all you. Thank you for that and about a million other things."

Maybe that's all I needed to hear – the acknowledgment that I've done well and that he's noticed because all the lingering resentment I've held on to from the past three years disappears with that statement. I'm hopeful that this really will be a fresh start for all of us.

"Also, for what it's worth, I think you should give the guy a real chance. He's definitely got Christian's seal of approval."

"What do you mean a real chance?"

Victor grins. "Don't write him off at the first screw up. You seem like you've already made up his mind for him." He holds his hands up defensively as I open my mouth to protest. Joel made his mind and feelings very clear. "Look, I know I have like no room to talk when it comes to self-development, but your tendency is to close off, bite your tongue, and stew in silence. That and my lack of balls is the reason this is the first time we've had a real conversation in three years."

"I can't force him to feel something he doesn't. And even if he did feel the same, what if he can't be what I need?" I voice my real concerns out loud. Being responsible for a tiny human means I can't settle or accept less than I deserve, even if I think I'd be willing to take any scraps Joel would give me if things were different.

"Then at least you can move on knowing you gave it your all. But right now, looking at you, I know you are still hoping for him to change his mind. Maybe he's having the same reservations."

The game ends late and at Nadine's insistence, I find myself in the guest room staying the night. Valley won, and I hold my phone over my face debating on texting Joel. I can't believe I'm about to take Victor's advice, of all people.

ME

Congrats on the game! Christian and I watched. We'll be cheering you on Monday!

My phone rings a minute later with a video call.

"Hey," I answer, heart in throat as Joel's face appears on the screen. It's the first time I've seen him in weeks.

"Hey yourself." He props a hand behind his head, and I can tell he's lying in bed.

"Shouldn't you be out celebrating?"

"I'll celebrate Monday night when we win. Until then, eat, sleep, ball."

I hear Nathan grumble in the background and Joel flips him off. "I gotta go, Kitty, just wanted to see your face. Tell little man I said hey."

"I will. Night."

He smiles into the phone, the sexy cocky smirk I fell in love with, and my heart squeezes. "Night, Kitty."

40

JOEL

Z's tears mix with my own. I'm crying like a baby and I don't even care. We won. Valley University has its first NCAA basketball championship trophy and our team has done something each one of us has dreamt about.

We take turns cutting the net down, there are interviews after interviews. It's the best type of insanity. The greatest moment of my entire life, one I'll never ever forget. My parents and sisters are watching down from their seats and there's a comfort and sense of contentment that flows along with the excitement.

It's late by the time the crowd clears, we shower, and head to the mixer for players, family, and whoever else was deemed important enough.

"Congratulations." Michelle moves to me first and hugs me tightly. She's covered head to toe in blue and yellow. So much Valley pride runs through her blood there's no doubt she'll be a proud Valley U student as soon as she graduates high school.

Bree doesn't hug me, but she does smile and tell me good game which is as much as I can expect from her. She's graduating high school this year and already stated loud and clear she's going anywhere but Valley. She hasn't applied anywhere else, so I'm calling bullshit.

"We're so proud of you." My mother places both hands on my face before pulling me to her. *"Estamos muy orgullosos de ti. Siempre."*

I remember Nathan is behind me, his family couldn't be here, and I realize how much it must suck to have no one here. I turn to him and wrap an arm around his shoulders and pull him into the circle before dropping my arm. "And we've got another shot to get back here next year."

"It was a hell of a year. One you should both be really proud of," my dad says in his official Valley president voice, but then softens as he says, "Don't spend too much time celebrating before you get back to work for next season."

Nathan smiles at that and holds up his arm and we bump fists. We make the rounds, saying hello to teammates, families, and anyone else that wants a moment of our time – which seems to be everyone.

When I can sneak away, I check my phone. Still nothing from Kitty. With about a million people patting my back and congratulating me on my contribution to the victory, it's her words I want more than anyone else. She'd sent me a good luck message before the game, her and Christian's faces pushed together, and I could tell they were both wearing their Valley shirts.

Nathan walks up as I'm staring at the picture and willing Kitty to call or text. "You ready to party?"

I nod. "Yeah, ready to get out of here for sure. I need to say goodbye to my family."

Nathan points to Shaw and Malone who stand by the door. "Want us to wait for you?"

"Nah, go on. I'll catch up."

My mom and sisters are nowhere in sight, but I spot my dad and make my way to him.

"We're taking off. Thank you for coming. Means a lot."

He places a hand on my shoulder. "You've grown into a good man. Hard working, smart, loyal. Nowhere else I'd rather be. Valley president or not."

Touched by his words but feeling awkward as hell at all the attention my talent and character has gotten tonight, I change the subject. "Where'd Mom and the girls go?"

"The ladies room. If it's anything like the trip they made at halftime, I wouldn't expect them back anytime soon. Go," he motions with his head. "We'll see you back home."

No further prompting is needed, I duck out and dial Katrina as soon as I'm far enough from the noise I think I'll be able to hear her.

"Hello?" she answers huskily, obviously woken from sleep.

"Hey."

"Congratulations." I can hear the smile in her voice.

"Thanks."

There's silence for too long, but I'm at a total loss. For someone that called her, I'm doing a shit job at talking. All the things I want to say and none of them feel right via phone.

"I was gonna text or call, but I figured you'd be celebrating with the team." She yawns.

"Still could have. You can always call."

"Christian drew you a picture. I, uh, promised him I'd get it to you when you get back."

Somehow that feels better than the trophy we accepted earlier. And thank you, little man, for providing a great excuse to see her.

"What about you? You draw me a picture?"

Her soft laugh makes my smile grow bigger. "No, but I've got coffee and muffins anytime you want."

"That sounds good." Except it doesn't. Relegating our time together back to the café where the counter serves as a literal and metaphorical boundary between us isn't enough. It's what I deserve, what I told her I wanted, but it just isn't good enough anymore. Winners want the ball. I want the ball.

I want Katrina.

———

Katrina

I yawn as I fill another cup of coffee. I wasn't the only one that stayed up late to watch the game judging by the long line that's been constant since the café opened.

Tabitha is next in line and she steps forward with what looks like yesterday's makeup smudged under her eyes.

"You too, huh?" She gets my first real smile of the day because smiling takes too much energy for those that don't require it today. "Seems like the whole university is running on three hours of sleep."

"Less than," she says and slumps on the counter. "Brody and I were up most the night rehearsing. Speaking of, I was just thinking of you on the way over."

I grab a large coffee cup and she nods. "Two."

I grab a second coffee and fill as I ask, "What were you thinking about me for?"

"Brody and I wanted to make sure you were going to make it tomorrow night for the costume fittings. They should have the backdrops ready then too. God, I can't believe the show is so soon."

"Cream or sugar?"

She shakes her head and I place the cups on the counter and secure lids on them. "Of course. I am beyond excited. It's already so much more than I could have dreamed."

I'm ringing up her coffees when University Hall breaks out in applause and cheers. Looking toward the door, I see him. He's wearing a Valley basketball t-shirt and athletic pants that show off sexy ankles – yes, sexy ankles. It's a thing. A Joel Moreno thing.

People crowd around him, pat his back and say things I can't make out. He takes it all in stride, smiling and thanking people but not stopping as he walks from the door to the counter. I hear Tabitha chuckle as I hand her card back without looking.

"Speaking of dreams coming true," she says to me and then looks to Joel. "Congratulations."

"Thank you." His gaze falls back to me and he smiles. "Hi, Kitty."

"What are you doing here?"

"I couldn't stop thinking about you and Christian last night. Wondering what you were doing and wishing I could celebrate by eating pizza and seeing that picture little man drew me."

Tabitha grabs one of the coffees and takes a sip, which draws Joel's attention to the fact we have an audience.

"Oh, don't mind me," she says. "Or the other fifty people hanging on your every word."

He chuckles and then jumps the counter. My mouth feels like I swallowed sand and I open to say something, ask what he's doing, or maybe I should just kiss the ridiculous smirk off his face like I really want. But I'm incapable of doing any of those things. The look he gives me reaches in and simultaneously tugs at my heart and excites my lady parts.

"I think you're holding up the line, Joel Moreno." Like I care.

"Coffee's on me," he says loud enough they can hear, "but first –"

I'm watching his mouth, waiting for the sweet words I'm sure are coming when his lips crash down on mine.

Hard. Cocky. Possessive.

For half a second, I consider where I am – at freaking work with a line of people, but when his tongue sweeps in and he grabs the back of my thighs to pick me up and bring me closer, I throw my arms around his neck and kiss him like I want to.

Like I've wanted to since the day he first walked into this café.

It's only when I feel his mouth pull into a smile against mine that I realize we're not just being watched, we're being cheered on.

He pulls away and rests his forehead on mine. "Might as well get used to it, Kitty. If we're going to be together, PDA is a requirement. No way I can keep my hands and lips to myself when I'm around you, no matter where we are."

"*If* we're going to be together?" My voice quivers.

He nods and sets me down, takes my hands and looks into my eyes. He has this way of looking from eye to eye like he wants to unravel the mystery of each iris – like each color has its own secrets to tell. "I love you. I love Christian. Give me a second chance to show what a baller boyfriend I can be?"

"Better say yes, or I will," Tabitha says.

"Me too," someone else yells.

Joel threads our fingers together, pulls me to him. "What do you say, Kitty? Go out with me?"

I say yes, like I wanted to from the first time he asked.

41

JOEL

he Tragic Love Story of Hector and Imelda's opening night performance closes to a standing ovation. Christian and I are in the front row along with Blair and Gabby and a bunch of Katrina's screenwriting friends. Katrina's family and the entire Moreno clan are coming tomorrow to the Friday night finale and I'll be right back here where I belong, watching Kitty become a star. The number of people coming to see the screenwriter probably outweighs the number for the actors and that makes me so happy. My girl has worked so hard and she nailed it.

I hold Christian up high as Katrina takes the stage for her bow. He waves the roses we got for her and she grins down at us. When the applause dies off, she walks down the side stage stairs and Christian and I meet her halfway. She picks Christian up, hugging him tightly and accepting the kiss I drop on her lips.

"Congradu…" Christian looks to me. We practiced the word a dozen times before the show because he wanted to get it just right.

"Congratulations," I say quietly near his ear.

He grins. "Congratulations, Mommy."

"Thank you, buddy. What did you guys think?"

"It was amazing," I say without hesitation. She killed it. I motion to where Blair and Gabby hang back. "The girls are waiting to shower you with praise. I'm gonna take little man outside to meet Karla."

Karla has no idea what she's in for. I predict Dylan and Christian will be thick as thieves in no time. And Karla may never agree to babysit again.

She kisses Christian and hugs him again. "Have fun tonight and be good."

He nods. "Dylan is gonna teach me magic!"

I snicker as Katrina and I raise our brows in unison. She hands him over and says, "Meet you in the lobby when I'm done."

"Take your time."

Once I get Christian in the car with Karla, I call Wes. "It's time to buzz the tower."

Silence.

"Dude. *Top Gun*? Never mind. Just pull around."

When the limo pulls up to the curb, I open the back door and laugh. Wes and Z are dressed up - a rare sight. They step out, Wes looking grumpy and Z out of place.

"You look pretty, Z."

He makes a strangled, gruff noise.

"That look in your eyes is a pain in my ass, you know that, right?"

He stares at me blankly and I shake my head. "*Mission Impossible*. What is wrong with you two tonight?"

"Nothing, just, why am I here again?" Z asks, pulling at his shirt cuffs, a poster board tucked under one massive arm.

"Because it was you or Nathan and I needed him to get the party going. All you gotta do is stand there and maybe smile. Well, and hold the sign."

Wes hands me a clear box, that matches one he and Z carry, and I smile. "Let's do this."

We head for the lobby. The theater has cleared out, only a few people still linger talking to the cast and crew. The girls are huddled in one corner talking and laughing animatedly in that way chicks do with their hands and facial expressions.

Gabby sees us first and I nudge Z. "The sign."

He groans, but unfolds the glitter bomb cardboard sign that reads, "Go to prom with us?" and holds it in front of his chest. I hear Wes snicker, but I focus on Gabby's face as she takes in the scene. Her mouth forms a little O and she turns red. We reach them as the other girls realize we're here and turn to face us.

"What's going on?" Blair asks.

"Prom do-over, babydoll," I answer and then look to Katrina. "What do you say?"

"Really?"

I hand her the corsage in the box. "Really."

The girls squeal as we lead them to the limo parked outside.

I open the door as Blair studies me. "How did you guys pull this off without us knowing?"

"I had some help." I motion inside where Vanessa and Mario sit waiting for us.

We pile in and I pop the champagne.

"This is amazing." Katrina looks me over like she's ready to reward me for good behavior. Excited for that, but first... we prom.

"You've got glitter sort of... all over you." Vanessa's voice temporarily distracts me from all the dirty plans I've got in store for later.

I look over in time to see Gabby biting back a smile as she tries to wipe glitter off the big man.

Tonight is gonna be baller.

The White House is madness. The eight of us pile out of the limo to an already wild party. A Thursday night party wouldn't normally attract this many people, but next week we're off for spring break, so everyone is looking to let loose before they head out of Valley for a week. Plus, the guys and I pimped the hell out of it to make sure it lived up to every expectation Gabby and Kitty could have possibly had.

Clutching my arm, Kitty smiles at her corsage and back to me. "Did you pick the biggest one you could find?"

"Custom ordered, Kitty. Nothing but the biggest and baddest for my girl's prom."

"What exactly awaits inside?" Gabby asks.

It's that moment that a group of squealing girls runs around from the back of the house covered in foam, stripping off clothes like they're about to go streaking through the quad.

"This may not have been the brightest idea you've ever had," Wes says as two girls stand in the front yard in their bra and underwear.

"Don't look at me." I chuckle. "This was all your girlfriend's idea."

"A foam party?!" Gabby screeches and jumps with such excitement even Z cracks a smile.

Gabby kicks off her heels and makes a run for it, Blair follows behind, and Wes and Z have little choice but to do the same.

"Impressive," Katrina says to Vanessa and I don't even try to take the credit for this because as long as that smile stays on her face, it's moot.

"Oh no, this was all Joel. I only kept it a secret so I could see the looks on your faces when we got here." She grins and holding hands, Mario and her, walk away.

"Shall we?"

Instead of following the others, I take her through the front door and up the stairs toward my room. She's quiet but wears a smile that tells me she thinks we're going to bang. I mean, maybe that too if there's time, but it's not why I'm taking her to my room.

"I know it's not quite as cool as the Zack Morris surprise prom, but..." I open the door and watch her expression carefully.

"Oh my God, what did you do, Joel?" She enters the candlelit room, hands covering her shocked face. She stops in the middle of the room and turns to me. "This is better. So much better."

"There's more." Taking her hand, I lead her out to the balcony. The music pumps and we've got a view of the foam party going on below. I pull her close and wrap my arms around her waist. "It wouldn't be prom if you didn't get to check out my awesome dance moves."

She rolls her eyes at me but places her arms around my neck and we sway to the music. "Were you always this cocky?"

"Always."

She lays her head on my chest and I wonder if she can feel my heart pounding inside. "Thank you for this. It's better than any high school prom could have possibly been."

"Only one thing that could make this night better." She lets out a little snort, clearly thinking I mean better by bringing my penis into the equation, but nah, I already mentioned I didn't bring her here for that. Summoning more courage than it takes to pull a spin move on Z, I drop to one knee all dramatic like.

"What are you—"

"Relax, sweetheart. I have a proposal for you, but not the kind you're thinking."

At least not yet. Took Zack Morris five seasons to seal the deal with Kelly, I don't have any intention of waiting that long, but I want that NBA contract first. Preferably in

LA. Not just because the Lakers is my dream, but because it's where she wants to be too. Not quite sure how we're gonna work that out yet, but I've got an entire year to figure it out and I think my dedication to getting what I want is clear.

"O-kay." My fearless girl looks nervous.

"Prom tonight." I pull out the key to my family's vacation house in Puerto Vallarta from my pocket. "Spring break trip tomorrow after the show?"

"Really??!!"

I expected a whole slew of questions about logistics for Christian – and I've thought of them all, but it's just excitement she wears as she jumps up and down. A whole lot of things she gave up to be the most amazing mom and still work toward her dreams. But I'm gonna give them all to her, one Thursday at a time.

And every day in between.

———

THANK you for reading The Fadeaway. You can read Gabby and Zeke's story in The Tip-Off.

Playlist

- Taki Taki by DJ Snake feat. Selena Gomez, Cardi B, Ozuna
- F**kin' Problems by A$AP Rocky feat. Drake, 2 Chainz, Kendrick Lamar
- Home With You by Madison Beer
- Bed by Nicki Minaj feat. Ariana Grande
- Shots by LMFAO feat. Lil Jon
- Whine Up by Kat DeLuna feat. Elephant Man
- Solo by Clean Bandit feat. Demi Lovato
- Gold Digger by Kanye West feat. Jamie Foxx
- In My Feelings by Drake
- Fine China by Future
- SWISH by Tyga
- Boo'd Up by Ella Mai
- Jackie Chan by Tiësto & Dzeko feat. Preme & Post Malone

- No Limit Remix by G-Eazy feat. A$AP Rocky, French Montana, Juicy J, Belly
- Post To Be by Omarion feat. Chris Brown & Jhene Aiko
- My Chick Bad by Ludacris feat. Nicki Minaj
- The Fall by Bryce Vine
- Lost in the Fire by Gesaffelstein feat. The Weeknd
- Without Me by Halsey
- Sunflower by Post Malone, Swae Lee
- Remind Me to Forget by Kygo feat. Miguel
- Wow. by Post Malone
- Close to Me by Ellie Goulding feat. Diplo, Swae Lee
- Ruin My Life by Zara Larsson

The Tip-Off Sneak Peek

1

ZEKE

Watching a grown man intentionally lose a game of PIG is downright embarrassing. The things people do for love.

I shake my head at Wes as I rebound the basketball from his weak shot attempt. The odds of him missing three in a row are as bad as my own and I could have made any one of those shots blindfolded.

I gotta hand it to him, though, he's a pretty good actor and his girlfriend is eating it up.

"That's G for you. I win!" Blair squeals and jumps up and down in front of my buddy, her ponytail swinging wildly like a whip. I toss her the ball and she brings it up over her head in victory and turns in a circle calling out to me and the rest of my roommates who are hanging around our half-court gym. "Reigning PIG champion, folks. You don't want any of this."

I chuckle and she steps toward me. "Come on, big guy. Let's see what the number one NBA draft picks got."

"Projected. He hasn't been drafted yet." Wes wraps both arms around his girl and tugs her to him.

"Thanks for the vote of confidence," I tell him dryly.

"Just want to make sure you don't start slacking, letting the media's hard-on for you go to your head."

I resist the urge to continue our banter by telling him to fuck off since Blair is present. My mom would lose her shit if she knew I was dropping F-bombs in front of girls. Besides, I know that underneath the jokes, no one has my back like Wes does.

"Let's go, senorita," Joel draws out the word, exaggerating the pronunciation as he pulls his shirt over his head and tosses it out of bounds.

"What'd I tell you about using the Spanish on my girlfriend?" Wes asks, not letting go of Blair.

Nathan sets his beer next to Joel's shirt and pushes him out of the way. "I got this. I'm three beers in and unbeatable."

It's a rare weeknight that we're all home at the same time. Since the season ended, we've each fallen into our own routines. Wes spending more time with Blair, Joel spending more time with his girlfriend Katrina, and Nathan doing whatever it is Nathan does. I've been right here making sure I do everything I can to get that top pick Wes is ragging me about.

In less than two months Wes and I will be graduating. He's staying in Valley as the team's newest assistant coach, so it's really just me that's leaving, and man that feels weird. Exciting too, though. I don't know where I'm going yet. East Coast, West Coast, Midwest. Honestly, I don't care so long as I can keep playing ball.

"Actually, I'm gonna have to take a raincheck." Blair bounces the ball to Nathan. "Vanessa and Gabby should be here any minute to pick me up for girls' night." She turns in Wes' arms and they get tangled up kissing and groping like she won't be back later tonight. She sleeps over every night.

My buddy has it bad and I'm happy for him. Blair's a solid chick.

"Speaking of," Nathan says and nods to the door as Gabby and Vanessa enter.

Joel and I hang back as everyone else walks over to greet them. I watch Gabby smile and hug Blair and then Nathan. She just moved to Valley, but she and Blair went to high school together and have remained tight, so she's quickly becoming a regular face at the house.

Her long blonde hair is down, and she keeps her chin tilted down ever-so-slightly so the long strands fall into her face. Her gaze meets mine over Nathan's shoulder and I hold my breath. I don't know what it is about her, but when she's in the room, my palms tingle with anticipation like I'm about to walk out on the floor before a game.

Completely unaware, Joel dribbles in front of me blocking my view of Gabby. I step to the side, but she's not looking at me anymore. "Hey, man, you busy tomorrow night?"

"No, I don't think so. Why?"

"Blair wants to have a party for Gabby. Thought we'd take it one step further and throw a surprise party for all the girls. One last big hurrah. You in?"

"Sounds good," I say absently and turn to the basket and shoot a jumper.

"I'm not even gonna tell Wes until tomorrow so there's less of a chance he slips and tells Blair."

"Good call." I glance back like I'm looking at the happy couple, but they're not who my eyes settle on.

"You and Wes are going to ride over and pick us up. The girls and I'll be at the theater for Katrina's play. Then we'll ride back to the house together. Cool?"

"I guess so." I dribble the ball and watch Gabby talk animatedly to the group – eyes bright and hands waving in the air.

Joel takes two steps backward to the door. "I'm heading to Katrina's. Don't forget about tomorrow. Oh, and wear something nice. The limo will be downstairs at eight o'clock. Be there or be lame."

"The limo?"

"Yeah, we're doing it up right. Classy as fuck." He winks and jogs backward a few more steps before turning.

Everyone leaves at once and the only one who offers me a goodbye glance is Gabby. She lifts one hand in a small wave, but my response is so delayed that by the time I get my hand in the air to wave back, she's gone.

With the gym to myself, I lift the headphones from around my neck and settle them on my ears, rack the extra balls, and start my routine. I've just finished my ball-handling warmup and am starting in on my shooting drills when Wes returns. I drop my headphones back to my neck.

"Are you getting in another workout?" he asks as he walks over to the rack.

"Nah, not really, just thought I'd get my shots in and kill some time until I can eat my last meal of the day."

He picks up a ball and smirks. "Sara still have you on that cutting diet?"

"Yes," I grumble.

My agent wants me to lean out before I start interviewing with NBA teams. I'm bigger than the average center, and though it hasn't been a problem up to this point, I don't want there to be any question, any slightest of reservations, about drafting me. If dropping weight proves that, so be it.

"How about a little one on one, for old time's sake?"

"Think you still got it? I just watched a girl with very little athletic ability – no offense to Blair – destroy you at PIG."

He smirks but doesn't answer as he moves to the top of the key and checks the ball. Wes and I played together for four years until an injury ended his college career. The boot he had to wear during recovery is newly off, but I'm not about to take it easy on him. Unlike him, I don't throw competition in the name of love or friendship.

Wes dribbles the ball, a cocky grin on his face. I know his moves as well as my own, so I'm prepared when he pulls a crossover. If I were anyone else, he'd be putting me on skates right now, but I hang with him all the way to the basket. He's forced to shoot around me but gets lucky with an off-balance jumper.

"Check," I say after I've rebounded the ball and taken it to the three-point line. I narrow my gaze on his and give him my best intimidating smirk. "I think you got slower."

He shakes his head. "Your smack talk won't work on me, Z."

"We'll see," is all I say before I crab dribble, backing him up with my large frame. The determination to show me he's still got it is written all over his face. And he does, but I'm still better. He's playing me close, chest pressed to my back to keep me from drop stepping low – my favorite move. Favorite, but not only. I go high and use my height and long arms to get a hook shot off and in.

"You've gotten even better," he says as he walks the ball to the three-point line. "Either that or I really have gotten slower. How many shots are you getting in a day?"

I shrug. "Six hundred or so."

Wes looks at me like I'm nuts, but lots of guys swear by shooting five hundred plus shots a day. Steph Curry and Kobe Bryant are just two in a long line of successful guys doing it. Next level skill and talent are earned with a lot of repetition and focus. It's the price of success and I'll pay it every day until I make it.

————

THE NEXT NIGHT at eight o'clock on the dot, I head downstairs feeling uneasy. Parties aren't generally my thing, but it's not that alone that has me unbuttoning my sleeves and rolling them up to get some air. Something about the plan for the night just doesn't sit right. A surprise party? A limo? What the hell have I gotten myself into?

Wes is already waiting in the living room and he shoves a clear box in my direction. There's some sort of flower inside.

"What's this?" I ask, noticing he has two other identical boxes in his left hand.

"It's a corsage." He watches my face for understanding. "It's for Gabby."

"What does she do with it?"

"You've never given a girl a corsage before?"

"I can't give her this." I try and push it back into his hand, but he won't take it.

"You have to. She can't be the only girl that doesn't get one. That's shitty. Besides, she's basically your date."

"What do you mean she's basically my date?"

Wes' phone beeps and he looks down at the screen. "Limo's here."

"Hold up," I say before he can open the door. "Explain."

Wes snorts and looks at me like I'm clueless. I guess I am. "Me and Blair, Joel and Katrina, Vanessa and Mario..." His voice trails off, allowing me to fill in the rest.

"What about Nathan? Where is he and why can't he give this... thing to her." I shake the box in my hand.

"Nathan's staying to get the party going. Would you rather stay here and play hostess or stand next to a pretty girl all night?"

He opens the door and I follow.

"That's what I thought."

Vanessa steps out of the limo. "Hello, boys." She gives us both a once over before nodding her approval. Vanessa, Blair, and Gabby are like the three amigos lately, so I'm surprised to see her without them.

"What are you doing here?" Wes asks. "I thought we were surprising you?"

"Surprising me?" She shakes her head. "Who do you think helped Joel put this together? I mean, honestly, like he was going to leave you two unsupervised to pull this off."

"Fair enough." Wes chuckles, steps past her and slides into the limo. I try to do the same, but Vanessa moves with me.

"Hello, Zeke," she says. "You clean up nice. I almost didn't recognize you without your headphones."

"Thanks, Vanessa. You look nice too."

"Let's talk strategy. This is going to be the best surprise party ever." She claps her hands and then climbs into the vehicle.

Strategy?

Once we're all in the limo, Vanessa's boyfriend Mario offers us a beer and a knowing look as Vanessa gets right to it. "Blair, Gabby, and Joel are all at the theater for Katrina's play. Joel's going to come out to get you two and you're going to storm in there looking all handsome and surprise the girls." She pulls out a rolled-up poster board and hands it to me. "When they see you, hold this up."

As I unroll it, glitter explodes. So does my head when I read what it says. *Go to Prom with us?* is written in big sparkly letters.

"Prom?" I'm not sure if I'm more thrown by the high school throwback or that this whole thing has been orchestrated as a big group date. Fuck, it's warm in here. I pull at the collar on my shirt. I'm going to kill Joel for leaving out some very important details.

Wes covers a laugh with his fist. "Uh, yeah, that's the other thing. Gabby and Katrina missed their high school proms so that's where the limo and corsages come into play. It's a surprise party with a prom vibe." He claps me on the shoulder and shrugs. A shrug that tells me he'd do anything for Blair and by extension, Gabby. "It's gonna be fun."

2

GABBY

THIS is why girls go to the bathroom together. So they can talk about boys, borrow lipstick, *and* so they don't get lost.

I push through the crowd careening my neck left and then right and walking on my tiptoes to try and see through the mass of people. There are a lot of great things about being short... not being able to see over tall people isn't one of them.

Relief washes over me when I spot my friends across the large lobby of the Valley campus theater. The front doors are open and the breeze filters through, bringing with it the sweet smell of spring. It's a beautiful night to be out, and though this is my first time watching a campus performance, I suspect the weather is partly responsible for everyone lingering after the show.

"I made it." I let out a long breath as I join Blair and Katrina.

"You got lost again, didn't you?" Blair asks with a teasing smile. Damn best friends, they always call you out.

"Not lost," I insist. "Delayed. There was a long line for the ladies and then I had to weave through a million people to find you. It's like a Beyoncé concert up in here."

"It's one of the best turnouts I've ever seen, and the show was fantastic."

At Blair's praise, Katrina blushes. Tonight's play was written entirely by her and all the actors were students too.

"It really was amazing. Congratulations."

"Thanks." She lets her shoulders droop. "I'm so glad it's over."

"We should celebrate."

No sooner than Blair says the words I spot Joel, Wes, and Zeke walking toward us with swagger that splits the room to let them through.

"I think Joel has something planned. He was being weird earlier when I asked what the plan was for tonight."

My throat is dry, and I have to clear it twice so my voice is more than a whisper. "Uh, guys."

I nudge Blair and she follows my gaze to the guys.

Going to college via online classes has one big disadvantage – no boys. No running into a handsome guy at a frat party – how Vanessa met Mario. No looking across the classroom and enjoying the eye candy – like Blair and Wes. And no running into your soul mate in University Hall like Joel and Katrina.

The whole soulmate thing I don't care about so much, but I am looking forward to the eye candy, and the three in front of me are some of the very best examples of why I decided to finally move to Valley for my senior year. The spring semester isn't quite over, but I thought I would feel less like a freshman if I got to know some people before Fall classes start. The next few months are my own version of orientation. Though the agenda is more social than academic.

My gaze flits over each of them. From Wes' blue eyes and crooked smile to Joel's jet-black hair and charm to Zeke's dark skin and large build... good God, my body shivers with appreciation as I get a good look at him.

Zeke Sweets, basketball king and NBA prospect, has traded his jersey for grey slacks and a black button-down shirt. My eyes trace the ink running up his left hand and disappearing into the rolled sleeve of his dress shirt. It's only when I'm giving that muscular arm a second sweep that I notice the paper in one hand and the clear box in the other.

He shifts the clear box awkwardly, so it's lodged between his side and elbow and unrolls the paper. It says something, but between the fluorescent lights bouncing off the glitter and the way Zeke's brown eyes lock on mine, I'm having a hard time reading it.

"What's going on?" Blair asks.

Joel responds for the guys by stepping forward, tossing me a wink, and handing Katrina a clear box identical to the one Zeke has. "Prom do-over, babydoll."

It's then that Wes nudges Zeke forward and the mystery box is pushed out in front of me. I giggle at the large corsage inside, a nervous reaction. A peek at Blair beside me confirms she had something to do with this. I missed my high school prom and it's never sat right with her. In all honesty, I'm more excited about starting over than trying to make up for the past, but I appreciate the thought.

With shaky hands, I take the box and Zeke looks like I've taken the weight of the world off his shoulders. "Wanna go to prom with me?" he asks with just enough humor in his tone that I think he might find this as ridiculous as me.

"Love to."

———

TURNS out this prom is better than whatever I missed in high school. The back yard of The White House, the nickname for the mansion Zeke, Wes, Joel, and Nathan live in, is packed. A DJ booth is set up in one corner with large speakers that vibrate my insides as we pass by it. Bodies push and grind to an old jam and I raise my arms with the rest of the crowd when Busta tells us to put our hands where his eyes could see.

"This playlist is killer," I yell over the music to Blair. "Way better than whatever you had at your prom. And I cannot believe you guys got a foam machine." On the other side of the party, people are disappearing into the foam and reemerging with big smiles.

"You said you always wanted to go to a foam party, now you have."

I throw my arms around her neck. "You are amazing."

"I can't take credit for this. I had a small idea for a party and Joel took it to a whole other level."

We find a spot somewhere in the middle of the party and set up in a circle – girls on the inside and guys hanging back. Wes stands two steps behind Blair, beer in hand. He's not dancing but doing a tiny little head bob to the music.

Vanessa has a similar setup – although V is turned toward her boyfriend Mario making it very clear she's dancing just for him.

Joel and Katrina have disappeared altogether, but that's not unusual for them. I think they spend more time naked than clothed when they have a night without Katrina's son Christian.

The sight of Mario and Wes watching their girls so possessive and adoringly makes me happy. But also, insanely jealous like if they weren't already my friends, I'd hate them for being so ridiculously in love.

In beat to the song, I turn to the side so I can see Zeke standing behind me. He's not looking at me possessively or adoringly. Actually, he's not looking at me at all.

What does it take to get Zeke Sweets' attention? Basketballs for boobs? And I don't mean huge boobs, I mean literal basketballs. The only time I've really seen him smile is when he's on the basketball court.

We've barely spoken to each other since getting in the limo to drive to the party, but I can't help but feel a little burst of pride being here with him. He's so handsome and big and strong and intense and handsome and... did I already mention handsome?

"Gabby baby!" Nathan shouts as he enters our couple circle. He tucks one side of his long hair behind an ear and then tackle hugs me.

I let out a surprised chuckle as all the wind is knocked out of me. "Good to see you, too."

Nathan and I have become friends in my short time at Valley, which is nice because I anticipate I'll be spending a lot of time at The White House since my best friends are dating jocks.

With a hand around my waist, Nathan moves us with the beat. The beer he's holding in one hand spills onto my arm and he backs up as he apologizes and then his gaze falls to my dress like he's just now seeing my outfit.

"Wow, Gabby. You trying to kill me in that dress?"

His words make me smile, but I swat playfully at him dodging the compliment like a boss.

Vanessa twirls, raises her hands, and yells, "Let's move up closer to the foam."

I nod and Nathan and I follow behind her. I peek over my shoulder to see if Z is following and he is, though unhurried and not all that enthusiastically. We're a train moving through the crowd. Mario holding onto Vanessa, me with a hand on V's back so no one can separate us and holding my other hand behind me grasping Blair's. Nathan is beside me and I don't look back again to verify but I assume Wes is back there pulling up the rear with Zeke.

Every step closer to the crowd dancing in the cloud-like substance makes my heart thump wilder in my chest. Now this is a party! It's not as packed in the foam, most people are staying on the outskirts of it, but I want in.

"I think this is as far as I go," Vanessa says and Blair nods in agreement.

"Sorry, Gabby, that foam freaks me out a bit," Nathan adds.

I mock pout but no one steps forward.

Wes shoves Zeke forward and my date's eyes widen in panic. The nice thing to do would be to let him off the hook, but my desire to get him to dance with me outweighs every nice bone in my body. Also, I find Zeke's presence a comfort, like I can be as crazy and reckless as I want, and he'll keep me safe. Stupid, I know, considering we've barely spoken. But if it came to blows, I think he'd at least step in front of me and block me with his giant frame.

"Let's go, big guy." I grab his hand and pull. He budges without me really having to put any weight behind it and we enter the foam, leaving our traitorous friends behind and joining a group of girls who look to be as excited as I feel.

They welcome us, widening the circle before getting lost to the music again. I do the same with Zeke standing behind me. He's closer now than before and maybe it's the foam or the way no one is watching us in here, but I grow bolder. I turn and place my hands on his chest, moving with the beat. I keep my eyes downcast until one of his hands finds my hip. My breath hitches and I move an inch closer and meet his gaze.

Zeke's eyes are a light brown, warm and soulful, and right now they're finally on me. Wow. The force of a thousand suns. All that intensity focused on me, I was not prepared for it. I reach down to the foam at my feet and scoop up a handful, stand, and blow it into his face. It takes him a moment to react, but slowly a smile spreads on his face and then he shocks me by reciprocating – tossing giant handfuls of foam at me, hurling it so fast and furious there's a cloud around us. I swat at the foam until I can see his smiling face and giggle, look down, and prepare to make another move.

He holds his hand up and says, "Truce."

"Okay," I say at the same time I move to grab for more, but he's quick and catches my wrist. His large fingers burn into my skin and he shakes his head, still smiling.

The foam builds between us and his touch disappears from my wrist only to be replaced by his fingertips brushing against the side of my face and pushing the foam away. It lasts only a second, but I feel it even after he's dropped his hand back to his side.

The song changes and the girls in the foam with us squeal in delight as the opening to Lizzo's "Truth Hurts" begins to play.

I feel on top of the world as I give myself over to the beat like I've only done in my bedroom for the past three years. Zeke doesn't exactly dance, but he seems more relaxed now and I'm patting myself on the back for pulling him in here. All he needed was a little forced fun.

One song turns to five and I'm drenched with a combination of foam and sweat when I turn back to face the middle of the circle. I offer a shy smile to the girl to my left. She returns it and then tilts her head and studies me. "You've got something…" She takes a step toward me, smooths a hand over her face at the same time she must realize the only thing on my face is… my face.

My scarred face.

Stupid. Stupid. Stupid, Gabby.

My hand flies to the left side of my face and I give her a reassuring smile. After all, it's not her fault.

They can make mascara that withstands a good cry fest, but so far, I haven't found a foundation that is as magical. Which means mine is gone with the foam and the lines on my face are more visible. The scars on my face from a car accident my senior year of high school are never completely hidden, but with several layers of concealer, foundation, and setting spray, it's not usually obvious enough that people gasp in horror – yep, that's happened.

"Sorry," she says and averts her eyes back to the middle of the circle.

I don't look around to the other girls. One thing I hate more than gawking – the pity. As if my life were defined by my face. As if I'm somehow less than because I'm not perfect. As if they're better than me because they wear their scars on the inside. And I flipping hate that I feel like they might be right.

I turn to face my date and hope he'll shield me from this awkward, awful moment or maybe whisk me away and tell me I'm beautiful no matter what. Cheesy, right? But I long to hear those words from someone even if it's not true.

Zeke's eyes are warm and understanding as his gaze drops to the scars on my face and then to the girls dancing around us. "Wanna head back?"

Well, it's not a profession of beauty or love, but it's an excuse out of here anyway. I grab his arm and duck behind him. With as much dignity as I can muster, I shimmy out of that foam like my pride didn't wash away with my makeup.

Man, I was stoked about a real-life foam party. I forgot one minor detail. Foam is made of water.

3

GABBY

Zeke leads me into the gym on the second story of The White House.

"When I said I wanted to go somewhere quiet, this isn't exactly what I had in mind."

"It's the only place off limits during parties."

He turns on the lights and grabs two basketballs from a rack. He extends one to me and I eye it curiously. He can't be serious.

"Really?"

He looks unsure as he gives a little shrug, ball still held out toward me. His eyes light up and he drops the ball to my feet. "Wait, I know what we need."

Confused but intrigued, I watch as he tucks the other basketball under his arm and takes out his phone. His head bounces from side to side as his thumbs tap on the screen.

"Here we go," he says as music pumps into the room. He pockets his phone and dribbles toward the basket.

I take a moment to look around the room, taking in the gym. I've seen it before, but never really appreciated how nice it is. The polished wood floor is a half-court version of the one at Ray Fieldhouse from the blue and yellow lines on the court to the Ray Roadrunner mascot painted on the wall. It's a sweet place. Joel's dad is the president of Valley U and he bought this place and outfitted it with everything the guys could possibly need – and way more. It's not as outrageous as some of the big university athletic dorms, but it's pretty over the top.

Moving up to the free throw line, I try to think back on what I learned in junior high basketball while I watch Zeke take shots. He's more relaxed than I've seen him all night. Even in dress clothes, he looks like he belongs with a basketball in his hands.

"It's a little intimidating shooting hoops with you."

"Don't worry about it, I make everyone look bad on the court."

I'm taken back by his words until I meet his gaze. He's smiling and wears a cocky grin he's never flashed my direction before. I feel that look in my toes. "You've got jokes, huh?"

He shoots, rebounds his ball and then dribbles to me. "Let's see what you got."

Under his scrutiny, I take my time getting into position at the free throw line and then shoot. I cringe as the ball doesn't quite make it to the rim. Airball.

Zeke gets my ball and brings it back to me. "Try again."

"Who knew the night could get more humiliating," I mutter under my breath, but I take another shot anyway. This one at least hits the rim.

After my fourth miss, he hands me the ball and then instructs me to widen my stance. "Good, now bring your right foot forward just a tiny bit."

Instead of trying to talk me through the upper body, he guides my arms up and into position and then moves my hands where he wants them. Goosebumps race to the surface at his warm touch. His hands are strong and steady, and it's a sad realization that this is the most a man has touched me since my car accident nearly four years ago.

"Alright, use your legs and really follow it through, let it roll off those fingertips."

With more concentration and focus than I've used since trying to read through Game of Thrones fan theories, I stare down the red rim and shoot.

"Yes!" I jump as the ball goes through the net. Freaking finally.

"There you go. Nice. Do it again." He sends the ball back to me with a bounce pass.

Intent brown eyes watch me as I line up and try and get into the same position.

"So, I've gathered parties aren't really your thing. Is this where you usually hide out?"

"Who says I usually hide out?"

"Everyone. Also, I was in town visiting Blair for the

party after the last home game of the season. I don't remember seeing you."

"It's not that they aren't my *thing*, I just don't party much during the season. What about you?"

"Are parties my thing?"

He nods.

"Yes. Well, I want them to be. I've only been to the one and I wasn't a student yet. So, this is my first official college party. I'm officially a fan, though. There's something so magical about the bass of the music and people dancing and having a good time. Well, everyone but you."

"I'm having a fine time."

"Wow, you really know how to make a girl feel special. You're having a *fine* time. At least I don't have to worry about you telling anyone how awful our date was."

"Why's that?"

"Because you don't talk much."

"Burn," he says and his lips curve into another smile. "I'm a man of few words." Palming the ball in one hand, he raises it toward me like he's pointing. "How about the best date I've been on in four years?"

"Well, then you'd just be lying."

He raises a brow and then turns to shoot without speaking.

I dribble and bring the ball up, pausing before I send the ball sailing to the basket. "This is the only date you've been on since then, isn't it?"

I remember the guys giving him shit once about never

dating, but I'd assumed they were exaggerating the situation.

He winks and keeps rebounding his ball and putting it back. He's gotten into it now and is shooting like he's at practice. Basketball in dress clothes – it's a good look.

"So, parties aren't your thing, dating isn't your thing, what is your thing?" He opens his mouth to tell me what I already know, but I stop him. "Besides basketball."

He shakes his head. "It's my only thing."

"If you had to give up food or basketball, which would you choose?"

He dribbles as he answers. "I'd die without food."

"Some things are worth dying for."

A deep chuckle echoes in the gym. "So, basketball for three weeks... maybe less since I'll be wasting away or a lifetime without it?"

"Mhmmm."

"That's savage."

"That's what makes it such a good question. You can learn a lot about a person by what they're willing to give up for the things they really love."

He agrees with a head bob and another quiet chuckle and goes back to focusing on the basketball goal.

"Peanut butter or jelly?"

"Both."

"That's cheating. You can only pick one."

"Peanut butter."

"Show up to class naked or knee to the balls?"

"Class naked." He shivers like the other option is too awful to contemplate.

I keep firing off questions and he answers – not in a lot of words, but I'm getting used to the subtle way his body language says what he doesn't. Right now, he's relaxed, and he thinks I'm at least a little bit funny. I can work with that.

I give up shooting and sit on the floor, ball in my lap, as I watch him. He's really something to take in. I've seen him play before, of course, but up close, all that testosterone and skill is just... well, it's a little breathtaking if I'm honest. This is almost better than the party.

As if he can read my thoughts, he looks over and stares at me a beat, sympathy in the way he takes me in. "Do you want to go back out to the party?"

I look toward the door with longing but shake my head. "I don't think so. Tonight is kind of a bust. This is not how I pictured it going down." Guilt steals the air from my lungs, and it burns as I let out a breath. "Please don't tell anyone I said that. Blair would be devastated if she thought I didn't have a good time tonight."

Zeke places the ball on the floor beside me and sits on it. "I won't say a word."

Now that I believe.

"What would you give up food for?"

I think for a minute. "I don't know. I don't have one big thing I want like you do. I want to do it all now that I'm at Valley, all the normal college things. That probably sounds dumb to the guy who is about to graduate and get drafted into the NBA."

"Not dumb at all. Certainly not any dumber than choosing a death sentence so I can play basketball for three weeks. Shit, I would probably be awful too without any food to give me energy." He looks really bothered by this, more so than the fact he'd literally be starving to death.

I laugh softly. "That is pretty dumb."

"Got anything specific in mind or are you just winging it?"

I've had a lot of time to think about this, so I nod. "I have a few things in mind."

He waits for me to continue, but I redirect instead. "Does no dating mean no anything? No kissing, no..." I'm a twenty-one-year-old woman, but I can't bring myself to say the word.

Thankfully he knows where I'm going. "I've hooked up occasionally, but it's hard—"

"I'll bet." I slap my hand over my mouth. "Oh God, I'm sorry, I didn't mean to say that out loud." I keep my head buried and wave him on. "Please continue."

Humor laces his tone, but the words are serious. "Dividing attention between two things like that... it stops you from being great at either one."

"Lots of professional athletes are married."

"Yeah and there's like an eighty percent divorce rate among them, too."

I start to laugh but realize he's completely serious. "What about casual relationships?"

He shrugs. "It's still a distraction."

I don't know why this hurts my feelings, but my face heats with rejection, which doesn't make any sense. We're on a date. He asked me to be his date. The man gave me a freaking corsage.

"If you haven't been on a date in..."

"Four years," he supplies as he stands and moves toward the basket. "Maybe five."

"Why tonight? I mean, obviously I'm amazing, but that's quite a streak to break for a girl you barely know."

He glances back and the panic in his eyes tells me everything. How did I not put it together before?

"Oh God." I cover my face with both hands as my emotions spiral. "Blair and Wes put you up to this, didn't they?" The words come out jumbled through my hands, but when he sighs, I feel confident he heard me. Of course, our best friends orchestrated this whole thing. How humiliating. I have no idea why he'd agree to go along with it.

"I'm sorry. They shouldn't have done that." I stand and pick up the basketball. His face is apologetic, the muscles in his neck tighten as he swallows. Full lips part and I wait in the excruciating silence to hear what he has to say. Like maybe tonight wasn't so awful, but he says nothing.

"Gabby! Z! Open up." Nathan pounds on the gym door, his smiling face is smashed up against the glass. At least one person is genuinely excited to hang out with me tonight.

Zeke looks conflicted, unmoving, while Nathan keeps yelling for us to let him in.

I hold up my basketball like it represents our time

together and toss it toward him. He catches it easily with one big hand, still holding his in the other. "Thank you for being so nice about the whole thing, but I don't need a pity date."

Also by Rebecca Jenshak

About the Author

Rebecca Jenshak is a USA Today bestselling author of new adult romance, a caffeine addict, and college basketball fanatic.

Be sure not to miss new releases and sales. Sign up to receive her newsletter at www.subscribepage.com/rebeccajenshaknewsletter

www.rebeccajenshak.com

Made in United States
North Haven, CT
26 June 2024

54096499R00202